Kill't Dead
...Or Worse

Sex, murder, and toxic waste: Nowhere Else But Texas

Nick Sibelius Series, Book 1

R. W. Hacker

Copyright © 2016 by Richard Hacker
All rights reserved
LifeJazz Media

Cover Art by Anna Hacker Downey

ISBN:0998203009
ISBN-13:978-0998203003

KILL'T DEAD OR WORSE

DEDICATION

To Sidney for all of her love and support, and to Bill Hacker,
who inspired my love of the written word.
Thanks, Dad.

KILL'T DEAD OR WORSE

CONTENTS

1	Starry, Starry Night	1
2	Showtime	3
3	Thank God for Duct Tape	8
4	The Rupture	13
5	A Visit to the Farm	18
6	2TH 4RY—One Year Ago	22
7	Carls Sets a New World Record	27
8	Feels Like Houston	30
9	Maybe It Was the Raptor	34
10	Jayson's Advice	40
11	Fishing Lunatic	42
12	Crazy Wild	47
13	Taking a Ride	49
14	Earl, Sr.	51
15	K-I-L-L	54
16	Standstill	60
17	Bridge Work	64
18	Bluebonnet Cafe	69
19	Taking a Nap	74
20	Date Night	77
21	Death Comes Floating	84
22	Junior Revisited	91
23	Handshake	95

24 Free and Clear   98

25 Lost and Found   106

26 ICU   108

27 Happy Reunion   112

28 Sands Motel   120

29 Beer and Peanut Butter   126

30 Wouldn't Want To Be You   130

31 Meeting the Pendletons   134

32 Bottoms Up   143

33 Escape from the Sands   146

34 Preparations   149

35 Holy, Wholly, Hole-y   151

36 View to a Kill   156

37 Marcus' Last Ride   161

38 Cost of Doing Business   163

39 A Break   168

40 Give Me the Finger   171

41 Dental Appointment   177

42 Chasing Reality   186

43 Hideout   192

44 Twitter Man   197

45 Hellfire and Damnation   200

46 Wish You Were Here   107

    About the Author   213

    Preview: All Hat and No Cattle   214

R.W.Hacker

Kill't Dead
...Or Worse

R.W.Hacker

1 STARRY, STARRY NIGHT

Carl scanned a night sky splashed with stars, while the din of rasping cicadas played the music of the Blackland Prairie and hot Texas breezes whispered through brittle cotton. A lanky, tall nineteen-year-old, he stood in a cotton field at the edge of his uncle's woods listening to a motorcycle's angry revs sputter to silence. With a rustling of oak and mesquite, a young black couple made their way deep into his world. He felt safe in this territory. Outside of this refuge he worked for his uncle, Earl Pendleton Jr., fixing fences, cleaning stalls, digging post holes. But at night, Carl would sneak away to his dimly lit secret place, his safe wooded haven, lying down in a small, ten by ten foot wide space he had cleared himself in a cluster of undergrowth surrounded by scrub trees. This night, seeing these intruders to his world, he slipped out of sight.

"Look at this, Ayisha." The man, lean and muscular in jeans and a khaki tee shirt, pushed into the space, pulling a girl, wearing short blue jean cut offs and a pale blue tube top, along behind him. "Somebody's done us a favor. This is perfect."

"I don't know, Delton. It's kind of spooky out here."

"You're with the Marines, pretty lady. Trust me."

Delton unfurled a blanket he had tucked under his arm, spreading the soft material across sun baked dirt. He sat down on the blanket, one arm reaching out for the girl, his eyes sparkling in scattered moonlight.

"Come here, Ayisha. See? You can see stars up through the opening in these trees."

She sat down, leaning back into his embrace, looking skyward. "They're beautiful, Delton. Like jewels tossed across a velvet sky."

For a long while Carl hid silently as the couple lay on their backs looking for shooting stars. Then the man began stroking the girl's face and neck, deftly sliding his hand down her top. Carl stood statue-still, mesmerized by

1

this young woman and the scene unfolding. The man soon had removed all of the girl's clothes as well as his own, her soft moans mixed with the rustling leaves and the couple's heavy breathing.

Carl knew he shouldn't be watching, but he quickly lost himself in the moment, voicing a soft groan. In a distant part of his mind he heard the girl's shaky voice. "Did you hear something? It sounded like a man moaning."

The man's voice tore Carl out of his moment.

"Sonofabitch. Who the hell's out there?"

Delton rose from the blanket, quickly pulling on his jeans. Terror rushed into Carl's chest. He could hear his Uncle Junior talking about his "pervert of a nephew."

He couldn't, he wouldn't let that happen.

2 SHOWTIME

Nick Sibelius tossed in his sleep, the ex who cheated on him, and his dead patrol partner calling out to him, reverberated in his skull, twisting his dreams. When his cell phone sang out *Miles and Miles of Texas*, the part of his less conscious self that had stayed awake jumped to his feet, pounding Nick's mind into conscious awareness. One blue eye opened.

"Damn, two-thirty."

He listened to the tune on his phone as it vibrated across the nightstand. The only call he could imagine receiving at this ungodly hour had to be somebody in a Bangalore phone center representing a credit agency. The caller, with a slight British accent, would want to know why Nick's credit card payment was three weeks overdue—again. The phone stopped playing the tune at "goin' to live here 'til I die." Nick bunched his pillow up, rolled onto his back and closed his eyes. The air conditioner in his 1962 Airstream trailer croaked like a frog on an LSD trip. However, given the night time temps in Central Texas hovered in the mid-eighties in July, he put up with the noise, telling himself he'd swing by the big box store to buy a new window unit over the weekend.

The phone came to life again, dancing to the same tune. "Okay. Alright. I'm coming."

The screenshot on his phone gave him pause. A woman with dark hair stared back at him, a spark in her eyes hinting at both her intelligence and passion. She always used to tell him with a tease in her voice, "You know Nicky, a hard man was good to find."

Apparently so. He pressed a green button on his phone, wondering when he'd have the courage to remove his ex's picture from the screen. She did cheat on him, but the thought of removing her picture made him feel very alone.

"Sibelius."

A deep, male voice asked, "Nick Sibelius, the private investigator?

"Look, it's two thirty in the morning. You need to call back during business hours."

"This is important, Mr. Sibelius. Urgent."

"Always is. Call back at nine."

He tapped the off button. Everyone thinks finding out who's cheating on them is urgent business. Nick knew from experience, namely walking in on his naked anesthesiologist of a wife taking a lunch break by sitting astride a trauma doc on their living room sofa. Sure, everyone wants to know if their wife or husband is cheating, but finding out does not constitute a win. More of a swift kick between the legs.

The phone rang again. Same number. After a thug named Jayson Moore murdered his partner, Denny, in a back alley, Nick wanted to hunt the son of a bitch down, but his Commander wouldn't hear of it. Too personally involved, he said. Now he heard on the news that Moore had eluded the police, vanishing somewhere in East Texas. He didn't have a partner or anyone else to protect anymore. All he had was his guilt at not bringing Moore down, an indentation where his wedding ring used to be, an old trailer, and a barely surviving private security business. He pressed the off switch to power down the phone, tossed it on the nightstand, and rolled over.

A banging startled him awake. Nick lifted his head off a stale, damp pillow case, the bed creaking as he sat up. Three fifteen. He slipped on some shorts and checked the safety on his Glock. The banging continued, which in his trailer sounded like Thor hammering on his head.

He shouted, "Who's there?"

"Reverend Anderson."

Nick didn't know a Reverend Anderson since he had no desire to step through the transom of a church anytime soon. This had to be the same guy who called. *Why would a minister go to this much trouble to wake me up?* He held the gun behind his back, opening the door to a large black man, six foot four, dressed in tan slacks, a green polo shirt and shoes with a shine that reflected the light from inside Nick's trailer.

"Did you call earlier?"

"Yes, that was me. I need to speak with you urgently."

Nick slipped the gun behind a cushion of the built-in seat by the door. "As I told you…" He searched for the man's name.

"Reverend Anderson. I'm the paster of Victory Church in town."

"Yes, mister…Reverend Anderson. Like I said, we can talk during normal business hours."

Nick reached to close the door.

"You shut that door and you're condemning my little girl to God only knows what."

"Trust me, Reverend. It can wait until the morning." Nick pushed the door closed, but Anderson stiff armed the door open. "You don't want to go down this path, Reverend."

"I've heard what people say about you."

"So I'm the talk of the town, eh?"

"They say you're rude, arrogant and a drunk."

"Well you can tell them to kiss—"

"And that you get it done." Anderson took a step forward, placing his large frame in the doorway. "Is that correct, Mr. Sibelius. Do you get it done?"

"It's Nick. And yeah, I suppose I do." He breathed a weary sigh. "Do we really need to talk about this right now?"

The Reverend stared at him. Nick eased away from the door, nodding toward the trailer's interior. Anderson took the two steps through the opening of the trailer, ducking to avoid banging his head against the doorway.

Nick said, "I take it I'm not going to get rid of you until you tell me what's crawling up your ass, right?"

"Yeah, that's right, Nick. I need your help."

Nick looked to the right at dishes piled in the sink, empty bottles on the counter and the remains of last night's dinner still sitting on the table, and then left, to a pile of dirty clothes and towels. He grabbed a barbecue stained paper plate off the table, folding it up and placing it in the trash under the sink. "So what's this burning issue?"

"It's my daughter. She's missing."

"Call the police."

"I did. They said I need to wait another twenty-four to thirty-six hours."

Nick cleared a magazine and a couple of tee shirts off one of the seats by the dining table. He motioned for Anderson to take a seat and then sat down across from him.

"How long has she been missing?"

"Five hours."

"Five." For a father to be this worried after only five hours, the girl had to be an infant or a toddler. Anderson looked like a man in his forties, but Nick figured having a two year old could be possible. "So how old's your daughter?"

"Eighteen, going on twenty-four."

Nick leaned back, shaking his head. He had just lost a night's sleep to some conservative religious fanatic who keeps his eighteen year old on a very tight leash.

"Look, with all due respect, eighteen year olds often don't listen to their parents. She's probably out having a good time and will back in the morning. Save your money and go home." Nick stood up to usher the preacher out of his trailer and his life.

Anderson didn't move. "She met this boy, young man really, a few weeks ago. Ayisha, that's my daughter's name. Ayisha met him one day at the Starbucks on the Interstate. She works there. She came home telling me she had a date with this boy. I told her she wasn't going anywhere with any boy until I met him. Then *I'd* decide if she was going on a date. Later that week, she brings this boy home, must be in his twenties with tattoos," the pastor's voice expressed his disgust, "on his arms and neck. His name is Delton, Delton Jessup. He said he had just returned from Iraq. I told him that I appreciated his service to our country and that he needed to stay away from my baby girl."

"So you don't approve of this Delton?"

"I know this kind of boy. Some punk kid who gets in a bind dealing drugs and joins the Marines to get away from some gang banger intent on killing him. Then he comes back, all covered in macho tattoos and the confidence walking around with a rifle will give you and he thinks he can come in here and steal my little girl. That dirty, filthy..."

A rage rose up from his gut, up his chest and then squelched at his throat, filling his eyes with tears.

"He took my little girl."

"You believe Delton kidnapped your daughter?"

"Kidnapped? He stole her! He has taken her soul and filled it with filth."

The pastor, with effort, stopped himself.

"How do you know this Delton Jessup has taken your daughter?"

"Last night I heard his motorcycle. It's one of those distinctive sounding things. And when I went to check my daughter's room, she was gone. He lured her outside and took her."

Nick didn't have any kids, but he did have a younger sister. Recalling her rebellious years, this sounded more like a teenage girl infatuated with a good looking guy on a motorcycle. And her father's disapproval only made her want it more.

"Have you seen this motorcycle? Can you describe it?"

"Yes, it's a silver and black motorcycle. One of those really fast racing bikes."

"And what time did you say she probably left with Mr. Jessup?"

"Ten or ten thirty. The local news was still on, and it was just after the weather, so probably ten twenty."

Nick imagined the two had decided to get a room for the night or they hit a wall doing a hundred. Of course he knew the preacher, or any father for that matter, wouldn't want to hear that kind of news. "Maybe they had a flat tire. Or they're partying a little late."

"He took her, Nick. Yes, she went willingly, but he still took her."

"So what do you want me to do about it?"

"Find her and bring her home to me."

The boy scout in Nick wanted to tell the man once more to save his money and go home. The girl would be back in the morning, maybe with a hangover or worse, but still, she'd be back home. However, Anderson had woken him up at oh-dark-thirty in the morning, he seemed intent on spending his money, and Nick's business could certainly use the cash infusion.

Nick reached out, shaking Anderson's hand. "Okay. I'll look into it. $500 a day plus expenses."

Anderson froze mid-handshake. "Five hundred?"

"Look, you can always call the police. But if you want me to look into this, it's $500 a day plus expenses."

"Okay. Fine. Just find my girl."

3 THANK GOD FOR DUCT TAPE

Ayisha stood in the dark, empty clearing, her lover having crashed through the undergrowth in hot pursuit of whoever had been lurking just out of sight. When she first sensed danger, she had screamed, but now in the dark and the silence, she could only hear her pounding heart.

"Delton? Delton, are you there?"

Cicadas and frog calls filled the emptiness as her panic increased. Branches snapped and brush rustled as if some large creature prowled just out of sight.

"Delton? Is that you?"

A light danced through the branches.

"Who's there?"

A white man in his forties crashed into the clearing only feet from Ayisha. He spoke first. "You look a bit lost young lady. What are you looking for out here?" He lifted his flashlight to her face, blinding her.

Ayisha tried to shade her eyes from the bright light. "You've got to help us. There's someone in the woods. My boyfriend just went after him."

"You don't say."

"Yes. Please, you've got to help us. I don't know what's happened to Delton."

"Delton. That your boyfriend?"

"Please. He needs your help."

The man laughed, scanning around the bushes with his flashlight. "I doubt Carl will cause your boy much trouble. Trust me."

Ayisha, making out through the glare the form of a shotgun cradled in the man's other arm, felt a deepened level of panic. She thought she recognized the man, but she couldn't be sure, as her eyes struggled to readjust to the darkness.

"Look, I don't know who you are, but something has happened. I've been calling Delton and he's not answering."

"I'll tell you what little lady." He lowered the flashlight, looking at her as if deciding something. "Turn around."

She recalled seeing the man's photo in the local paper attached to a story about how he shot and killed a trespasser on his property. *Junior Pendleton.* He lifted the gun up in her direction.

"What? No, please. I thought..."

"You thought wrong. Now turn around or your boyfriend will be picking up little pieces of you all over these woods."

Junior pulled out a roll of duct tape from his pack, taping her mouth shut. Ayisha tried to scream, but only a muffled sound came out, cut short by a slap across her face.

"Hush up. I'm not interested in your FBI trickery, sending signals to your man out in the bushes. So be quiet or else."

Her face stung from his slap, but his words about the FBI didn't make any sense at all. As he wrapped duct tape around her wrists, her heart raced, fighting a panic building within her. With the muzzle in her back, he walked her through the undergrowth toward the pond until they found her Delton lying unconscious by a tree and a white boy, also unconscious, in some nearby brush.

Junior looked over at the white boy who appeared to be alive, his chest rising and falling.

"Carl, you stupid..."

He looked back at Ayisha.

"He's not my kid, you know. No, my brother, my dear brother Caleb kill't hisself. That boy's mama," he pointed to Carl lying unconscious in the brush, "she ran off with some rodeo cowboy and Caleb tried to dull the pain with a load of beer and a bunch of whiskey. Sonvabitch got drunk and rolled his truck. Now I've got his boy, Carl, in my business. You got kids?"

Ayisha shook her head "no."

"Figures. You FBI types probably don't have time for family. Well let me tell you what. It ain't all it's cranked up to be. I mean, look at this situation. I've got you people," he waved the gun across at Ayisha and toward Delton on the ground, "federal agents, snooping around my property and where's Carl? Face down in the dirt. I tell you, the boy makes a cedar post look smart.

He checked the man's pockets, coming up with a driver's license.

"Bet this is a forgery. You FBI people know all the tricks."

He taped Delton's wrists and ankles, as well as his mouth, and then tried to heave the dead weight onto his shoulder, only to drop to his knees under the weight, letting Delton fall back to the ground. Ayisha stepped toward Delton, but Junior had his gun back on her.

"Your boy here weighs a ton. You're going to have to help me."

He walked over to Ayisha, cutting the bindings on her wrists and then directing her at gunpoint to Delton.

"You try to run and you're dead. Understand?"

Ayisha nodded her head in agreement.

"You're going to help me get your boyfriend to the barn so we can sort this all out. You take his feet and I'll take his shoulders."

Ayisha lifted Delton by the feet while Junior cradled him around the chest holding the shotgun with both hands. Her arms burned with fatigue, but she held on, not sure what Junior would do if she faltered. Once at the barn, he bound Ayisha again, tied the two intruders to chairs and put burlap sacks over their heads. Ayisha, fear and exhaustion gripping her, the musty odor of burlap on her face, listened to Junior's footsteps move away and the steady breathing of Delton tied up in the chair behind her.

~*~

With the feds incapacitated to his satisfaction, Junior stepped out of the barn to sort out his next steps. When voices and the sound of snapping limbs had come from the woods he just knew someone was poking around in his business, looking for evidence. He grabbed a flashlight and his gun, determined to keep the trespassers away. He figured he actually had the law on his side. You just can't walk onto a man's property without permission and not expect some consequences, even if he does have a meth lab hidden in an out building and toxic waste buried throughout the property. What he hadn't expected to see was a teenaged girl in skimpy clothes. Since Waco, the Federal Government couldn't be trusted, but sending out young girls to do a man's job seemed a bit over the top, even for the feds. And the girl kept going on about Delton. Which led to the second surprise of the evening, a half dressed black man out cold on the ground and Carl knocked out just a few feet further down the trail. He wondered how on earth Carl could have knocked out both himself and a man built like a running back for the Dallas Cowboys.

Now, as he stood in the warm night air with two people tied up in his barn, the difficulties in his plan as executed to date became clear. If they were feds, he was going to have to kill them. And if they weren't feds, he wasn't sure what to do. While lately people kept dying all around him, he actually didn't like the idea of killing people outright. In his mind there was a distinct difference in walking up to a dog and putting a bullet in its head versus the stupid mutt walking in front of your speeding car. For some reason Junior found himself plagued by stupid people intent on his speeding car rolling right over them, but at least he wasn't just going around killing people for the hell of it.

As he thought about his situation he urged himself not screw this up. If his boss, Barry Swenson, got wind that he had let a couple of *federales* get in Barry's business, there would be serious hell to pay. Junior knew he had anger management issues, or at least that's what the court appointed doctor had told him, but Barry was a whole a different beast. In fact, because of what Barry had done to his half sister, Junior liked to think he had a personal obligation to one day kill the bastard and spread his body parts over the great state of Texas. However, Junior had a twofold problem with trying to kill the man right now. Barry had a crazy, vicious streak that could easily lead to Junior being buried alive, head first in a post hole. Not the best of circumstances. But more importantly, Barry provided a very generous income, which Junior could never match working the farm or even selling meth.

He needed more expertise. He needed somebody who actually liked putting bullets in dogs. Someone like Jayson Moore. Somehow, without knowing what he had done, which seemed to be an increasingly common thing with Junior, he had become friends with Jayson Moore. And when he found out the extent that Jayson was one evil sonvabitch, he threw up and then started shooting shit with his shotgun just to man up. Besides murdering a Houston cop, word was that Jayson's favorite way of killing people involved slicing them open with a box cutter, then wrapping their intestines around their neck so tight they strangled to death. The whole thing seemed a little far fetched, but Junior had no intention of discovering if he would survive such an encounter.

The other disturbing thing about Jayson was his politics. It wasn't so much that Jayson had a position, and he definitely had a position, but that he ranted on and on about all sorts of conspiracies and perils. Just last week he had been in room with Jayson, waiting to talk to their mutual boss, Barry.

"You do understand the great peril this country is under, don't you Junior?"

"Peril? You mean the liberal media, rap music, and all the Mexicans gathering at the border?" Junior didn't understand Jayson, but he did faithfully watch cable news when *Pimp My Ride* wasn't on.

"Yes, but that's only the tip of a conspiracy that has plagued our nation from the very beginning."

Jayson then began a long rant about the founding fathers, worked his way through the Revolutionary War, the Northern Aggression, which he explained to Junior was the same as the Civil War, the two World Wars, Korea, Vietnam and the Middle East to the present, identifying critical points when the nation had taken a wrong turn.

"You see Junior, I used to deal in drugs and protect my interests by busting heads as needed."

"You don't do that anymore?" Junior initially felt relieved, but then a bit confused, since Jayson was working for his boss who dealt in drugs and who also liked to bust heads.

"Yes, I still deal in drugs, but for a higher purpose. The country is broken, Junior. And Barry Swenson has the vision to fix it."

Standing outside now with two civilians, or worse, crafty *federales* tied up in his barn, Junior felt in way over his head and realized, even though the man scared him, he needed Jayson to keep this thing from blowing up in his face. Stepping onto his porch he paused at the door. Looking up to the sky where he figured the Lord lived, he prayed, "Thank you for duct tape. And if you're listening Lord, I'd appreciate it if you'd keep Jayson from stomping my ass into the ground. Amen."

4 THE RUPTURE

After the black guy in the woods gave chase, Carl, in a panic, ran like his now deceased daddy had the belt out and a drunk on. Carl's consumption of beer had slowed him down a few steps, so even though he knew every log, tree, and path through thorny mesquite, the husky breathing of what in Carl's mind was an increasingly large angry black man swiftly gained on him. He could hear the man yelling, each footfall sounding like one of those huge dinosaurs he had seen in the movies, branches snapping, briars tearing at his pant legs. He could feel the man's hands almost upon him, blood pounding in his head, lungs burning. Then as if some great African hunter fired an elephant gun fitted with a silencer from a great distance, the beast suddenly crashed to the ground, skidded across the leaf covered floor of the woods, and finally came to an awkward twisted rest against a live oak. Carl paused only long enough to see his pursuer, who appeared to be cold stone dead behind him. Turning to run, he smacked full force into a tree, falling unconscious into the thick undergrowth.

When he awoke, he found himself face down and tangled in a thick growth of brush. Tearing his tee shirt in the fight to extricate himself from the brush, he held his head in both hands in a failed attempt to keep the throbbing at bay. He looked up, but the dead body of the pursuer he heard crash behind him was nowhere to be found. The body was gone, like some goddamn zombie! In a panic he bolted upright, running blindly as fast as his feet would carry him.

Once out of the woods he wasn't sure what to do. At first he hid in a nearby shed thinking maybe he'd be safe there. A siren wailed in the early morning air, the patrol car's lights creating a kaleidoscope of colors through the cedar board slats of the shed. He felt scared, but he also felt something else, something new. Seeing that girl make love in the dirt right beside him left him feeling strong, forceful. Dangerous.

Tires screeched and doors slammed causing Carl, curled up in the dark corner of the shed, to involuntarily jump.

"Dammit!"

He didn't want to be his usual chicken shit self. No, he wanted to be a man. A real man. Rats scratched the eaves above his head, the sweet and sour pungency of manure and hay thickened the air. Carl peered across the darkness. *A real man don't hide in no shed. No sir.*

Carl stood up, bits of hay falling away, as he moved to an opening in the back of the shed. He meandered in the dark through a field to his pickup on what had been his dead granddaddy's property and then, taking the back roads, found his way onto Interstate 35 north to Dallas.

As always, this main corridor between San Antonio and Dallas, seemed like some insane parking lot in motion where the cars, only inches from each other, hurled themselves down the road at 70 miles an hour. Settling into the drive, Carl still felt the adrenaline of the evening coursing through him.

"That girl, *damn*, she was so pretty. *Jesus.* And that big ol' Marine. Shit. That ol' boy just about had my ass. Then to just up and be gone like that. I was sure he was dead. Sure sounded like some big ol' white tail buck crashin' to the ground. Wonder where he went off to?"

He pondered the disappearing Marine for some time, his mind wandering here and there until his thoughts rested on his mom. Carl loved Mama although she didn't seem to like him much. So when she ran away with the rodeo cowboy he felt a little guilty about not feeling too sad. Then his daddy up and died by flipping his pickup. When family and friends had gathered for the wake at granddaddy's, Carl had imbibed in a bit too much of Junior's hooch. It was a special batch Junior had flavored with Fredericksburg peaches. Damn, it was good. But after a mason jar or two, Carl had gotten in touch with his true feelings about his parents, how much he loved his mother, in spite of the cowboy, and how pissed off he was that his daddy left him in the lurch with a dilapidated trailer, no cable, and the rent about three months past due for the trailer park. He drove up the interstate crying, the tears making it difficult to see the traffic in front of him. Then the memories of his dear departed mother suddenly answered his question about the disappearing Marine.

"Of course! Shit! Wouldn'tcha know. The Rupture! Mama always said I was such a good for nothing that when the Lord ruptured, I'd be left holding the bag. The Rapture. That's got to be it. Sure as shit!"

Only a few miles down the road past Round Rock he realized he was angry about the Lord leaving him behind, hungry, and out of gas, so Carl pulled into a BBQ joint for some breakfast tacos and a fill up. Standing in line, a beautiful young woman with short, fine red hair stood just in front of him. She wore a bikini top, like she might be going to a lake, and cut off jeans, the threads dangling between her thighs. Carl held his breath thinking about how easily he could just lean over and kiss her soft milky white shoulder. His blood pounded. Carl felt on fire.

The girl turned, smiling. "Hi."

Carl struggled to pull back from his fantasy. "Uh, oh, yeah. Hi."

Her neck and shoulders looked so soft and the curve of her breasts reminded him of his grandmom's bone china. He imagined that if he cupped one of her breasts in his hand, he'd be able to see right through, just like one of those china tea cups.

She filled the pause in conversation, saying, "A breakfast taco is going to really hit the spot this morning."

Carl hesitated, stunned by a woman, any woman, and in this case, a really good looking woman, talking to him.

"Uh, yeah. Nothin' like breakfast tacos." Carl immediately wishing he had said something else, he didn't know what, just whatever guys who got laid all the time said. "You get taco's here often?" He felt good about having a follow up question.

"You know," the girl's eyes, emerald green, sparkled as she talked. "I stop here every time between Austin and Dallas without fail. I just have to have my taco hit and some caffeine to make it the next hundred miles. And I always get the same thing. I mean, one of these days I guess I should try something other than sausage, egg and cheese, but I get up to the counter and before I can say something else, I just blurt out sausage, egg, and cheese."

Carl, a little light headed with the rarified air of this encounter heard some of what she said. Something about tacos. But more to the point, he could feel the eyes of the others in the restaurant wondering how he got hooked up with such a fine looking woman. There was a moment of silence and the girl looked to him as if waiting for something. For a reply. Of course, a reply!

"I like the breakfast tacos here, too. Try to stop by every time I come through."

She asked, "Where're you from?"

Carl, without thinking, said, "New Sweden," immediately wanting the word back. He didn't want her to know about New Sweden, or Junior or how he shoveled shit for a living. He needed something better, something she wanted to be around.

"East of Pfugerville, right? What on earth do you do in New Sweden? I always wonder when I drive through little towns like that what people actually *do* who live there. So what do you do?"

Carl hesitated for a moment and then blurted out, "wind farmer." He had seen the title on one of Uncle Junior's farming journals. The cover had a picture of a big fan that sort of looked like the GE fan his mom had used in the trailer to keep it cool, only this one was about a hundred feet tall. He wasn't sure what "wind farming" meant, but it sounded important, hopefully important enough for her.

She frowned. "Wind farming. I figured that was more out in West Texas."

Carl knew he had made a wrong turn, his mind working to find some explanation that would make sense to this girl.

"Well, I'm not a wind farmer yet. I'm studyin' wind farmin'. Yeah, I'm a student."

"Oh. My. God."

"What?"

"You're an Aggie, aren't you." The words sounded more like an accusation than a question. "No need to lie about it. We're outside of the Austin city limits, so I guess this is neutral territory."

Carl stood still, not sure what to say. The student thing had just come to him. Being college educated seemed better than just saying he was a wind farmer, whatever that was. Now she thought he went to Texas A &M University. He wasn't sure what the A and M stood for, but he lived close enough to the University of Texas campus to know the ongoing rivalry between the Aggies in College Station and the Longhorns in Austin. He tended to root for UT because Aggie jokes always felt like they were somehow about him. She playfully punched his arm, an electric jolt pulsing through his body.

"I'm just teasing. I go to UT, so I have to give you some hell."

"No, that's OK. Happens all the time. I think folks are just a little jealous."

She laughed, turning to place her order. He liked her laugh. She was nice.

They both ordered and over the hot sauce dispenser decided to sit down together, Carl still in wonder with this woman spending time with him. The two chatted about football, the weather, the traffic on the Interstate, and then she balled up the foil which had held her taco, rising from the table.

Carl asked, "Where ya going?"

"Got to get on down the road. If I don't get to Dallas before noon my daddy will have the Texas Rangers out looking for me."

"You don't need to go right now though, do ya? I mean, we just met."

The girl suddenly looked uncomfortable, like she had just drop kicked a puppy. "Look, it was good to meet you. I enjoyed talking with you, but I need to get on to Dallas."

Carl grabbed her wrist firmly. Her eyes moistened as if the crushing pressure of his grip had squeezed bodily fluids right out of her.

"Just stay a little while longer. I think you'll change your mind."

"Change my mind about what?"

Carl briefly met the flat stare of a police officer sitting at the far end of their table. Carl eased his grip and she wrested her arm away.

"How about this?" She hissed at Carl. "How about you stay the hell away from me." And with those words she stomped off. Carl watched her leave, following the hypnotic shift of her hips as she walked, wondering how he had lost her so quickly. Left alone, he glanced back down the table. The police officer still had eyes on him.

5 A VISIT TO THE FARM

Even though Nick had been in Pflugerville for almost six months, he still couldn't get over how easy it was to get out of town. In Houston he would drive for miles and miles as the city and the surrounding suburbs sprawled out across the land. In Pflugerville, a left turn at the stop sign by the HEB supermarket led out to the east and the soft rolling farmland of the Blackland Prairie. A right took him to the highway and downtown Austin. Today he drove down a bumpy two lane road between fields of corn, stunted and dead brown from lack of water. A pendulum, a silver chain with a small St. Sebastian medallion, swung on his rear view mirror. The necklace had been Denny's, his partner on the Houston Police. Denny wasn't a Catholic, but his wife had given him the necklace "to keep him safe" just a week before the last time he'd ever see his friend alive.

As Nick's pickup rattled up to Junior Pendleton's white framed farmhouse, two ferociously barking cow dogs came running. At the front door a man in his early forties, looking like a survivor of the 1930's dust bowl, wearing worn cowboy boots, faded jeans, a soiled tee shirt and a straw cowboy hat, stood silently on the porch holding a twelve gauge shotgun. Nick cracked open his window, shouting over the sound of the dogs.

"Mr. Pendleton. Call off your dogs. I'd like to ask you a few questions."

Nick's pulse quickened at the distinctive two part sound of a 12 gauge shell being chambered. He threw the car in reverse, the big V-8 roaring, tires eating into the dirt track, a cloud of dust enveloping him, as he put the truck between himself and the shotgun. A blast, shattering the passenger side glass, sprayed across the seat, but Nick had already opened his door, rolling out onto the ground. He made his way to the back tire, listening for Junior Pendleton's position. Junior made it easy.

"Get the hell off my property, goddammit! You got no right to be here."

Crouching, Nick used the rear of the truck for cover. Junior had walked up to the pickup and, at the moment, had his head stuck through the shot out window. Nick rushed him from behind, slamming Junior hard into the truck, the shotgun firing into the ground by Junior's feet.

Junior screamed, "Sonvabitch. My damn foot. Son-of-a-bitch!"

Nick kept Junior jammed into the window, ripping the gun away from the farmer's hand. As Junior continued to struggle and curse, Nick noticed several pellet holes clearly visible in the man's worn cowboy boots.

"I don't think that's how you want to start this conversation, Junior."

"Who the hell are you?"

"Just somebody who wants to ask you a few questions. You don't mind now, do you?" Nick kneed him in the butt, shoving him deeper into the truck window, suspending Junior's feet off the ground."

"Sonvabitch. What'cha want? That thief I kill't had it comin' and the court agreed."

"Not here about a thief."

He paused struggling. "Then what are you here about?"

With Junior stuck in the window, Nick ejected the shells from the shotgun, then tossed it like a baton, end-over-end, past a barbed wire fence, while a curious shaggy brown goat looked on. He grabbed Junior by the belt with one hand and the nape of the neck with the other, hauling him out of the car window and slamming him up against the side of the vehicle. Junior's tough facade had evaporated into something like a hunted animal, eyes darting, lips quivering uncontrollably in abject fear. Nick held him in position, staring at him as if deciding whether to eat his heart right out of his chest or cook it first. Junior licked his lips, his breathing shallow.

"Mister, I didn't mean nothin' by the gun. Thought you were a thief or something."

"A thief. Driving up to your place in broad daylight and asking to talk with you."

"Well, yeah, I guess I may have overreacted."

Overreacted. Nick could understand now why Junior had so many encounters with the local police. "Junior, have you noticed anything out of the ordinary around your farm in the last few days?"

"Out of the ordinary?"

"Yeah, unusual. Like maybe some people you don't know hanging around your property?"

Junior's mouth opened, but it took awhile for words to form. "Mister, if I saw somebody, they wouldn't be hangin' around here for long." He choked down a chuckle, then offered a grimaced smile.

"So you haven't seen anyone?"

"No. What's this about?"

"Well, I imagine it will come to nothing, but a young couple disappeared last night and the young man's motorcycle was found abandoned on your property."

"A motorcycle on my property? What the hell you talkin' 'bout?"

"They got off a motorcycle, maybe walked into your woods and then disappeared. They're probably sleeping off a bottle somewhere, but I'm making a few inquiries. You wouldn't know anything about it, would you?"

Junior's eyes darted around as if he was looking for the emergency exit in a burning theater. In a desperate, high pitched voice he asked, "But why me? You a cop?"

"A private investigator. What do you know, Junior?"

Junior let out a breath, his courage coming back, "Kiss my ass, Mr. Investigator."

Nick stomped hard on Junior's pellet riddled foot. Junior cried out, collapsing into Nick's grasp.

"Aw, goddammit! Damn it to hell. Why'd you have to go do that?" He shook his head and in a whisper said, "Damn Carl."

"Carl. What about Carl?"

Junior got nervous again, the sudden burst of courage having just as rapidly retreated from him. "Nothin'. We done?"

"Were you around here last night? Say between 10 pm and 4 am?"

"I was in bed. What about you? Anyone with you last night?"

Nick realized he hadn't had anyone with him in six months of nights. "I don't have an abandoned motorcycle on my property and I'm not shooting at people for no reason. Where can I find this Carl you mentioned?"

"Carl?" Junior chuckled. "I've known golden retrievers brighter than that boy. He won't be able to tell you much of anything. Besides, I haven't seen him this morning, the lazy good for nothing…"

"Junior, three things are going to happen."

"Three? Okay." Junior kept his weight off the injured foot.

"First, if you hear anything about this couple disappearing, you're going to call me immediately. Second, you're going to pay for my window and the bodywork to get the dents out of my door."

"What? Are you out of your mind?" Nick continued to stare at Junior with an intensity wilting Junior like a plant in the hot sun. "No, right, mister. I should pay for that."

Nick glared at him.

"You mean now, don't you." Junior dug into his back pocket pulling out a black wallet that smelled something close to a dead animal. Nick forced himself not to gag, as Junior handed him a one hundred dollar bill.

Nick glared. Carl, mumbling unintelligibly while shaking his head, fished four more bills out of his wallet. "Good enough?"

Nick pocketed the money, wondering why a farmer walked around with five hundred bucks in his worn out jeans.

"And third, if you ever threaten me with a gun again, I will personally shove it so far up your ass that when it goes off you won't be able to hear the shot. Are we clear?"

"This is America, dammit. I know my rights."

Nick stood motionless, inches from Junior, staring him down until Junior looked away. "Are we clear?"

"Yeah, sure. We're clear. I've learned my lesson. You can count on me."

Nick walked back over to the shotgun, picking up the weapon, then stepped to the driver's side of his truck. "And you can buy back your shotgun on eBay."

"You can't sell guns on eBay."

Nick tossed the shotgun in behind the seat. "Exactly."

Driving away he smiled to himself. There's a certain freedom to not being a cop. If his encounter with Carl had been caught on tape in Houston, his Lieutenant would have had him directing traffic for months. More importantly, he had some information to go on now. First, a man doesn't lead with a shotgun unless he's got something to hide. Nick couldn't be sure Junior's defensiveness had anything to do with the couple, but it did make Junior a primary suspect. And second, Junior had given up the name Carl. He'd pass that on to Alice and see if she could locate him. Yes, Junior definitely had something to hide. Nick just needed to figure out what, exactly, Junior was hiding.

6 2TH 4RY—ONE YEAR AGO

Ever since Junior's brother, Calab, fatally rolled his Ford F150 into a ditch, Junior found the world increasingly just pissed him off. Instead of looking up in wonder at the occasional brightly colored hot air balloon floating over the farm, the colorful airborne behemoths created an itch that only firing his twelve gauge seemed to scratch. He found himself swerving his truck into the path of hitchhikers and cyclists just to see their panicked looks. And on occasion, he had peppered the back sides of trespassers with buck shot, including an asshole with a Confederate flag tattooed on his butt who made out like Junior was trying to kill him, or something. Then that incident with the Mexican happened. His first shot at what he figured had to be a wetback trespasser, had been fired above the man's head to scare him off. The other shots were a complete accident. Sure, he pulled the trigger, but the weight of the .45 semi-automatic in his hand, the explosive sound, and kickback of the gun led him to instinctively wince. Unfortunately, Junior hadn't accounted for the "automatic" component of a .45 semi-automatic and so, with his eyes still closed, the thing just kept firing. When the hunk of metal in his hand finally rested with an empty clip and a hot barrel, he opened his eyes to the sight of a dead man shot in the back several times, blood pooling around his lifeless body. At first he felt a rush of adrenaline, his senses sharp, each second lasting forever. Then, as the rush subsided, he thought of the man, his family, possibly a wife, maybe some kids. Junior knew he had done something he could not take back.

After the incident with the Mexican, Junior found himself once again in the wood paneled office of John Mathers' of Mathers, Smiley, and Pritcher, Attorneys at Law, who had successfully defended him regarding the hot air balloon incident and flag butt guy.

"Junior, you have got to get a grip. I got you off the hook when you shot up the balloon and the guy with a flag on his butt, but when you start killing people, its time to put on the brakes."

"I know, Mr. Mathers. I didn't mean to kill him."

"I know you didn't, Junior."

"He shouldn't have been there anyway. Damn trespasser, that's what he was and I was well within my rights. Yessir."

The attorney sat behind a large mahogany desk, a painting of Earl Campbell scoring a touchdown for the Longhorns behind him, defensive linemen straining to stop the inevitable, as a determined Campbell exploded across the line, his huge piston like thighs powering through the ultimately impotent opponent. John Mathers swiveled back in his leather chair, looking at the painting and then back to Junior, as if comparing the two. Junior figured he didn't stand much of a chance against the god-like running back from Tyler.

"Listen to me, Junior. I consider myself a damn good lawyer, but I can't get you off when you're obviously guilty as sin, over and over again. Once? Certainly. Twice? Sure. He trespassed on your property. The third time on a potential murder charge? We were lucky and I was brilliant. Four or more times in the same county? Its not going to happen. Hell, that judge sees you again for a parking ticket and I can guarantee you he'll be trying to find a way to strap you down on a Huntsville gurney and give you a lethal injection. Do you understand what I'm saying, Junior?"

"I need to stop shootin' and shit?"

"Yeah Junior. You need to stop shootin' and shit. Maybe hanging around the farm with Earl Sr. running the place and your nephew Carl doing all the work is just giving you way too much free time. If you want my advice, and you might as well take it 'cause you're paying me by the hour for it, you need to find something new to do. Go to school, start a business, do something to utilize your strengths and abilities, if you have any."

Junior left Mathers, Smiley, and Pritcher, Attorneys at Law, with the firm conviction he had to come up with some new scheme that, as Mr. Mathers suggested, would give him something else to do other than shoot at people. Then about a year ago, the kid who used to eat his own boogers in first grade, Barry Swenson, showed up like the goose that laid the golden egg. He could still remember Barry driving up to the house in a pearl white Audi TT with "2TH 4RY" tags. Even as an adult, Barry played the part of the nerd. His pants pulled up high on his waist, the dark rimmed glasses and red hair making him look like a combination book worm sex offender garden gnome. At the time, Junior didn't recognize the booger eater. Despite his conversation with Mr. Mathers, he almost unconsciously reached for his twelve gauge, rising from the porch swing, shotgun at hand.

"Do I know you? I ask 'cause if I shoot you for trespassing, my lawyer says the judge will have my ass and I want to know who to blame."

The red headed man, holding a white Panama hat, raised his hands in surrender. "Bernard Swenson. Dr. Bernard Swenson. You'll remember me as Barry. We went through twelve years of school together, Junior."

"Bernard Swenson. Barry Swenson? The booger eater?" This was the guy who had hurt Junior's sister. He rested his finger on the shotgun's trigger.

Barry grimaced, his eyes squinting. "It was a stress behavior from a difficult family life, Junior."

"Stress behavior? You should jack off like the rest of us."

"I was eight years old."

"Whatever. But really, Barry, it was nasty." His trigger finger tensed.

"I think we've spent enough time on the subject, Junior. I actually came here to talk with you about a business proposition."

Not what Junior expected. He lowered the gun slightly. "Business proposition" sounded just like the thing Mr. Mathers wanted him to do.

Junior's decision not to shoot him just yet, seemed to encourage Barry to step toward the porch.

"I understand you're working at your daddy's farm on a regular basis."

"What of it?"

"I only bring it up because, and I imagine you've been giving this some thought, there will be significant changes in your tax position once you inherit your daddy's farm. The county assessor's tax estimate on this farmhouse alone will definitely set you back a bit more significantly than your trailer, not to mention inheritance taxes, and paying off the outstanding liens on the property."

"Liens? Look I don't know who you get your information from, but when I inherit this farm I'll get it fair and square."

"No doubt. But you'll still have to pay those debts and taxes."

Junior didn't know he had a 'tax position', whatever it was. "How much we talkin' about?"

"With the lien on the farm and the back taxes, I'd estimate something in the range of $150,000."

He dropped the gun to his side. "What? I can't afford that. That's crazy!"

"Yes, quite tragic really. How a small farmer, or for that matter, an independent dentist, can survive in this economic environment is beyond me. But that's why I'm talking with you today, to give you sufficient time to build up the necessary reserve of cash. Mind if I join you on the porch? Your rocker there looks quite comfortable."

With Barry gently rocking on the porch, Junior rested his gun against the the house and grabbed a couple of cold Shiners from the ice chest he kept handy by the porch swing. Passing one to Barry, Junior, with a quick turn of the wrist, twisted the cap off the brown beer bottle, tossing it, Frisbee style, into the yard. He noticed Barry strained a bit trying to open the bottle, finally taking out a handkerchief to protect his hand and give him a better grip. Having opened the bottle, they both kicked back for a moment, enjoying the cold brew.

Junior looked out at Barry's car, once again noticing his tags, 2TH 4RY.

Junior read out slowly, "Second-th Four Are Why."

"Excuse me?"

"Tags on your titty car."

"Titty?"

"Audi TT. Get it? Titty." Junior let out a quiet chuckle at his own wit.

"What about the tags, Junior."

"It reads, Second-th Four Are Why."

Barry set his beer on the armrest of the swing. "That's Tooth Fairy. Two-T-H, Tooth. Four, R-Y, rey, Fairy. Tooth Fairy. Get it?"

"How do you get Fairy out of 4-R-Y?"

"You can only have so many letters, so it's as close as I can get. Is that alright with you?"

Junior guzzled the last third of his beer, then tossed the bottle across the yard perilously close to Barry's Audi. "Not my tag, Barry. Just wonderin' is all. So, tooth fairy, you a dentist?"

"By training, but the same pressures you feel today have destroyed what was a viable business."

"So kinda like you were sayin' to me, you inherited your dentist thing and had to pay taxes?"

"Well, no. I built my practice from the ground up. Then I had a couple of clearly passive aggressive patients sue me because of simple misunderstandings. I suppose I can't expect laypeople to understand the technical issues involved in performing a root canal."

"Root canal? What does diggin' ditches have to do with teeth?"

Barry stopped rocking.

"Surely you've heard of a root...Its a dental procedure, Junior."

"Never been to a dentist. What, did you screw it up, or something? Drill here when you shoulda' drilled there? That sort of thing?"

"I really don't think we need to go into it. Let's just say, even though they had to take nourishment through a straw for several months, root canals always come with certain risks. Both patients signed documents prior to the procedure releasing me from responsibility, but you know how crafty lawyers can be." Barry leaned forward, condensation from his beer bottle dripping on the wood porch between his legs. "Look Junior, I'm really not here to bore you with my professional challenges. I came here today with a business opportunity."

Junior let his eyes wander past the weathered porch of his white framed farmhouse, to the cedar barn across the yard and an old Ford tractor parked by the split rail fence.

"Barry, you need to look around. I ain't no dentist."

"No, no, you misunderstand. My business proposition has only the barest connection to dentistry. After the lawsuits and an unfortunate sexual harassment claim by a conniving bitch of a receptionist, my debts required I find a new direction for my entrepreneurial spirit and creativity. I call it environmental resourcing."

"Keep talkin'."

"Did you know dentists happen to be one of the most prolific users of mercury?"

"Prolific. You mean they shoot it up and shit?"

"No, Junior. Prolific, as in they use a lot of mercury in fillings. Up until six months ago, disposing of the mercury could be done rather cheaply. However, the city council added some regulations around the disposal of toxic waste and the cost skyrocketed. That's where I come in. I provide a low cost solution for my colleagues. Once I got into dental environmental resourcing, I discovered if I simply avoided some of the unwarranted government regulation and oversight, I could offer a low cost environmental resourcing solution for many small to medium businesses."

"I don't mean to be slow here, Barry."

"I'm sure you don't."

"Yeah, well, first of all, what is environmental resourcing?"

"Toxic waste disposal, Junior. Toxic waste. What else could environmental resourcing be?"

"Okay, toxic waste disposal." Junior said the words, images of comic superheroes and barrels of green radioactive sludge crept into his mind.

"Environmental resourcing, Junior."

"Okay. So this resourcing thing, how do I fit into your little scheme?"

"I'm glad you asked, Junior. One of the keys to a successful low cost environmental resourcing system happens to be an unregulated, off the grid, if you will, landfill. That's when I thought of you. Here you are working on a big farm and I know for a fact you weren't really ever into farming. Wouldn't you like to make a steady income off the land you will one day inherit, without having to lift a finger, other than keeping prying eyes away, of course?"

On the one hand Junior knew he must one day get justice for his sister against this man. On the other hand, he couldn't turn his nose up at the idea of making money without doing anything. Besides, didn't his daddy, Earl Sr., always say keep your friends close and your enemies closer? Yessir. Junior willingly shook hands with Barry, the booger eating dentist, that very day.

7 CARL SETS A NEW WORLD RECORD

Carl, stung from the girl's sudden rejection, picked up a few tall boy malt liquors to smooth over his pain. He had tried various drugs in his teenaged years when his world just seemed to be too much to handle, but he always came back to alcohol. He liked the gradual buzz to full blown drunkenness malt liquor provided. Besides, it was dirt cheap compared to the weed those two old guys sold by the BBQ joint. Opening his truck door he pulled one of his tall boys out of a bag, tossing the rest on his passenger seat. Popping open a can, he poured cool liquid down his throat, less for thirst than for effect. *I may shovel shit, but nobody's beating me in a chuggin' contest.* Before turning the key, he had already started on tall boy number two. Completely distracted by his encounter with the girl, he absentmindedly drove back to Pflugerville. By the time he reached Lake Pflugerville Park, he had downed six cold, mind numbing, pain relieving cans of malt liquor. He tossed his last empty behind the seat, his bladder urging him on with an overwhelming need to pee.

He pulled off the road coming to a halt in a small paved parking lot straddling two spaces, punctuated by his front tires bouncing up over a concrete barrier, just missing a long hair chihuahua by a couple of inches. The dog's tethered owner glared at Carl, yelling something at him about being a stupid jerk endangering Annabel's little life, but Carl, in an alcoholic haze fueled by a raging need to piss, didn't pay much attention to where or how he parked. He popped his door open, which then rebounded, slamming the door window against his head exactly where he had nailed himself with a tree the previous night.

"Shit!"

For a moment the pain of glass against skull pulled him out of his haze, but like a hiker caught in quicksand, with each movement he felt himself being pulled back down into the soft, gooey warmth of inebriation.

Stumbling across the lot he made his way to a toilet only to be distracted by a family eating lunch at a concrete picnic table under a burr oak's shade. Carl remembered his boyhood love of road trips and especially rest stops. Looking out a car window offered its own pleasures as new and exotic places like Marble Falls, Abilene and Amarillo passed by. However, rest stops always gave Carl a chance to interact with the wonders unfolding around him. Sometimes a cow or a horse would be in a field, separated from the rest stop by only a few strands of barbed wire. He used to marvel at how shit would just pop out the rear end of the beasts, while the other end ate grass as if nothing was happening.

One place he recalled had a trail climbing to a scenic view. He remembered the steps as if he ascended them right in this moment, finally reaching its pinnacle, looking out on an expanse of flat, arid desert. Opening up his fly he pulled his member out, peeing freely into hot Texas air. For a moment, standing above the vast openness of Texas, warm breezes blowing over his prick, and the intense release of what Carl imagined could be a *Guinness Book of World Records* quantity of pee, he felt at peace. A man on a mountain marking his turf in the sight of God.

~*~

Sergeant Quentin Matthews of the Pflugerville Police Department had been on the job for over five years after a stint in the Houston Police. During his time in law enforcement he had seen his share of horrors, lame excuses for speeding, and the absurdities occurring when two or more human beings gather in a single place, like the interior of a car or a rest stop. So when he noticed a man he had seen harassing a young woman at a barbecue joint down the highway peeing off a picnic table with a shocked family sitting around him, he knew today would just be another day at the office.

"Sir!" Sergeant Matthews used this same command voice to get his golden retriever to stop peeing on the carpet. "Sir, you need to get off the table. Now."

The man didn't seem to hear him, staring out into space with a goofy grin on his face and an unimaginable amount of urine continuing to gush forth from his member he held with purpose in his hand.

"Sir!"

Carl turned to follow the voice interrupting his ecstasy. "What?"

"Duck, Sammy!" A mother screamed to her ten year old boy who sat directly in the path of Carl's now pivoting penis. The boy, who had been experiencing a full body paralysis induced by the visage of a crazy drunk guy standing on his peanut butter sandwich peeing between him and his sister, Michelle, dove under their table just as a spray of urine passed overhead.

"Sir! Stop peeing!"

Sergeant Matthews clearly understood his duty to serve and protect. However, he also had just started his shift and had no intention of wearing a urine soaked uniform for ten hours. Maneuvering tactically behind Carl, he tapped the father's shoulder to move. Young Sammy crawled past him, while the mother had inserted herself between Carl, whose back was now turned to her, and her daughter. With a ferocity only hours of labor in childbirth can instill in a human being, she swung her purse, which weighed in at about fifteen pounds, at the crazed pisser's legs.

Her first blow made Carl think maybe a goat had gotten out from behind the fence and climbed to his lookout point. But then he felt an impact from the other direction and then a third time against his knee. His world began spinning, the vastness of Texas devolving into a couple of pickup trucks, several cars and a trash barrel. Holding fast to his penis, still completing the piss of a lifetime, he came crashing down in a cloud of dust, sandwiches, chips, and moon pies. Feeling the weight of something much larger than a goat, who had professionally flipped him onto his stomach and handcuffed him, Carl remembered just how much he liked moon pies.

Sergeant Matthews sat astride the drunk pisser, rising to pull him to his feet. He turned to the family, who looked shaken by the bizarre turn of their picnic, telling them he'd want a statement. He grabbed his captive by the arm, escorting him to his patrol car. Girls giggled and boys laughed, then one father, his face contorted in a combination of rage and disgust, yelled out, "Officer!" Looking straight at Sergeant Matthews, he then directed his eyes to Carl's crotch, which at this point featured a rather generously proportioned penis dangling through an opening in his jeans. Moving Carl quickly to his car, he freed him from the cuffs.

Sergeant Matthews peered into Carl's dazed face. "Why don't you stuff your prick in your pants. I think its seen enough of the light of day, don't you?"

Carl dutifully pushed his member back into his jeans, zipping up the fly.

"What, what happened? Am I under arrest?"

"Put your hands behind your back." Sergeant Matthews re-cuffed his offender.With one hand on Carl's head, he guided him into the backseat. "What happened? Well, you decided to stand on a picnic table and with your dick flying in the breeze, pee all over the place. And yes. You're under arrest."

"But..." The slamming patrol car door cut off Carl's protest.

Sergeant Matthews had seen a text his good friend Nick Sibelius' assistant had sent him about Carl Pendleton. He'd have to be sure to remind Nick to never say he hadn't given him anything lately.

8 FEELS LIKE HOUSTON

Nick drove back into town, then picked up the tollway into Austin. He expected to hear any moment from Alice about their missing motorcyclist being found in a barn somewhere. At least he'd make five hundred dollars today, not to mentioned expensing his breakfast tacos.

He pulled into an industrial park looking like the good old days were somewhere in the late 50's, or early 60's, if he felt generous. Peeling, faded paint layered in shades of blue, exposed cinderblock walls. Rusted chain link fencing, some sections topped with coiled razor wire, protected small garage-like warehouses topped with corrugated steel roofing in various states of rusted repair. He had a great rate on his lease since the EPA would be shutting the place down in nine months to begin a toxic waste site clean up. Hopefully he'd have some clients and wouldn't be glowing in the dark before the nine months were done.

Nick pulled his truck into one of three spaces reserved for him in front of the Sibelius Detective Agency, LLC. The business to one side rebuilt old fork lifts and the other, a purveyor of wholesale plumbing hardware, had recently been evicted after Austin Police found him selling kilos of weed from his loading dock. Across the road, AusTex Anachronistic Industries, Inc., made swords and armor for people who apparently liked to pretend they lived in the 14th Century. After visiting his new neighbor, Nick decided he'd take his Glock over a broadsword any day.

The door creaked open on rusty hinges. Alice Coleman stood at an ancient Mr. Coffee resurrected from a garage sale, in white go-go boots, pink hot pants, and a tee-shirt tied in a knot at her hairy midriff. The whole get-up instinctively stopped him in his tracks, then he remembered Al, or Alice, as he insisted on being called now, hadn't started hormone therapy yet. Six months ago he hired the late twenties-something six foot tall Iraq vet to be his office manager. Three months ago, Al sat Nick down to explain, while he currently had the body of a man, he knew in his heart he was a woman. The whole thing seemed a little strange to Nick, but he figured either Al or Alice could do the job, so he was okay with whichever one showed up at work. Looking at the fashion train wreck before him, Nick made a note to himself to get Alice a subscription to a women's fashion magazine ASAP. She looked up from the pot, tilting her head flirtatiously.

"Nicholas."

Nick walked in, grabbing a dinged mug off a table by the coffee pot. "No one calls me Nicholas. Not even my mother."

"I just thought, maybe, Nicholas could be our special name."

The only thing worse than Alice's feminine fashion sense had to be her coffee, which always seemed too dark and more disturbingly, thick. He poured some of her potent brew into his mug.

"Alice. We work together. My name is Nick."

She frowned, putting her hands on her hips. "You don't think I'm a real woman."

Alice had been bringing this up on a regular basis over the last several weeks, possibly because Nick had no intention of returning her affections, but more likely because her world wasn't recognizing the change she felt in herself.

"Alice, you can be whoever and whatever you want to be. I like you as a person, you do good work in the office and…"

"Yes?"

He picked up a container of powdered cream, shaking it over his mug until his coffee looked less like sewage and more like muddy river water. "I'm not into you."

"You just need time. I understand. You see a man in a dress, not the woman inside."

"Can we move on? Please." Nick moved toward his office in back.

"Sure, Nicholas, uh, Nick."

His sparsely furnished office consisted of an old grey metal desk, a brown leather swivel desk chair with a light leftward lean, and a worn wood side chair with arms darkened by decades of use. Institutional white walls stood unadorned, except for a few nails and a white board Nick had brought in a couple of weeks ago. A small wood bookcase, holding only his prized Nolan Ryan autographed baseball on the top shelf, leaned against a wall behind his desk. A two inch thick manila file sat in the middle of his desk near a small framed photo of his dog, long since dead, a Springer Spaniel named Fisher.

Alice brought Nick a file with information she had gathered on Junior Pendleton, as well as information on Carl, who turned out to be Junior's nephew. Opening Junior's file he reviewed his recent history. Pendleton Jr., known by the name Junior, had no prior record, not even a parking ticket, until his brother died. Which either meant Junior had been an upstanding citizen or Earl Sr. had the previous Pflugerville Police Chief in his pocket. The file exposed a life slipping into craziness—something Nick could relate to. A photo of a human rear end tattooed with a Confederate flag, bloodied with bird shot. From a notation Nick worked out this must have been a homeless guy wandering onto Junior's property. Then a hot air balloon basket, its wood bottom splintered from twelve gauge shot. Nick imagined the balloon pilot was grateful Junior "dove hunter" Pendleton hadn't punctured one of his propane tanks. Nothing like falling five hundred feet to a fiery death.

The last photo could have been from Nick's days on the force in Houston. In Junior's file photo, his victim lay on a barn floor, blood soaking into soil around his head and chest. Junior's .45 semi-automatic left four bloody holes in the man's neck, shoulder and back. A machete lay about ten feet away. Just from the photo Nick put together a probable scenario of Junior surprising a machete wielding thief. Given the victim had entry wounds in his back and his machete having been flung some distance away, it looked like this fellow was much more focused on running away than attacking Junior. Maybe one bullet in the back could be attributed to fear and adrenaline on Junior's part. But the second, third and especially fourth shot came from a man intent on killing, not defending. Junior must have some kind of fancy lawyer to have gotten out of it. Now two people had disappeared in proximity of Junior's recently inherited property.

Alice stood at his office door. "Call for you, line one. I think Quentin must have gotten my text about Carl."

Nick and Quentin Matthews went way back, all the way back to playing football in high school, staying connected through college, grad school, and the police academy. After the academy, they joined the Houston Police Department. Within a couple of years Nick had gotten married to his future unfaithful physician wife and was a street cop, while Quentin, following his wife, who got a gig with a start up dot com, joined the Pflugerville Police Department.

"How's the PI biz working out for you Nick?"

"Quiet and peaceful. Just the way I want it."

"So you've gone from arresting murderers and drug cartel leaders to following cheating husbands with a video camera. You do missing gerbils too? I might have something for you."

Nick knew Quentin would do anything for him, even be there for him when his life went right down the toilet. He was the one who talked him into moving to Austin. Quentin just needed a bit of banter both for old time's sake and probably thinking it would help Nick feel like his dump of an industrial park office was a career choice, not a rehab option.

"Your guy Al texted me this morning."

"Alice?"

"Yeah, whatever. Anyway, he wanted me to keep an eye out for a man named Carl. You won't believe this, but I just picked him up at Lake Pflugerville. I found him standing on a picnic table, his prick out attempting to pee into a trash barrel."

Nick smiled at Quen's description. "His little communion with nature should at least give him an overnight stay in jail."

"I'd agree, if it wasn't for the fact that at the time, there was a family of four with a six and a ten year old sitting at the table with a crazy guy standing on their sandwiches pissing over their heads."

"Any chance I could talk to him? I've got a client."

"A client? Well, that's good news."

"Yeah, thanks. Anyway, this Carl guy might know something about my case."

"He's in lock up. I'll let them know you're coming."

As Nick hung up, Alice came through, a cup of coffee in her hand. "Hey boss. You forgot your coffee." Nick hadn't forgotten, but he took the cup anyway.

"I need to go talk to Junior's nephew who's having a pajama party in lock up. Do you happen to know anyone we could bring in to nose around the area. I want to be sure this couple isn't sleeping off a party in a barn out there."

"I'm you're woman."

"You do realize you can't go tromping around fields and cow pastures in hot pants and go-go boots, right?"

"Definitely. The sun would be brutal on my skin. No, for this particular job, I'll go back to my old ways of jeans and boots." She put a finger to her chin in deep thought. "Hmmm. I might just add a tasteful scarf to contrast my cowboy hat."

"Do be careful out there, Alice. And I'm not talking about rattle snakes."

"Don't worry about me. I can be as butch as the next girl."

"Yeah, exactly what I mean. Be careful."

9 MAYBE IT WAS THE RAPTOR

Walking back to the Justice Center jail, Nick found Carl curled up in a fetal position on a cell cot. Clanging metal to metal as the cell door opened didn't rouse him from what appeared to be a very deep, restful sleep.

"Carl. Carl! Time to wake up."

Carl tightened his position around his pillow, his less conscious self not ready to relinquish control.

"Carl, wake up." Nick banged his cot a couple of times, startling Carl awake.

"What? What? Jeeze, what is it?"

"I'm so sorry Carl, did I wake you up?"

"Well, yeah." Carl pulled himself up to rest on his elbows

"I just wanted to see if we could schedule a massage for you, maybe a skin treatment."

Carl rubbed his face. "Gosh a massage would be great."

"Don't be an idiot, Carl. Have you ever heard of a prisoner getting a massage in a town lock up? Now get up. You and I have some talking we need to do."

"Sure."

Carl lifted himself up into a seated position on one side of his cot. Nick pulled up an aluminum metal chair sitting down across from him. The young man reeked of alcohol, fluorescent light or maybe Carl's alcohol levels giving him a pallid hue. Nick hoped he'd hear some good news, like "Oh, the couple you're looking for? They're asleep at my house." If only.

Carl wiped across his face with the palm of one hand. "I already told you people I didn't mean to get drunk."

"I'm not here about your urological issues, Carl. I've got a few questions for you.

"I'm sorry, Sheriff."

"I'm not a sheriff, Carl. And what are you sorry about?" Nick realized his hands had a tremor. A little too much of Alice's sludge coffee today.

"Sorry about the rest stop thing. You know, peein' on that family?"

Nick splayed his hands across his knees to steady himself, then looked directly into Carl's blue eyes. "Oh, the part where you were driving your truck down a road under the influence of alcohol, parked at Lake Pflugerville to expose yourself to children, and then urinated in public?"

Carl held tightly to his cot's metal frame, his knuckles turning white. "No! You're puttin' words in my mouth. I ain't done nothin' to children. I wasn't drunk while I was driving."

"You weren't."

"No. I was not drunk."

"So you got drunk at the park and then exposed yourself..."

Carl leaned toward Nick, his eyes filled with the panic of a trapped animal. "No! I got drunk while I was drivin' down the highway and then I pissed all over...I mean I stopped to go to the bathroom." He paused, then sat back, resignation seeping into his words. "Only I missed."

"By about twenty five yards, Carl."

Carl fidgeted nervously, wrapping his arms around his chest, his hands tucked into his armpits. Nick stared at him silently until the young man squirmed. "Son, you are in a heap of difficulty."

Carl looked weary from his adventures. "I know. I know. She just made me mad, treating me that way. I got upset and yeah, I guess I drank too much. But Sheriff..."

"Nick."

"Yeah, okay, Nick. It was all an accident. I didn't mean to do it."

Nick's senses immediately heightened when Carl mentioned a girl.

"Why don't you tell me what you didn't mean to do, Carl."

"I didn't mean to drink so much."

"No, I mean with the girl. What didn't you mean to do with her?"

"The girl? I didn't get to do nothin' with her. She blew me off and just walked away."

"When did this happen?"

"This morning, at the barbecue place off I-35 goin' outta town. Ask your cop friend, who, by the way, put those handcuffs on kinda tight. He saw me."

"So your drinking and the excitement at the park had to do with this girl you met at a barbecue joint?"

"Yessir."

Nick, knowing Carl's alibi could be easily checked, felt some relief. Maybe his couple would still be found alive and unhurt. Of course Carl might be telling the truth about the girl this morning, but what about last night.

"Where were you last night Carl, between 10 pm and 8am?"

"I was at my trailer alone. Watched some TV, had a couple of beers, then went to sleep."

Nick had no way of knowing if Carl had been in his trailer or not, but he decided to wind him up a bit, just to see if something broke loose. "You're lying to me Carl."

"But I was in my trailer."

"I'm going to ask you for a DNA sample Carl. When I get a match and know for certain you're lying to me right now, I will personally hunt you down." He, of course couldn't ask Carl for anything and he didn't have any DNA evidence, but since Carl seemed to think he could, Nick played the card.

"A match. A match to what? I told you, I didn't meet that girl until this mornin'."

"I have a feeling Carl you were busy in the woods last night. Sound familiar?"

Carl looked shocked, blood draining from his face, then flushing red again, resignation overwhelming him. "Aw hell! I'm goin' to hell, aren't I? Just like my mama said. 'Put that thing back in your pants,' she said. 'God in Heaven, are you some kind of pervert?' Daddy beat the crap out of me for that one. But I don't know, I have these urges. You know, Sheriff?"

Nick wished he had no idea what Carl was on about, but he had urges too. Yes, indeed.

"I don't have no regular girlfriend, so I just gotta, you know... How'd you get hold of my jizz anyway?"

Nick had to keep from smiling at Carl's notion of a police evidence bag of his semen. "I'll ask the questions. You sticking with your story or are you going to tell me the truth? Believe me Carl. The truth may not set you free, but it will certainly reduce your jail time."

Carl looked up at the ceiling, either to pray to Jesus or stare into bright fluorescent lights. "Okay, I was in the woods last night."

"And?"

"And I jacked off. Is choking the chicken a crime now?"

"It is if you kidnap and kill two people in the process."

"What?" He rose off the cot.

"Sit down, Carl."

He lowered himself back down. "No, no I have nothin' to do with any killin'. I don't know what happened to them, but I didn't do it!"

Them. Finally, Nick felt like he might be getting somewhere with Carl. "Them? So what did you see in the woods last night?"

Carl began rocking back and forth in his cot, springs creaking with each movement.

"Come on, Carl. What did you see?"

He stopped rocking, taking a hard swallow. "Okay. There was this black couple. Real cute girl. And the guy was pretty ripped."

"What happened, Carl?"

Carl nervously picked at his fingernails, staring intently at his work.

"I know this is difficult for you Carl, but we're going to sit here until you tell me what happened."

"It's embarrassin'."

"I've heard it all. Trust me." Actually Nick hadn't heard it all, and those times he had heard it, he usually wished he hadn't.

Carl hesitated, then looked up. "Okay. I've got a place in Uncle Junior's woods. A little clearing all my own where nobody can bother me." Carl looked to Nick for confirmation.

"I can understand why you'd want your own private space, Carl."

"So I'm walkin' near the woods last night when I hear this motorcycle stop, the two voices come toward my place. I hid a few yards away in some brush. The guy put down a blanket and they spent some time just lookin' at stars. The girl was really cute. I liked her."

"Then what happened?"

"He started takin' her clothes off. She wanted it. It wasn't a rape or nothin'. They were doing it right there in front of me." Carl leaned back, his eyes closed, savoring his memory. "Man, she was so pretty. I've never seen a black girl naked. It was just, I don't know, I just..."

"You decided you wanted some."

"Well yeah, I wanted her. I didn't mean to hurt nobody. It's just she was so pretty and I'm so, well...so alone."

Nick could hear tumblers on the combination lock of this case begin to fall into place. "How did you hurt her Carl?"

"I guess watchin' her do it. That's not right, is it?"

"No, that's not right, Carl. But why don't you tell me what else you did to hurt them. Did they hear you? Did they catch you and you had to keep them from talking?"

"What? No!" Carl looked around his cell nervously. "They heard me, but like I said, the guy was really ripped. Had a marine tattoo. I'm a little slow, but I'm not goin' to take on a nekked Marine in the woods."

"So what happened then, Carl? You just let them go?"

"The Marine? He chased me. I heard the girl screaming and then everything went silent."

"What do you mean everything went silent?"

"I mean he was crashin' through the woods about to kick my sorry ass with his girl standing there screaming, when he got kill't. And then I ran into a goddamn tree."

As quickly as Nick had sensed victory, the combination had been spun again by some hidden hand. "Slow down, Carl. What happened to the Marine? Are you saying the man died? How do you know?"

"Like I said, I'm runnin' like a dog with my ass on fire when I hear him crash to the ground. Musta tripped on a rock or somethin' and well, I ran into a tree. Knocked me cold out. When I came to, the woods were silent and the Marine was gone. Gone! I'm tellin ya, I've never seen anything like it. Gone!" He wiped a hand down his face with a deep sigh. "At first I thought zombies."

"Zombies." Nick tried to push back the image of a zombie Marine, eyes wide, arms outstretched, roaming the woods. "Come on, Carl."

"No really, Chief. I mean the guy's dead as road kill, then he just walks away? But then I remembered my mama. She used to go on and on about the Lord rupturing."

Nick paused a beat. "Help me out here, Carl. What are we talking about?"

"Maybe it was the raptor. Yeah, that's what Mama used to go on about. The raptor. You know?"

"The raptor?" Nick knew for certain Carl's mom hadn't been admonishing her boy about extinct dinosaurs.

"Mama always said I was a good for nothin' and when the Lord came I'd be standin' there in a field and she'd be going on to heaven." Carl paused, letting out a deep breath. "I guess she was right."

"The raptor? Do you mean the Rapture, Carl?"

His eyes lit up with recognition. "Yeah, the Rapture!"

"That's your story? You're standing in the woods and the Rapture occurs."

"I'm telling you the truth. One second he's about to kick my sorry ass and the next second he's gone. Gone! It's the god's honest truth. May Jesus and all the angels strike me dead if I'm lying. He was gone!"

Nick rose from his chair. "I tell you what. While you're waiting for whoever's going to bail you out of jail, think about your story." He put a business card in Carl's hand. "If you think of anything, Sgt. Matthews will let you call me." Nick moved to the cell door.

Carl sat back up grabbing a pillow from his cot. "Hey, Nick?"

Pulling the door open, Nick looked over to Carl.

"I guess at least I won't be in hell by myself."

"How you figure, Carl?"

"Well, the Lord took all the good people, so you must be bad like me. I guess we'll be in hell together."

Nick started to tell Carl to shut up, but then on second thought, he realized Carl had a point. Even though he didn't believe for one second the Rapture had or would ever occur, if there was a God and a Rapture happened, given his current track record, he'd probably be left behind with all the other losers. He had let his partner get killed, watched his wife leave him, and forced his boss to fire him. He either had some really bad karma, a run of bad luck, or maybe Carl had it right.

"Maybe so, Carl. Maybe so. Try to stay away from the malt liquor for a few days, okay?"

Nick let the door shut behind him, sensing his easy money case turning ugly right in front of his eyes.

10 JAYSON'S ADVICE

Junior's hip and back ached from being shoved into the window of Nick's car. His right foot throbbed from several pellets he had to pry out of his flesh with a cork screw and a pen knife. He poured some whiskey on his wound to keep it clean and the rest of the bottle down his throat to settle his nerves. He had a private investigator nosing around, a hole in his foot, and Jayson Moore driving up to his house in an enormous black pickup. And if this gun snatching investigator could be believed, he had two civilians, and not two federal agents in his barn. This day was not going well.

The big hemi engine of Jayson's enormous black Dodge Ram truck rumbled as he came to a stop beside Junior's house. He opened his door, making the three feet down from his perch in one leap, the ground thudding under his weight. Jayson, with his shoulder length blond hair, bulging muscles, and bulbous beer gut, looked like a knocked up professional wrestling action figure. His grungy dirt colored tee shirt displayed the wonders of modern textiles, the fabric contorting around solid, ripped biceps, and straining to hold Jayson's generous gut at bay. Junior had no way of knowing, but he suspected Jayson kept a loaded .38 hidden under a fold of his stomach. He had called the beast, Jayson, for help, but his own stomach ached just thinking about the blood curdling mayhem which followed Jayson around like the Tasmanian Devil Junior used to watch on Saturday morning cartoons.

The beast spoke, "What's the story, Junior."

"Well, like I said on the phone, I've got this couple…"

"I know all about your couple, Junior. What do you want to do about it?"

Junior took a step back, confused. "That's why I called you, Jayson. I figured you'd know what to do."

He frowned with a shrug. "Shoot'em and dump the bodies."

"What? Well, I suppose I could, but I'm not altogether sure who they are. Isn't there something about killing cops. I was watching one of those crime shows last night where this guy kills a cop. Dumbest damned thing he could have done. Had the whole police force after his ass."

Jayson glared, his hands on his hips, which were way too close in Junior's mind to the imagined .38 under Jayson's stomach.

With an urgency in his voice, Junior said, "I'm not talking about you. No, you were righteous in killing your cop. Definitely. What I mean is, if these two are *federales* and I kill 'em, then I'll bring the whole FBI down on us."

"Then leave 'em tied up in your barn. They'll die eventually."

"I can't. I've already got some private investigator snooping around. I think he's some kind of undercover cop, too. Texas Rangers or some such. No, I need to get them away from here. "

"Then take them to Barry's compound. He'll sort it out."

The compound was one of Barry's properties east of Austin hidden in the piney woods. Besides his meth operation, Barry's compound had a hanger which would provide an out of the way place to hide two FBI types until he could figure out what to do. Hiding them away was the upside. Of course, Barry seeing two feds in his hanger was the downside. Junior consoled himself with the notion he was showing some initiative. *Yessir. Barry's gonna see me taking care of business.*

They hitched the trailer, which Junior most recently used when he was painting houses the previous year, to Jayson's truck. Under Jayson's direction, Junior had loaded his captives into the back, keeping the vents open so he wouldn't succumb to paint fumes. Jayson agreed to haul the trailer over to Barry's compound, depositing Junior's prisoners in the hanger, while Junior stayed behind to clean up any evidence on his property. When he finished, Junior opened up a new bottle of Jack Daniels for breakfast. The gold liquid burned his throat going down and a familiar calmness settled over him like a morning fog settles on a pond.

11 FISHING LUNATIC

Harlan Jones was a "goddamn fucking fishing fanatic"—or at least his ex-wife thought so, screaming at him while she tossed out his clothes, box of blues vinyl LPs, sleeping bag, 12-gauge shotgun he got for his eighteenth birthday twenty years ago, and a black velvet painting of a joint smoking Willie Nelson wearing a red bandana. But most hurtful in the "tossing all of his shit in the yard" extravaganza occurred when Dolores screamed, what Harlan considered to be true words about his fishing addiction, but in a very negative tone. Then to heap pain on his hurt feelings she tossed his graphite rod with titanium guides and prized spinning reel with graphite body and stainless steel bearings, into the air. He had to literally do one of those horizontal dives like Ricky Williams used to do when he'd catch a pass to score a touchdown for the Longhorns. He did manage to catch his reel before her beautifully constructed aluminum and graphite body hit his driveway. Unfortunately, Harlan took the brunt of his driveway's rough concrete nature, scrapping up his forearms pretty good. He still lay prone holding his precious reel when his now dead daddy's tackle box landed on his back, popping open, scattering more treble hooks and spinners than God had ever intended one man to lie amongst.

Driving away in his 1993 Ford Bronco, Harlan couldn't believe how long it had taken him to extricate himself from the minefield of lures, hooks, and other sharp implements of his craft. At least Dolores had slammed the door shut, so he didn't have to listen to her go on anymore. He had tossed all of his belongings into the back of his Bronco, heading off to where, he didn't know. Then the idea for doing a little fishing on a Saturday morning came to him the way Galileo figured out the Sun sat in the middle of our Solar System as depicted on the Discovery Channel. He decided right then and there to swing over to Junior's fishing hole, figuring since Earl Sr. had died in an unfortunate power take-off accident, and Junior didn't pay much attention to his farm anyway, he'd pretty much have the run of the place to fish for a big lunker bass he just knew had to lurk somewhere in those dark waters.

Working his way through the woods he finally reached the pond's shore, its surface calm and still in the morning air. He leaned his rod and reel on a nearby tree, then set down his tackle box, which now had a new dent, thanks to Dolores. Harlan grimaced to see a jumbled mess of tackle in what normally was a very neat, organized display of bobbers, lures, sinkers, hooks, and line.

"Damn, Dolores."

He searched through his box until he found a nice purple rubber worm, a hook impaling the serpent through one end, coming out about a third of the way down, and then curling back towards the head with its point imbedded in the worm's body to keep it from snagging on every weed in Junior's pond. Harlan unclipped a swivel hook already tied to one end of his monofilament line, attaching the purple weapon he would use to lure his lunker from the depths. Standing on the pond's shore, he gracefully flipped his rod, the worm arcing across a glassy surface, landing with a plunk beside a stand of grass peeking out of the water. A shotgun shell being chambered broke the peace. Harlan turned to see Junior standing about ten feet away, looking at him intensely, as if Junior was trying to burn a hole through him with his mind.

Harlan turned to his childhood friend. "Why hey, Junior. I didn't see you standing back there."

Junior stared at him.

"I guess you're wondering what I'm doing on your property this fine Saturday morning."

Harlan looked to see if he had guessed Junior's agenda correctly. Getting no feedback, he decided he better just keep talking.

"Normally I wouldn't just walk onto your property like this Junior, it's just that, it's just that, well, you know Dolores?"

Still no response from Junior.

"Dolores, she's my ex-wife. Well sort of. See we got ourselves a divorce 'cause I guess I'm a bit of an ass hole and she's definitely a bitch. So we got this divorce, but then I guess you know that. Well, after about six months, she took me back in. Love is a strong bond, ain't it, Junior? Anyway, I moved back in, 'cept once I was there, I remembered the only good thing about Dolores was the sex. Otherwise she's harping on me about this and that and the other. The kind of thing that can just break a man down. So I packed up my stuff all orderly like and left. She was crying and wailing, trying to take my stuff back into the house, but I just told her a man cannot be disrespected like that. Right, Junior? I—"

BOOM!

The explosion from Junior's gun so startled Harlan he dropped his rod on the ground, leaping about a foot in the air.

"Jesus, Junior! What the hell! I don't mean no harm. Look, I'll just pack up my shit and get on my way. Jesus! Scared the holy crap outta me."

Junior chambered another round. "What you nosin' around my place for? Who put you up to it?"

"Nosin' around? What the hell you talkin' 'bout? Like I said, Dolores tossed my ass out of the house and I just decided to do a little fishin'."

"Bullshit. Who you with? EPA? FBI? Some damned UT professor? Those people who chase whale boats?"

"Junior, I don't know what you're smokin', but I definitely want some. I have no idea what the hell you're talkin' bout. There's not a whale around here for miles." He pondered the whale thing for a moment. "Wait a second. Is 'whale' code for lunker?"

"I'm not messin' around Harlan. I don't care if we've known each other since elementary school, I'm goin'a count to three, so you had best start talkin' or I'll be dragging your dead carcass to a shallow grave. You understand?"

"Junior, Junior. Calm down man. Like you said, we go way back. No need to start shootin' and shit." Harlan decided maybe reminiscing about old times might lower the volume on this situation. "Hey, remember Emily in the second grade?"

"Emily? Sure I remember Emily. She was pretty at eight and downright illegal in her twenties."

"No shit, Junior. Hey, remember the time you put that big ol' earthworm on her plate at lunch and she off and walloped you? Damn! I can still hear the smack!"

"Oh, I remember, Harlan. Even at eight she was tryin' to fight her primal attraction to me."

"Primal attraction?" Harlan laughed. "She pretty much succeeded, didn't she? I mean she married Colson, the quarterback, remember?"

Juniors eyes narrowed. "I know what position he played."

"I didn't mean nothin' by it Junior. Just saying he's the guy she married. I hear he's some kind of heart doctor or somethin'."

Junior moved his hand closer to the trigger. "Why we talkin' 'bout Emily, Harlan?"

"I don't know. Just standin' here with you made me think of old times. All the good times we've had over the years."

"So the first thing you think about is some girl who wouldn't give me the time of day my entire life? Jesus Christ, Harlan. What kinda friend are you?"

"You're the one pointin' a gun, Junior. We are friends, right?"

"Up until the point where you started nosin' 'round my business for the EPA or some such shit."

"Junior, I don't know nothin' 'bout any EPA. Like I said, Dolores kicked my ass outta my house this morning, so I thought I'd do some fishin'. You know. Calm the soul."

I'm countin' to three Harlan. Start telling me the truth or start dying. Your choice."

"Junior..."

"One."

"Come on Junior. I don't know what you're talkin'bout."

"Two."

Harlan looked desperately around for an escape route, but he realized Junior would be able to cut him down any direction he went, unless...

"Three!"

Harlan dove for the water just as Junior reached three. Sinking underwater Harlan could barely hear the muffled sound of Junior's shotgun, as pellets sprayed across the pond's surface. At the same moment, a six pound lunker bass attacked Harlan's purple worm, the fish's swift movement to deeper water firmly embedding the hook in his jaw, as the weight of rod and reel dragged behind. Harlan tried to swim underwater, convinced Junior would blast him if he surfaced. Moving through the water, his clothes and boots weighing him down, his mind wandered to the world of the fish he had spent many of his thirty eight years hunting down. Eyes open in green hued surprisingly translucent water, he came to a firm conclusion he needed to definitely use silver spinners to get those lunkers to pay attention. Suddenly a big bass swam right by him, a purple worm dangling from his jaw. *My lunker! Goddamn, I caught my lunker!* Letting out a holler, he instead, took in a lung full of pond water, bringing a level of panic to his chest. He flailed to reach the surface, but the damn hiking boots Dolores had given him last Christmas were so heavy he might as well have had weights tied to his feet. His lungs, now completely full of water, burned. Blood pounded in his head. He looked up to the surface above to see his lunker bass, still holding his worm, swimming free from his line. Harlan couldn't believe he had somehow lost his lunker. Then his mind went blank and the pond embraced him.

~*~

Junior stood at water's edge looking for his longtime friend to surface, enjoying how effectively he had just scared the holy crap out of Harlan. He considered those thoughts for a minute, then two, then three, until he realized Harlan might not be coming to the surface at all.

"Sonvabitch. Gawddamn it!"

Junior paced the shoreline, scanning for Harlan to break the surface, cussing at Harlan for scaring the hell out of him. They'd go out for a beer and Junior would make things right.

"Harlan! Damn it! Come on man, float." The surface remained calm and smooth. "Shit. Harlan."

Junior tossed his gun to the ground, squatting by the edge of the pond, holding his head in his hands.

"Jesus, Harlan, I weren't goin' to shoot you, you stupid sonvabitch. Harlan?"

Junior couldn't believe Harlan, his friend since elementary school, might be lying at the bottom of his pond by now. Dead. Memories flooded over him of shooting spit wads in school together, beating up some new kid who moved in from New York or Boston or wherever, double dating, smoking weed, those fishing trips they took, and the time they both made out with Suzy Holmes in the cab of his Daddy's Ford F150, at the same time. Damn! Tears welled up in Junior's eyes as the reality of his loss took hold of him. He sat in the dirt crying for some time.

Then anger replaced his grief.

"Why is everyone intent on totally screwing me over? First that damn Mexican with the machete turns his back just as I decide to shoot him in the chest. Should have been pure self defense, but instead that asshole made it look like I tried to murder him. Next, Daddy doesn't have the good sense to keep his balance when I pushed him into a power take-off. If Daddy hadn't been such a stick in the mud about my business I wouldn't had to fight with him in the first place. Then a couple of FBI agents start creeping around my woods forcing me to kidnap them. Now Harlan," grief crept back into his throat, "Harlan has managed to drown hisself. Shit."

Junior realized he was having a really bad run of dharma, farma, karma. Whatever the hell that eastern hocus pocus was, he was having a bad run of it. He waited by the pond for another ten minutes on the off chance Harlan floated. Then he tossed Harlan's tackle box into the water, figuring if the cops ever found Harlan's body, they'd assume the old boy had committed suicide in deep despair over Dolores kicking him out of the house.

The pond's glassy surface exploded, a huge big mouth bass leaping skyward. Junior could have sworn a purple worm dangled from the lunker's gaping jaw.

12 CRAZY WILD

Returning from the Justice Center, Nick pulled his rental car into a convenience store near Main Street for some gas.. One pump over he noticed the soft curves of a woman's rear end filling out a pair of jeans. His eyes scanned up her hip to a tight fitting tee shirt flowing above her waist, then to dark brunette hair falling to the middle of her back. She looked over, as if sensing his attention, offering a playful smile, then turned her attention back to the business of filling her blue Prius with gas. Nick, momentarily forgetting why he stood in the middle of a convenience store parking lot, startled to an ad for liter bottles of Pepsi blaring loudly from a speaker by his pump. He fumbled for his credit card, pushing buttons on cue, then placed the nozzle in his rental's gas tank. He looked back across to her pump again, a blue Prius still in place, but the dark haired woman no longer there.

He finished pumping gas, then went inside the store. On his way to the beverage case, Nick spotted her again, this time holding an empty coffee cup by a coffee maker. He didn't want a cup of coffee, but he still found himself standing beside her, pulling a cup from its dispenser. Without looking in his direction she said, "I wonder which of these pots is the freshest."

"Good question. Of course, drinking Alice's coffee, I don't think I could discern good coffee from bad anymore."

She chose a pot on her right, lifting a glass carafe from its burner. "You shouldn't talk about your wife like that."

"Oh, he's not my wife. If I was talking about my wife, well my ex-wife, I'd be saying worse things than criticizing her coffee."

"You call him your wife. That's really sweet. I always thought 'partner' seemed a little too generic for love."

"What? No. I'm not... My office manager—he's a woman. So is my ex."

Nick didn't know how he had gotten himself into this Mobius of a conversation.

"Actually, see, my office manager was a man…"

She pour coffee into her cup, then stirred in some sugar with a straw. "It's okay. Really. I don't need to know the details. I'm a 'live and let live' type of person. So whatever you're into, no need to explain."

"No, I just don't want you to have a wrong impression."

She snapped a white plastic lid on top. "Oh, about your girlfriend's coffee. Maybe you could buy her a good coffeemaker?"

"He's not my girlfriend. I mean *she's* not…"

She placed a hand on Nick's arm. He felt an electricity of her touch through his shirt sleeve. Even dull fluorescent light danced in her hazel eyes.

"Really, it's okay."

Then she stepped over to the counter, paid for her coffee, and walked out the door. Nick stood by the coffee maker, stunned by how badly his attempt to meet this woman had gone. Before his ex-wife, he had been capable of engaging women in meaningful conversations. Somehow his plan to take advantage of this serendipitous meeting had turned into a failed explanation of how the man who is his office manager is not his girlfriend. He set his empty cup back down, then scanned the refrigerated case, pulling out a bottle of water. A chunky man in a corporate blue vest stood behind the counter, ringing up Nick's purchase.

"Struck out there, eh, man?"

"What? Oh, yeah. I guess I did."

"I think you lost her when you started talking about your girlfriend. Probably a bad move."

Nick looked at the pasty white man with tattoos running down both arms. He imagined the guy hadn't had a date in awhile. Then he noticed a gold wedding band.

"Married?"

"Yeah, ten years tomorrow. Best damn thing I've ever done."

"Ten years." Nick and his ex had only managed eighteen months. "Good for you."

"Thanks, man. Have a good one."

As Nick turned to walk out the door, the cashier said, "Hey, don't take it too hard. When you find the right lady you don't have to have the right words. Trust me, man. Love is just crazy wild like that."

"Yeah, thanks. Crazy wild."

13 TAKING A RIDE

Delton's conscious awareness shifted from running in the woods, the sounds of his quarry crashing through undergrowth to total darkness to an enclosed feeling of something smelling like gun oil covering his face. His heart pounded with labored breathing. A hard, cold surface slapped against his back. For a moment he kept running. Best to stay moving. Don't let whatever was happening get a lock on him.

Slowly his body gathered new data. He must be on his back. Something cold and hard. A shed? No, there's movement. A van. Maybe a trailer. He tried to reach for his face, but his hands were bound behind his back. Panic rose up to his chest as he writhed in place to no effect. *Ayisha. What about Ayisha?*

"Ayisha. Are you there? Ayisha."

Someone moaned nearby. The surface he lay prone upon bounced, slamming his head hard against it. The stunning blow interrupted a panic, as if someone had hit the pause button. He took a few deep breaths. Paint fumes left him dizzy. An engine rumbled. Radials on asphalt sounded like a needle caught at the end of an old vinyl LP. Another moan to his right.

"Ayisha?"

"Delton? Are you okay? I thought you'd never wake up."

"What's happening Ayisha? The last thing I remember is the woods."

"Its been hours, Delton. A man kidnapped us. We've been tied up in his barn for at least a day. And now..." Ayisha's voice trailed off.

Delton spoke into darkness feeling his hot, moist breath inside whatever covered his face. "Are you okay? Are you hurt?"

"I don't know. I don't think so. Delton, what's happening?"

"I don't know. Are you tied up? Do you have something over your head?"

"Yes." She took in a deep breath, then exhaled. "Delton, I saw the man who did this. It's Mr. Pendleton. Junior Pendleton. He locked us in his barn for awhile, then put bags over our heads and put us in the back of this trailer. Delton..."

He could feel a panic he had just brought under control in himself beginning to well up inside the girl.

"We're okay, Ayisha. I don't know what's going on, but I'm not going to let anything happen to you."

"Delton..."

He shifted his body across the floor toward her voice until he came in contact with what he assumed was Ayisha. At his touch she screamed, writhing to get away from what she could not see.

He spoke calmly. "It's okay, Ayisha. It's me, Delton. Shhh. You're okay. It's me."

She stopped her desperate struggle, gasping for air through her hood. "How can we be okay? We're all tied up. Mr. Pendleton, he had a gun. Why would he do this?"

"I don't know."

They sat together for a few minutes, the contact of their bodies giving each a thread of reality to grasp, while a roaring sound of the vehicle's engine provided a soundtrack.

"Ayisha. I don't know what's happening, but you have my word. As long as I've got breath in my body, I will never let anyone hurt you."

Delton felt her rest her head on his shoulder, the warmth and fragility of her body heightening his instincts to protect her.

"I know you will, Delton. I do."

Time passed, Delton couldn't be certain how long, until the vehicle turned off an asphalt road onto a dirt track. He could hear rocks and dirt kick up in the wheel wells as they bounced, sometimes violently, back and forth in their metal prison. Then they stopped, the engine shut off, doors slammed, a door latch beside them let out a hollow metallic sound, and warm, humid night air enveloped them.

14 EARL SR.

Leaving Harlan to the fishes, Junior jumped in his pickup to get to Barry's compound, hoping all would be right once Barry realized moving his feds off Junior's farm was in everybody's best interest. Being an environmental resource executive carried with it more responsibility than Junior had ever had or actually wanted. He had imagined his life getting simpler as money and women gathered at his doorstep. Instead, his world just seemed to get more complicated with each passing day.

The first few months of being in business with Barry went off without a hitch. Every other day Barry would come by with a barrel of "environmental resource" gathered from his many clients, hand Junior a hundred dollar bill, and Junior would move Barry's barrel to a secluded part of his Daddy's farm. Then one day at the Bluebonnet cafe, he heard some guy talking about how cops were spotting marijuana fields with airplanes. Upon hearing the news, he made a point of planting his weed in smaller, harder to find plots. He also realized a bunch of barrels in the middle of a field might be a bit too obvious. In a lucid moment he came up with what he considered to be one of his best ideas, namely rolling the barrels into a livestock water tank. Unfortunately, the first barrel floated, necessitating a revision to his original plan. Then Junior came up with his second best idea — punching holes in the barrels in order to fill them with water until the steel drums willingly sank. For a moment he considered how putting holes in his barrels might leak "environmental resource" all over the place, which he figured couldn't be a good thing. But since he didn't have a better idea, he went with his instincts.

Everything went smoothly for a few weeks until Earl Sr. began sniffing around, finally confronting Junior in their barn just as he got back from brush hogging the south pasture.

Earl Sr. raised his voice over the rumble of his still running tractor, "Junior, I went out to the stock tank for a little fishing yesterday and found all of our fish belly up. At first I thought there might be something leaching into the tank."

Junior shifted nervously. "Leaching into the water? I doubt it."

"Then I found a pile of barrels out in one of our fields while I was checking the fence line today. So I need you to be on the lookout. Some sonofabitch who thinks he can dump his crap on my property has something else coming."

"What you goin' to do, Daddy?"

Earl Sr. tapped a wrench in the palm of one hand. "Well first off, I'm going to call the police. Then I'm going to have those barrels hauled off my property."

"You don't want to call the police, Daddy. No need to get them involved."

"Why the hell not? What, you want me to just let some lowlife dump garbage on my land. For all we know it's some kind of toxic waste."

Junior stood up straight, taking a step toward his father. After all, he was a successful businessman now. "Maybe people need to have a place to dump their toxic waste, I mean their environmental resources. Have you ever thought about that? Maybe they're willin' to pay a good price to get rid of it."

Earl Sr. tossed his wrench into a grey toolbox sitting by his tractor. "Environmental resources? What are you saying, Junior? You saying you dumped toxic garbage on my property?"

The boy in him wanted to step back, but the environmental resource executive in Junior held his ground. "I'm saying you need to get with the times, Daddy. While you slave away growing corn or sorghum or cotton, I've found a way to make money without hardly workin'. Did you know dentists use a lot of mercury?"

Earl Sr. stood firm, hands on his hips. "I can't believe the words coming out of your mouth, son. My father's father worked this land. I've put my entire life into keeping this farm alive. And now my son, my very own blood, stands before me talking about making money by storing toxic waste on land that has provided crops and income to several generations of Pendletons?"

Standing with his back to the tractor he poked Junior firmly in his chest with an index finger, emphasizing each syllable of his rage. "You're here to tell me you're dumping toxic waste on my land, without my permission?"

"It's as much my land as yours, Daddy. I'm your only son. It's gonna be my land one of these days. And it's not toxic waste. It's environmental resources!"

"So you think being my son gives you the right to poison our land?"

"Poison? You just don't get it, do you Daddy? You're just an old farmer set in his ways. I'm talking about the future."

Earl Sr. pushed Junior away. "Get out of my face, you ungrateful..."

Junior felt a coiled spring of rage suddenly unwind within him against the man who made his Mom run off with a vacuum cleaner salesman because Earl Sr. kept his half full chewing tobacco spit can on the coffee table, leaving Junior alone with his Daddy, trapped on this damned farm. The rage exploded from his gut, through his chest, and down his arms. He gave Earl Sr. a mighty push. The force of Junior's shove took Earl Sr. off his feet, slamming him against the running tractor. Without warning, his jacket caught in the rapidly spinning power take-off. Junior saw his father instantly realize the danger, glare fiercely at his errant son, and then acquiesce to the physics of farm machinery. Junior turned his eyes away, hearing only a single resigned "damn" and then a sickening thud, thud, thud, thud, thud, thud of his daddy's body spinning and slapping the ground like so much meat on a spit.

Junior had definitely meant to hurt his Daddy. He just didn't mean to hurt him quite so much or so permanently. However, once Rev. Hatcher had buried Daddy's bits in the family plot, Junior realized he had finally come into his own as both sole owner of the family farm and a 21st century environmental resource executive. Everything seemed to be falling into place, finally.

Until the proverbial shit hit the fan. As Junior drove to Barry's compound outside of Thrall, he fantasized about a simpler life. A life in which Junior Pendleton had lots of money, women on call, and body guards like movie stars have so he wouldn't have to deal with FBI agents and private investigators and fornicating couples and stupid fishermen ever again. By the time he pulled up to Barry's compound, Junior had a vaguely formed plan to get out of the environmental resourcing business before he had to spend his remaining cash stashed under a pine floorboard in his bedroom with Mathers, Smiley and Pritcher, Attorneys at Law.

15 K-I-L-L

Delton felt hands grab him. He fought back, but a quick punch to his face told him he needed to wait for his moment, rather than give these people an excuse to incapacitate or kill him. Lifted up by his arms on either side, his kidnappers dragged him for a distance into some kind of building. The air shifted from cedar and dust to oil, fuel, and metal. His captors pushed him down into a chair, duct taping his ankles to its legs. Someone abruptly pulled his hood away to reveal a hanger, a small airplane to one side, while a large industrial fan generated a breeze of hot air. While his eyes adjusted to light from several fluorescent lamps hanging from a high ceiling, a plump red headed white man in Bermuda shorts and a Hawaiian shirt looked at him with an intensity reminding him of his first drill sergeant. His look said, "I'm going to break you, you pathetic little shit." Yeah, he knew the look and all it implied.

The man leaned forward, hands on his knees, inspecting Delton like a prize bull at a county fair. Then he stood up, pursed his lips as if pondering what to do next, and spoke.

"Well, my friend. I'm afraid you showed up in the wrong place at the wrong time. We didn't intend for you," he walked out of Delton's vision, "and your girlie here, to get caught up in this. I suppose I could get all righteous and say it's what you get for fornicating in public, but we're all men here. Well, all of us except for this pretty little thing."

"Leave her alone!" Delton fought against his restraints.

"Or what? Son, hell me and my boys could have our way with her right now and there's not a damn thing you could do about it."

"Delton..." Ayisha's voice trembled.

Two other men shifted in the shadows.

"But I want you to know I'm not the kind of person who would take advantage of this situation. Unless, of course, you force my hand. No,

I'm just an American businessman, an entrepreneur, and patriot trying to make a living in difficult economic times."

"What do you want?" Delton spoke defiantly, pulling against his bindings.

"I don't think I like your tone." The plump man turned on him with surprising force, delivering a crushing blow to Delton's stomach. Breath exploded out of his lungs, the force of the punch slamming him into Ayisha, then toppling him sideways to the floor.

Ayisha cried out, "Delton!"

The plump man said, "Shut up girl, or I will let my boys have some fun right now. Understand?"

Ayisha, panicking to the point of hyperventilation, struggled to catch her breath.

He repeated, "Do...You...Under...Stand?"

"Yes. Yes."

"Good."

Delton lay gasping for air. He could take a beating, but provoking this asshole would only get them killed. Somehow he had to find a way to keep the attention on him.

"Look...mister." Delton spoke, laboring to breathe. "I'm not sure what you want with us, but we were just walking in the woods. Why don't you just let us go. We won't look back."

"I'd certainly like to son, but I think you'll understand, being a trained soldier and all, I just can't let you walk out of here."

"We'll just walk away. We'll just walk away and you have my word we won't tell anyone."

The man leaned over to look at Delton, his stark white legs covered in freckles. "I'd like to believe you, but there's just too much at stake. You've seen me, so I'm afraid there's no possible way I can let you leave." To someone out of Delton's view he said, "Stay here and don't let them out of your sight. You two dumb asses come with me."

A man in blue jeans and a plaid shirt holding a semi-automatic stepped out of the shadows. Beyond Delton's line of sight he heard footsteps of the two who must have brought them here, walking out of the hanger, probably trailing behind their pudgy red headed leader. Delton tasted dirt from the hanger floor and blood in his mouth. Ayisha cried softly somewhere close behind him.

~*~

Outside of the hangar, Junior and Jayson met with Barry Swenson under the shade of a large live oak. Barry, his red hair, fair blotched skin, and bloated appearance in his plaid Bermuda shorts and yellow Hawaiian shirt, looked like Humpty Dumpty recuperating from tuberculosis at a resort spa.

He said, "Boys, we've got a problem."

Barry looked directly at Junior, so he spoke up first. "I agree. I don't know how, but the feds are crawling right up my ass. First, those two show up outta nowhere with some lame excuse for being on my property late at night, then some private investigator threatens me at gunpoint."

"An investigator?" Barry stroked his chin in thought. "What did he want to know?"

"Well, I think he's an undercover agent. Maybe the Texas Rangers or some such. He was asking about the couple and if I'd seen them around my farm. That sort of thing. Left me his card. Nick Sibelius."

Jayson asked, "Sibelius? The partner of the cop I killed? What the hell is he doing around here?"

"Well, what do you think, Jayson?" Barry glared at the big man. "He's looking for you. Must have made some kind of connection. Did I not tell you two to keep a low profile?"

Jayson protested, "There's got to be another reason he's here. No way he could have hunted me down."

Junior could see an opening to his redemption. "It's beginning to sound to me like the FBI is crawling around my place because of you, Jayson. I told you he was trouble, Barry."

Jayson protested, "Like hell. You must've mouthed off at the cafe or something."

Barry, his face a crimson red, screamed, "Enough!"

Junior, trying to calm the situation down, offered, "Maybe we just need to lay low for awhile. Just long enough for the cops to stop messin' in our business."

Barry's contorted face eased into the bare hint of a smile. "You want to lay low for awhile?"

"Yeah, lay low. Just for a little while."

"I've got clients expecting me to secure a safe haven for their toxic waste and if I recall, you made a commitment to provide the secure haven. Am I right, Junior?"

"Well, yes, but the situation has changed."

"Has it?" Barry pulled out what looked like a small electric razor or one of those drills you use for craft projects from his pocket. "The situation for environmental resourcing has changed?" Once Barry turned his small machine on, Junior was transported to the only time he had been in a dentist chair, a ten year old squirming under a dental drill. For a craft tool, it sure sounded nasty.

"Calm down, Barry. I'm just saying, let's take a few days off, until things settle down a bit." In another time and place Junior might have laughed at Barry, red hair, glaring eyes, Hawaiian shirt, and red socks moving toward him looking something like he imagined Bozo the Clown would look like on vacation in the Bahamas. But his whirring drill gave the dentist a horror flick quality. Barry trapped Junior next to a tree. Jayson stood back, arms crossed with a grin on his face.

"I don't give a damn if Beelzebub and all the fucking fallen angels are after your ass, we have a deal, and I expect you to keep it. And if you don't..."

Barry's drill whined to a shrieking pitch, then slowed as its bit ate into tree bark beside Junior's left ear. Bits of tree stung his face and the odor of burning wood filled the air. Junior wasn't sure who this Beelzebub guy was, but Barry's dental drill by the ear said everything Junior needed to hear.

"Shit, Barry. Okay, okay. Don't get so wound up."

"Do you have any idea of the stakes here?"

"Well, I guess, well no..."

"Between our toxic waste and the meth businesses, this little enterprise is worth millions."

"That's a lot of money."

"Damn straight it's a lot of money. Do you have any idea why I'd bring Jayson Moore into this business?"

He looked to the cop killer who stood arms crossed, a blank look on his face.

"Jayson? I don't know, 'cause he knows how to cook meth?"

"Because he believes in our movement and he's a damn sado-masochistic, psychopathic killing machine. That's why." Barry whirred the drill so close to Junior's eye he could swear he smelled his eyelashes burning. "Mess up this business Junior and I'll have Jayson pull your brains out through your nose. And trust me, he loves that kind of shit. Do you hear me?"

"Through my nose?" Junior peered past Barry to Jayson. "You can do that?"

The big man nodded.

"Yes, he can, Junior. And worse. So get your shit together. I will not allow you to fail."

"Sure, Barry. It was just a thought. A stupid one."

Barry looked over his portable drill. "Damn."

"What?"

"You see what you did, Junior. You made me dull my drill against a tree."

"I'm really sorry, Barry."

"I think you'll need to take a few barrels at no charge to pay for the damages."

Barry's face, just inches from Junior's, softened. However droplets of sweat on his forehead hinted at his crazed rage. Junior thought about protesting, but Bermuda Bozo was still armed with a drill.

"Sure, Barry. No problem. About what I said, it was just a thought. No harm in thinking, right? So we'll just pretend I didn't say a word. Okay, Barry?"

"Sounds like a good idea, Junior."

Junior wanted to let their conversation end right there, but Jayson, who had been mostly silent the entire time decided to speak. "So Barry. What's the plan?"

Barry had closed his eyes, a hand rubbing one cheek, thinking through his next steps. He stood between the two. "Here's what's going to happen. Jayson. I want you to take out the investigator, Sibelius. Whether he's looking for you or me, he needs to go."

"Consider it done."

"I do Jayson. I do." He turned to Junior. "And Junior, you're going to kill our lovebirds, then bury the evidence."

Junior reached up to rub the back of his neck, a throbbing headache journeying down his spine. "Wait. Barry, what are you saying?" He looked at Jayson, hoping to get some support, but Jayson had his arms crossed in bored agreement. "Oh, come on man. I can't start killing people. Not on purpose."

Even standing outside, Junior felt his world closing in on him. He looked to Jayson. "You saw his tattoo, right?" From Jayson's non-response, he turned his attention back to Barry. "He's a Marine. We can't kill a Marine."

Jayson came to life. Finally, but not in the way Junior had hoped. "Marine? What a load of left wing crap. The traitor who let the black man in the military should have been strung up."

"Clinton?" Junior guessed, hoping Jayson's little rant would somehow keep him from having to kill anyone.

"Clinton? No you dumb goat herder. George Fucking Washington! Goddamn, you don't even know your history."

Junior focused on a tree in the distance, wishing he could beam up like they always did on Star Trek reruns. Jayson had definitely become more intensely crazy than ever.

Jayson broke the silence, "Do I need to kill them?"

"Will you two shut up." Barry poked a finger into Jayson's gut, the finger partially disappearing with each jab. "No, you little Nazi, you don't get to kill them. Junior needs to do this." Barry turned to Junior, a hand on Junior's chest, shoving him as he spoke. "Did you know your nephew got arrested for pissing on people?"

"What?"

"Oh, you didn't know about his little adventure. Well, it turns out your nephew, Carl, is in jail." Barry turned deep red shouting, "And guess who he's talking to?"

"I, I don't know, Barry."

"Nick Sibelius. You're damned nephew might be giving us up right now. So you're going to leave here, bail his ass out of jail, then bring him to me."

"Carl?"

Barry screamed, veins bulging in his neck. "Bring him to me!"

"Yes, yessir."

"And Junior, what kind of stupid waste of space brings two people into the middle of a damned operation. I don't care if they're Marines or cops or your damned cousins. When you get back with Carl, get rid of them. Permanently."

Junior said, "Can't we just cut 'em loose. They'll keep to themselves. Hell, they don't know much anyway."

Barry pushed his glasses up on his nose. "Cut them loose?" Barry's crimson face filled Junior's vision, spit flying with every word, making Junior flinch. "Did you just tell me to cut them loose?" Barry turned to Jayson. "Grab him."

Jayson took hold of Junior's arms, pinning them behind his back, his feet just touching the ground. Pain shot up Junior's shoulders. He felt a warm trickle of pee run down his leg.

"Listen carefully you little pea-brained imbecile. You do what I say, when I say."

Barry's intense gaze inspected Junior like a surgeon scanned an x-ray looking for a tumor. But more urgently, he could feel Barry's hairy red hand squeezing his balls with the force of a steel vice. Immobilized, nausea swept over him.

"Kill them, Junior. K-I-L-L, kill." Barry's hand pulsed with each letter, the word kill emphasized with crushing intensity. "Is that clear enough for you?"

Between clenched teeth, he yelped, "Yessir." Then fell to the ground once Barry released his death grip and Jayson let go.

Barry waddled away, wiping his hand on his pants. "I do not want to know, see, or hear anything about those two ever again. Period."

Junior lay in a fetal position, holding his traumatized crotch protectively, rocking to ease his pain.

Jayson looked down at his whimpering colleague with disdain. "Pathetic. Don't say I didn't tell you to kill them in the barn, asshole."

16 STANDSTILL

The day after Nick questioned Carl, his investigation slowed to a standstill. From experience, he knew his hope Ayisha and Delton had just partied a little too hard evaporated with each passing minute they failed to be found. At this point, all he had was Carl, whose somewhat deviant and quasi-religion addled mind, struggled to maintain a grasp on reality. The likelihood this slow farmhand with a drinking problem took out a Marine fresh from active duty seemed a bit far fetched. He wanted to feel optimistic, but his intuition told him otherwise.

A knock on his door preceded Alice, all six foot two of her, stepping into his office. He lifted a folder off his desk. "Alice, I've got to say I'm impressed. Looks like you checked every possible hiding place in the vicinity. Good work."

"Aren't you sweet." She let out a sigh, moving her hand across her forehead to wipe imaginary sweat from her brow. "Thought I was going to melt right into the ground out there. Sorry I didn't find them for you."

"Yeah, well, I'm sorry too, but not for your lack of trying."

Alice, wearing a sensible sundress, towered in her heels. She must have gotten her chest waxed earlier in the day, which helped sustain her desired effect.

"Sorry to disturb, but I just took a call you'll want to know about. Dolores Jones, her ex is an old fishing buddy of mine, called all frantic about him. She says he's disappeared."

"Disappeared? If he's an ex, maybe he just doesn't want her to know where he is? He is a he, isn't he?"

Alice cocked her head with a frown. "You're so silly. Of course he's a boy. No, she used the word 'disappeared'. She tossed him out of their house, but said he always comes back."

"Alice..."

"I know, Nick. I wouldn't be bothering you with this if it wasn't for the fact another vehicle has been abandoned by the Pendleton farm. It matches Dolores' description of Harlan's car, a faded brown 1993 Ford Bronco. And the plates match."

"How long?"

"He's been gone since Saturday morning. Seems like he went into those woods and never came out."

Nick rose from his desk, tossing the file into a desk drawer. "I'm going to go out to have another visit with our friend Junior Pendleton. Call Quentin over at Pflugerville PD."

~*~

Nick dropped in on Junior to discuss this most recent, far too recent to Nick's thinking, disappearance from his property. This time Junior chose not to brandish a gun in Nick's presence, instead holding a broom as he swept his front porch.

"Howdy, Nick. These visits are becoming regular events."

Pendleton sounded overly cheerful. Nick said, "Well I wish I could say this was a social call, but I'm afraid we've got more to talk about."

Junior stopped sweeping, leaning against his broom. "Look, I don't know nothin' about no motorcycle on the road."

"Been a quiet day today?"

"Well, yes. Why?"

Nick walked toward the porch, stopping at the bottom step. "Nothing happen out of the ordinary? No noisy kids or trespassers?"

"No, nothin'. Of course I've been in my barn most of the day tryin' to get my tractor to run. Damn fuel pump. So what, you catchin' trespassers for me now?"

Nick ignored his question. "Do you ever have any trouble with people coming onto your property? Maybe trying to fish in your pond without permission?"

Junior grasped his broom handle more firmly. "I'm not sure what you're gettin' at. Yes, I get dove hunters in my fields or somebody with a fishin' pole down at my pond. I've told them it's not safe to be loitering around this farm. This is a workin' farm. Anything could happen. I might run one of 'em down with a harvester or something."

"Has Harlan Jones ever been on your property without an invitation?"

Junior looked out across his yard as if conjuring memories of his old friend. "Harlan. Let me think. Yes, I believe Daddy used to talk about what a pain in the ass Harlan was. Had some hair brained idea our pond held a giant bass or something."

"Has he been around since your Daddy died?"

"Harlan?" Junior brushed his broom across floorboards a few times. "Nope, not to my knowledge. But if you see him, would you tell him its trespassing to fish in my pond. Maybe he'll listen to you. You have a way of making a convincing argument."

"So you haven't talked to him at all."

"Not anytime recently, but I know Harlan. We've known each other since we were kids."

Nick put a foot on the first step. "When you did talk to him, did you threaten him in any way?"

"Threaten? Look, I don't know who you've been talkin' to, but I don't go around threatenin' people. Besides, Harlan's a friend of mine. So maybe I've warned him of the dangers, this being a farm and all, but that's it."

"So was this farm more dangerous than usual yesterday morning?"

"This farm's always dangerous. We've got heavy mechanized equipment, sharp tools, mean pigs, all kinds of ways to get into serious trouble. Like I said, this is a workin' farm, not some playground for sportsmen."

"And where were you yesterday morning?"

"I don't think I like what you're implying with your question."

"I don't care what you like or don't like. Just answer my question."

"In the barn, like I told you. In the barn. And before you ask, no, I don't have any witnesses. Since the cops have seen fit to arrest Carl for simply exercising his bodily functions, I run this farm alone. Accuse me of whatever it is you think I've done, but you're wasting your time."

Nick looked over to Junior's barn. "Mind if I take a look in that barn of yours?"

"Yes I do mind. Hell, you're not even a real cop. Even cops need a warrant or something before they go invading my privacy."

"You're right Junior. I imagine the police will have a warrant next time they drop by."

"For what?"

"Harlan Jones has turned up missing. Funny thing. His car has been abandoned on the shoulder of the road right beside your property. That's the second abandoned vehicle and the third missing person in two days. Are you sure you don't want to tell me what's going on? Sounds like you may have gotten yourself into some serious trouble."

Junior swept his broom back and forth in jerky motions, not focused on sweeping anything in particular. "Thanks for your concern, but there's nothin' to say. Now get the hell off my property."

~*~

As Nick's car pulled away, Junior, angry at the trouble Harlan and those two he had stashed away with Barry were causing him, raised his broom, swinging with all of his might to smack the handle across a porch pillar. The handle bounced back off the solid beam, a vibration sending bolts of pain into his hands and up his arms.

"Shit, shit, shit!"

He slammed his broom down on his porch in frustration. Junior knew he had set the wheels in motion and there was no turning back.

17 BRIDGE WORK

Nick drove back towards Pflugerville in the rental car Junior had grudgingly provided, while a body shop repaired the dents and shot out window of his pickup. The small, four door sedan seemed agile enough, although Nick missed the rumble of his V8. His ex had kept her BMW, leaving him the pickup. While the big Ford drank gas, he didn't have the heart to part ways with his ride. He had lost enough.

~*~

Nick and his Houston Police patrol partner, Denny, had been gathering evidence, building a case against the big man who stood with his back to them. Jayson Moore, a drug dealer and walking time bomb of mayhem turned as they approached him. Blood dripped from a baseball bat still gripped in his right hand. Bits of his victim and splattered blood covered his barrel chest and face. He smiled as if happy to see he had witnesses to his atrocity. Nick, a hand on his weapon, turned in response to a metallic clang behind him. The jolt of a taser pulsed through his body, knocking him down, his gun skittering across asphalt. Coming to, he tried to rise, but a tire iron wielded by an accomplice slammed down on his shoulder, snapping his collar bone. A second hit broke his right arm. A crushing kick to his abdomen took his breath away.

He lay on the ground, sour garbage thick in the air, his body throbbing with pain. He lifted his eyes to a repetitive banging noise to see Moore holding Denny by his collar, bashing his partner's head against the hood of their patrol car. Across his muscled arm a green blue tinted tattoo, designed like an American flag, pulsed with each movement. Only in this flag, a field of swastikas replaced the field of stars on Old Glory. He laughed, taking Denny's gun, then pointing it at Denny's head. Nick called out, but his unseen attacker stomped his face down into hard asphalt with a heavy boot.

A gunshot rang out. Nick screamed to his partner, but another swift kick broke his jaw, silencing him. He came back to consciousness, immobilized and helpless. Jason Moore knelt over him, his face inches away. Nick could smell his stink of sweat and alcohol. Multiple sirens wailed. They sounded like dying whales to Nick, crying out as whalers murdered them one by one. He wanted to dive deep into a cold abyss, away from this horror. Someone tugged on his name badge, "I should kill you, Sibelius. Just like your partner."

Another voice from behind said, "Come on, Jayson. Let's get outta of here before the cops are all over us. He's as good a dead anyway."

"Yeah, I suppose you're right. What kind of a man lets his partner get killed, eh, Sibelius?"

Nick spent weeks in a hospital recovering from broken bones and contusions. Mercifully, a skull fracture slipped him into unconsciousness for several days. He was told he was lucky. If a unit hadn't pulled up when they did, Jayson Moore would have finished him off. Denny left a pregnant wife and all of his dreams for life. He never saw or spoke to Barb after Denny's death. The funeral happened while he lay in ICU. The only evidence he had of his friend's existence, and his wife's impossible forgiveness, was a St. Sebastian necklace, left without his knowledge, on his hospital nightstand. Nick tried to go back to work, St. Sebastian dangling from his neck, but questioning looks from his fellow cops, wondering how he let his partner get killed, burned into his flesh. Whenever he closed his eyes, he could see the door of their patrol car, Denny's blood covering over the words "to Protect." Yes, he had definitely lost enough.

~*~

His visit with Junior puzzled him. The little twerp should have been more nervous than their first meeting, given every instinct in Nick's body told him this guy knew about his missing couple and also had something to do with Harlan. But instead, Junior was all laughs up to the point when he had directly accused him of having something to do with Harlan's disappearance. Nick had to meet with his client, Reverend Anderson, later in the day and really wanted to have something, anything, to tell him.

Turning onto Kelly lane he drove past a golf course. A foursome stood on a fairway tee box, while several golfers practiced putting on a green near a small clubhouse. Nick had never gotten into golf, even though his ex liked to play. Why a anesthesiologist would want to chase after a little ball half the day, just to have an excuse to drink a couple of cocktails on the 19th hole eluded him. Of course, the few times he had played, he spent most of his time in bushes or ponds looking for his ball, which he admitted only to himself, probably tainted the game for him.

Driving past a high school he glanced up at a tollway overpass down the road. He noticed something odd, something on the overpass. No, make that someone. A kid? Probably some high school kid standing there on a dare.

Then he caught a flash. Sunlight reflected off a mirror? Or a rifle scope. A man, not a boy, stood on the overpass, a scoped rifle in his hands, pointed directly at Nick. Instinct kicked in. Swerving onto the shoulder, a bullet exploded through his back side window. Crushing the accelerator, his car's small engine pushed into red, screamed. Another bullet pierced his windscreen, impacting the seat beside him.

He raced through a light, clipping an SUV. The impact set off his airbag, its concussive bang lost in chaos. Time slowed, as Nick, thinking offense, jumped out of his battered vehicle. An angry driver yelled, but Nick's focus moved to the man above him with a rifle. He had to keep gunfire away from a now crowded intersection. A daylight assassin would make no distinctions between his intended target and innocent bystanders.

Running up a concrete embankment he angled upward to get to the overpass. His attacker had jumped a side safety wall, apparently hoping to get another shot. Seeing him, Nick fired in his direction before the gunman could set up. The shooter, a large man with shoulder length blonde hair, vaulted back over the wall. Jayson Moore?

Nick got to the edge, knowing his attacker might be standing feet away, he waited, listening. Hearing only traffic, he took a chance, popping his head up to see Jayson Moore jump into a black truck, then drive away in a cloud of burnt rubber and exhaust.

Jayson Moore was in Pflugerville trying to kill him—again. Nick had heard the son of a bitch had gone into hiding somewhere in East Texas. He had even considered searching East Texas himself, except Quentin had talked him out of going. Why would Moore take the risk of coming out in broad daylight to kill him?

Nick looked down the embankment at a small crowd gathering around his bullet riddled rental car. He'd have some explaining to do at the rental agency. A Pflugerville PD officer stopped in the intersection and from Nick's position he could tell the officer was Quentin. He needed to get away, avoid a delay with police, and hunt Jayson Moore down before he had a second chance to kill him. Instead, he walked down the embankment toward Quentin, if for no other reason than to keep his friend out of the line of fire.

~*~

After finishing his investigation, Quentin offered Nick a ride to the car rental agency. Burnt rubber and fuel still permeated the air. Moore must have hit the gas tank with one of his shots.

"What the hell is going on, Nick?"

"Damned if I know. Probably some kid with a hunting rifle making some mischief."

"Mischief." Quentin looked over Nick's shoulder to the wrecked car. "This is what you call mischief. This wasn't some random shooting, Nick. Somebody's intent on killing you."

"Look, I appreciate your concern Quentin. But really, I'll bet it was some kid or maybe a nut case out to create some drama."

"Did you get a good look at him?"

"No. Didn't catch his plate either, but I did see a large, black pickup truck drive away."

Nick, feeling Quentin's eyes drilling into him, scanning him for clues, peered out his window.

"Well you've narrowed it down to a few thousand vehicles. Nick, seriously, what's going on? That was no random shooting. Someone is intent on killing you. Do you think this might have a connection to a case you're working on?"

"No, I don't tend to work on things leading to hit men. Strictly small time."

Quentin broke off his questioning, focusing on the traffic ahead. A group of buzzards circled in an updraft, roiling cumulous clouds billowing behind them. Nick wondered what road kill had attracted their attention.

Quentin said, "So you talked to Carl and I assume it didn't go anywhere. I take it you've also spoken to Junior Pendleton?"

"Yeah, he's a certified nut case, by the way."

Quentin shook his head. "Yeah, in a sneak up and shoot you in the back kind of way. What does Junior have to do with this girl you're checking up on?"

"You know I have to protect my client's privacy, Quentin. I've said too much already. Look, I'm fine."

Quentin drove his patrol car into the rental car lot, pulling up to the front door. He kept his engine running. "You're holding something back, Nick. I don't know why, but you've got somebody trying to kill you. Don't you think it might be a good idea to bring me into the loop?"

"I appreciate your concern, Quentin. Really. But I can take care of this myself."

"Like today."

"Yes, like today. I'm sitting here talking to you, aren't I?"

"After someone with a rifle shot the hell out of your car. If you had reacted just a bit slower, I'd be standing over your dead body in a morgue, and you know it."

Nick reached for the door handle. "It's a one off, Quentin. But if I see the pickup or remember anything else, you'll be the first to know."

"I better be." He shook his head. "I am the law around here after all."

"If it doesn't break confidence with my client."

"Well, I think you know more than you're letting on, my friend. But if that's the way you want to play it, so be it."

Nick stepped out of Quentin's patrol car, wondering how things got so complicated. Beyond trying to explain a bullet riddled 'economy' rental car, he wasn't sure what to say to Anderson about his daughter. But more troubling, a nightmare from his past had attacked him in broad daylight. Dark cumulonimbus clouds towered eastward, a warm, moist front of Gulf air colliding with dry Hill Country air from the west. The massive anvil shaped beasts would probably bring little relief to Austin's ongoing drought, but would provide a dramatic show of lightening.

18 BLUEBONNET CAFE

After his run-in with Jayson Moore, the car rental manager, noting how her bullet scarred vehicle now resided in a police impound, expressed her regret Lone Star Car Rentals would not be willing to provide a replacement car. He was able to rent an old 1980 Cadillac from Harvey's Rent-a-Wreck. Other than anticipating a Navy jet coming in to land on the deck of his land bound aircraft carrier, the old beast did move forward and had a decent air conditioner. This morning he pointed his ship to a breakfast joint.

The Bluebonnet Cafe had it all. Thick, coffee stained ceramic cups, booths with red plastic seats, small chrome juke boxes filled with tunes from the 60's and 70's at each booth, and staffed with a number of the original waitresses, now in their sixties, with high piles of platinum grey hair and brightly painted nails. An aroma of bacon fat mixed with slightly burnt coffee met him as he pushed open the cafe door. The place buzzed with activity. Moving past tables to sit at a far end of a formica counter, Nick picked out pieces of conversation.

"I'm telling you, T.J., this is some kind of serial killer. I'd keep the wife in the house until this blows over. I sure tell you, I never thought I'd live to see the day where we had to lock our doors."

"Aliens. Got to be aliens. Think about it. Three people disappear. Not murdered or kidnapped. They disappeared! Sounds like an alien abduction to me. You know last night I thought I saw some kind of UFO. It came in low, lights flashing. At first I thought it was a small airplane, but there was no sound! Absolutely stone cold silent. I think people know. They've seen things like me, they're just afraid to speak up. Afraid the government is going to come and arrest them. But what are we supposed to do? Just sit here while aliens pick us off one at time?

"There's evil in those woods. Evil. Reverend Anderson knows there's evil in there. Satan, he said. It's Junior Pendleton. His pagan ways, God knows what perversions he has committed in those woods, paving the way for Satan to take hold. And that mindless boy, Carl. An easy target for demons. He just doesn't have the mind or the faith to fight. But we do. We're not going to let Satan get a foothold in Pflugerville. Remember how Jesus made demons leave the body of one who was possessed, moving them into a herd of swine? Well that's what we need to do. Just like Jesus, we need to drive those demons right off the edge of a cliff."

"Morning there, Nick." Stacey, a veteran waitress with tall hair, greeted Nick at the counter.

"Morning, Stacey. This place is really buzzing today."

"Yeah, they're all convinced they have an inside track on these disappearances." She shook her head in amused disbelief. "I've heard some crazy things this morning. Coffee?"

"Absolutely. And the breakfast plate with..."

"Eggs over easy, sausage and an extra biscuit." Stacey winked at Nick.

"You know me too well. Sounds great."

Stacey put a weathered ceramic cup in front of Nick.

"You know, I have a theory about what happened."

"You too? Okay, what's your theory?"

"Sink hole."

"Sink hole?"

"Think about it, Nick. Those woods have been perfectly normal, then three people just disappeared. Well its either the mumbo jumbo some of these folks are coming up with or its science, pure and simple. And what could be more straightforward than a sink hole."

Nick had been expecting another crackpot explanation, but Stacey had surprised him with an idea he now admonished himself for not considering. Caves riddle limestone formations in this part of Texas, so some kind of collapse could actually be possible. Of course, Carl still offered the best hope of a suspect. A sink hole might be responsible for one disappearance, but three? Carl had guilt written all over him. He felt sure Carl had been hiding in the woods, watching Delton and Ayisha make love. He must have knocked the young Marine out with a rock, then in a panic, killed them both and hidden the bodies. And Junior had to be hiding the truth to protect Carl. It was a theory, at least.

So much for the first disappearance, but what about Harlan? Maybe these disappearances weren't connected. Maybe the couple died at Carl's hand, but Harlan could have fallen into one of Stacey's sink holes.

Well, if there's a sink hole out there, we'll certainly find it. And maybe the bodies of my couple too.

"You just might have something there Stacey. Sink hole. Could explain a lot. Of course we have to find it."

She poured steaming coffee from a glass pot into his cup.

"Here's your coffee, Nick."

"I tell you what, Stacey. You mind getting José to turn my order into a couple of breakfast tacos? I'd like to get back out to those woods and see if a sink hole might have something to do with this."

Stacey flashed a collegial smile. "No problem, Nick."

While he pondered potential geological causes for recent events, a woman in her thirties sat at the counter on a stool next to him. Nick's eyes wandered from his hot steaming coffee mug past a sugar shaker to the gentle curve of her breasts rising and falling with each breath. His mind seamlessly shifted from sink holes to his lips softly kissing the base of her throat, then moving up her neck, brushing away her dark, full hair as he caressed a soft spot behind her ear lobe with his tongue.

"...about the disappearances."

"What?" A part of Nick's consciousness knew someone out beyond his mind had spoken to him, but he couldn't come back to awareness quickly enough to hide the fact he had lost himself in this woman's form and scent.

"Excuse me. Hello?" A woman's voice, assertive with a soft edge, gently pulled Nick out of his dreamtime.

"What? Yes, uh, yes, hello. Sibelius. Nick. I was..."

"In deep thought?"

Damn! She had seen him staring at her. He couldn't believe how out of control he was feeling. Nothing like an awkward encounter with a beautiful woman in the most public place in Pflugerville. God she was beautiful. And somehow, familiar. He could see flecks of gold and green in her hazel eyes.

He turned to his coffee. "I'm sorry about that ma'am. I think I just, well, I suppose I just didn't expect...you."

She pursed her lips with a cock of her head. Nick assumed she was trying to discern whether he was a misogynist jerk. Putting him out of his anguish, she leaned over close enough for Nick to feel the warmth of her body.

"It's okay. I'm flattered. Really. Besides, I believe we've already met."

Nick knew without a doubt they had met, but tried to be nonchalant. "At the convenience store. Yes, I believe you were getting a cup of coffee."

"Yes, and you were complaining about your girlfriend's coffee making skills." Before Nick could initiate a new defense, she continued, "I hear you're some kind of private investigator."

"Yeah, I provide security and do some investigating as well. Didn't know I was the talk of the town."

She put a soft, yet firm hand on his arm. "You might be, but I asked, Stacey." She looked over to the waitress, who acknowledged her with a smile. "She told me. So are you investigating these disappearances?"

Nick's heart sank. This beautiful woman must be a reporter or given her looks, a television sound biter. He shifted into business mode.

"You have an interest in the disappearances? May I ask in what capacity?"

"Well of course. I'm a reporter for the Houston Chronicle. Thought I'd try to cut through all the hype this type of story generates. Get to the truth of the matter."

He chuckled. "The truth?" Nick's skepticism melted across his words.

"Yes. You do believe in the truth or are you one of those jaded, burned out types?"

He took a sip of coffee, recalling all the times in Houston a story got twisted around by a reporter. "No, no. My job's all about finding the truth. I'm just surprised to hear you're interested."

"Ah, you are jaded. Well, cable news will be homing in on whatever they think will generate viewer ratings -- alien abduction, serial killer, coyotes."

"Coyotes?"

"You haven't heard that one? I'm surprised. Yes, an expert biologist at the University of Texas thinks these disappearances may be linked to a recent sighting of a group of coyotes. They've taken down several cattle in this area." Nick opened his mouth to speak, but she continued, "I know what you're thinking. Coyotes? Don't they make howling noises? And how could they take a full grown adult down without leaving a trace? Well, Dr. Samuelson, the UT professor? He describes this very possibility in his paper *Texas Coyotes: Silent Killers or Ecological Necessity.*"

"Does he."

"Yes, he does. They tend to go right for the throat, which would explain the lack of screaming." She paused. "What a horrible way to die."

"Well, Ms., I'm sorry, I don't believe I caught your name."

She reached out to shake Nick's hand, her face brightening into a smile. "MaryLou."

Her hand, velvet soft with slender long fingers belied a strength he sensed in her eyes. He vaguely remembered feeling embarrassed about his ogling, but the memory slipped away as he formed her name with his lips.

"MaryLou."

They both paused, Nick sensing a tidal pull between them, yet both anchored from its effect by the business at hand.

"And you are?"

"Nick. Nick Sibelius." He paused for a moment to gather his thoughts, then continued. "MaryLou. I'm a private investigator, so whatever I know or find out, well it's private, for my clients eyes only."

She squeezed his hand, lightly touching his thumb and forefinger with her other hand.

"Maybe I should hire myself a private investigator."

They paused again, time moving ever so slightly, then released their clasp on one another. Nick turned away, then back to her. "Are you always a reporter or do you take some time off now and then?"

"Yeah, now and then."

"Would you be taking some time off this evening, say around seven o'clock?"

She studied him for a moment. "Funny you should ask. I've been planning on taking some time off at exactly seven tonight."

"Good. That's really great. Well I can't let you take time off in our town without showing you around a bit. How about if I pick you up at seven for some dinner?"

"Sounds good. I'm staying at the Alamo Inn on the Interstate. I'll be waiting outside the lobby."

Nick hardly believed he had just asked a woman reporter, albeit a stunningly beautiful woman reporter, out on a date. What puzzled him more was he knew her looks had hardly anything to do with it. Nick opened the door to leave when he heard Stacey's voice.

"Hey Nick! Don't forget your tacos!" She waved a small white bag in his direction. He stepped back over to the counter, taking the bag from her.

"Thanks Stacey."

"No problem Nick." She glanced over at Mary Lou. "You've got a lot on your mind these days."

19 TAKING A NAP

Dining on a now cold breakfast taco in the middle of Junior's woods on a Monday morning did not rank high in Nick's list of things to do. However, Stacey's thought about a sink hole had some merit to it, so the sooner he either confirmed or denied the possibility, the sooner he could move closer to solving these disappearances. At mid-morning, a summer fireball of a sun hung in a cloudless blue field, inching temperatures into the upper eighties. By mid-afternoon, the temperature would rise to a blistering one hundred degrees or more. These woods would be a very hot, humid, and miserable place to be.

Nick made his way through tangles of undergrowth to Carl's wooded hiding place. A red tail hawk screeched overhead at bold sparrows attacking the large bird of prey like a squadron of fighters swarming a lumbering bomber intent on making its target. Nick tried to place himself in Carl's "room" on the night of the disappearance. While his version with Carl sneaking up on the couple to clock Delton with a rock seemed most probable, to date, the police had been unable to find a blood encrusted rock or a weapon of any sort.

Nick walked through the scenario from Carl's perspective. Carl sits in his secret spot looking at stars, when he hears a couple coming through his woods, so he hides in some brush. While he didn't like having strangers discover his secret place, he didn't mind once Ayisha lay naked a few feet away. Then sometime during the couple's lovemaking, Carl makes some noise, startling them and exposing him for the sick little pervert he is. Carl said he ran, Delton fell dead, then the Rapture occurred.

If I can figure out which way Carl ran, maybe I'll find a sinkhole and a rational explanation for Delton's disappearance.

So which way did Carl run? An opening to the north provided an obvious exit. Nick pushed through scrub and low hanging branches following a very narrow path which eventually ended at the edge of a large pond. Carl hadn't mentioned a pond, so Nick backtracked, trying one path after another. No sink holes.

Finally he settled down in a small clearing by the pond. His resting place, a grassy slope in dappled sunlight, offered a soft bed. He leaned back to take in the blueness above marked only by the white contrail of an airliner on its way to anywhere but Pflugerville.

~*~

In his dream he laid on his back, MaryLou kissing him deeply. He took in the warmth of her body next to his, her lips parted, longing for him. He opened his eyes expecting his new lover, but instead he had two cables from a taser stuck in his chest. A jolt of electricity sent him into convulsions, his body becoming a neon kaleidoscope of color flopping around on the ground in perfect rhythm with the eighties band, Cameo singing *Word Up*. The singers, all wearing only cod pieces, riffed off the tune, while young women writhed in contorted dance moves. He struggled to move, to get away. Jayson Moore pinned Denny to a wall, a gun, god, more like a cannon, pointed directly at him. With a massive explosion his gun fired, ripping Denny's chest open, blood and viscera flying in all directions. Nick flailed, sharp, jagged pain searing up his legs and torso, his hands contorted and paralyzed. Looking to his right, his wife Sarah naked on all fours, her trauma doc lover doing her doggie style beside him, moaning and crying out, "Do me. Baby, do me." Her nails dug into Nick's leg. They all laughed at him while Reverend Anderson, in a Fred Astaire top hat and tails, rode a Ducati around Nick screaming over and over again, "Where's my little girl, Nick? You promised you'd find my little girl!" Moore stood above him now, Nick's gun in his hand, pointed directly at Nick's head. He cried out for help, but Sarah, her lover, Denny, Reverend Anderson and Benjamin Franklin only looked on, laughing. Franklin's courtesan, a young French woman in a long, formal dress and too much make up, cloyed at his side, gasping for air, recognizing the impropriety of laughing at a man just before a .45 caliber slug violated his head. She stepped up to Nick, placing in his deformed hand a key with a string which rose up disappearing into a dark, angry sky.

He looked up at Franklin's courtesan. "What is this for?"

An corpulent Franklin, twirling a St. Sebastian necklace on a finger, a cold Corona with a lime in the other, partially held back a giggle. "Dead men make good lightening rods, don't you think?"

Nick took hold of Franklin's antique iron key the size of a tennis racket, as Moore pulled the trigger.

"What? No!" A bolt of lightening arced down the string engulfing Nick in flames.

~*~

"No. No. No." Nick sat up, his face flushed with sunburn on a sticky, hot afternoon.

"Damn."

He hadn't meant to go to sleep. Drenched in sweat from heat and his dream, he checked his watch, not believing it was after 1 pm. If his dreams were a measure, he had to get this case sorted before somebody shipped him off to a looney farm. Rising to his feet, he knocked dirt and leaves off his pants feeling a renewed loneliness. Even in his dreams Sarah had looked right through him as if he didn't exist.

20 DATE NIGHT

With Stacey's sinkhole hypothesis coming up short, Nick drove into Pflugerville to visit Carl one more time in the local jail. After dropping by a drug store for some aloe gel for his face, he pulled into the Justice Center. To his surprise, Carl had been bailed out by none other than Junior Pendleton. Part of him wanted to go back out to Pendleton's to see if he could find Carl, but he had a date, something which hadn't happened in quite awhile. So Nick made his way to his trailer and a much needed shower. When he finally pulled into the Alamo Inn parking lot in his Rent-a-Wreck Cadillac, he congratulated himself for being on time—tardiness being something Sarah had adamantly thrown in his face every time he had been late, which had been pretty much every time. MaryLou stood just outside the lobby door in a blouse, jeans and cowboy boots. Nick pulled his car up and getting out said in an over the top Texas accent, "Good evening Ma'am. Would you be the Miss MaryLou I'll be taking to Bucket 'O Brisket tonight?"

"Yes I am, Nick Sibelius." MaryLou played along with her own over the top accent. "Odd name for a cowhand."

Coming around to open MaryLou's door, Nick followed the line of her shoulder, down her back to her perfectly rounded rear end held lovingly by 501 Levis. Nick could have just stood there watching her all night long. He pulled himself together to continue the conversation.

"There's a long tradition of Sibelius' in Texas. There was Nathan Sibelius at the Alamo, the fur trader Hannibal Sibelius and who could forget Betty Sue Sibelius, best sharpshooter in the state."

"Really."

Standing at the open door, he followed the contours of her throat down to the top button of her blouse and soft curve of her breasts, looking up to see MaryLou's deep, dimensional hazel eyes playfully alive.

"Well, I may be prevaricating a bit, but there is my sister Kate Sibelius. She's an attorney in El Paso."

Closing her door, he came back around to the driver's side, his heart pounding as if he had Peggy Wilson in the front seat of his Dad's car again, his hands exploring a once forbidden realm underneath his classmate's blouse.

He spoke firmly to himself. "Get ahold of yourself, Nick. You don't even know this woman."

Pulling away from the motel, Nick drove down a county road into town.

"I'm glad you're joking, Nick. Bucket 'O Brisket? Where did you come up with that?"

"Oh, well, I'm afraid the Bucket 'O Brisket part is true. When the couple who owned Pflugerville Barbecue got divorced three years ago they had one hell of a fight about the business. He kept the family name and she kept their original location. Unfortunately, the husband, while a gifted meat smoker, was one lousy businessman. The wife had told him he was such a pathetic loser she could call her business Bucket 'O Brisket and still beat him right into the ground."

"I'm guessing she did exactly that?"

"Yep. But I understand they're getting along better after their divorce. Once he lost his business she hired him back as pit master, which was what he was doing before the divorce."

"So a happy ending. And some good barbecue too."

Bucket 'O Brisket had the look of a building having stood for a hundred years, every pore and crevasse of the structure deeply smoked with mesquite. Long, pine picnic style tables had squeeze bottles of barbecue sauce and a roll of brown paper towels in a vertical holder at each end. Servers behind a wood counter placed sliced brisket and sausage on white butcher paper resting on worn, chipped brown trays which looked like they had been manufactured back when the Beatles invaded The Ed Sullivan Show. Nick and MaryLou found an open spot at the end of a table, several trophy bass and a couple of deer heads watching them from the walls.

For a moment they ate in silence, taking in the smoked peppery flavors and mesquite aroma of the place. Nick noticed how the tip of MaryLou's nose subtly wiggled each time she chewed.

"Pretty good barbecue, but being a Houston girl, I imagine you have your own favorite barbecue joints."

When MaryLou looked up from her plate of beef, Nick lost himself in her eyes, how her nostrils gently flared, her soft full lips. Part of him wondered why he felt so connected to her and another part told him to shut up and enjoy the ride.

She said, "Well, my Mom was originally from Tennessee, so growing up, her version of barbecue was always pork."

Nick winced, a true believer confronting a heretic. "Oh my god. You eat pig! You do realize pig's not really barbecue, right? I mean in Texas, barbecue is beef."

She teased back, "Are you kidding, Nick? There's nothing like a big barbecued pork sandwich."

They both laughed, Nick a bit more nervously because he knew he'd really like this woman no matter what she ate.

"Fortunately, my grandparents lived in East Texas. We used to go out to their old farmhouse in the woods and Granddad would make real, honest to god, smoked Texas brisket. God, I loved their farm. Deep in East Texas, away from everything. It was as if we went to another planet. No one would ever be able to find us out there."

"Sounds like quite a refuge."

"Yeah, it was. I'm going to get out there again one of these days and hide away. Of course, I'd probably enjoy it more if I had someone to hide away with me."

Nick wanted to be cocky or at least a little hard to get, but with those words and a look, Nick lost himself in the woods of East Texas hiding away with a naked MaryLou, covered in barbecue sauce. Her voice pulled him out of his savory moment.

"So, what do you think about this missing couple? Any new developments?"

No matter how hot and bothered she made him feel, MaryLou's words reminded him she was still a reporter. "No, not really. The police have a farmhand, Carl, in detention, but so far I haven't been able to get much out of him. Here, " Nick lifted a small piece of sausage on a fork toward MaryLou, "you've really got to try this jalapeño garlic sausage." She leaned forward, holding Nick's wrist to steady his fork's path to her mouth, her grip firm, her touch soft. "We can definitely put him at the scene, but I'm having a hard time imagining Carl overpowering a trained Marine."

MaryLou slowly pulled meat away from his fork, taking in his hot, spicy morsel, then sweeping her lips with a soft, pink tongue. Nick felt himself become firm.

MaryLou said, "What about the guy who owns the farm?"

"Junior? He certainly has a history of aggression and violence. It's possible he scared Carl away, then killed them. Although without bodies or a weapon, I'm a bit hard pressed to make it stick."

"Yes, its difficult to imagine a farmer suddenly turning into a kidnapper or a murderer."

MaryLou reached across, her fork piercing a cut of brisket, dipping his meat in some sauce on Nick's plate, then bringing the manna to her lips.

Nick asked, "Why not? This guy does have a bit of a history, Mary-Lou."

She chewed slowly, carnally, then swallowed. Nick could physically feel the motion of her throat.

MaryLou said, "I don't know. I guess I think of farmers being focused on making things grow, not killing. Just intuition on my part."

Nick reached across with his own fork, pausing to search out a sliver of meat which would satisfy. At the point his fork penetrated a link of sausage, its skin burst, hot juice spraying across her plate.

"This is why I'm the investigator and you're the reporter. If you do what I do long enough, you learn some of the most innocent looking people are just sadists waiting for an opportunity. My intuition tells me Earl Pendleton Junior is trouble."

MaryLou hovered her fork above Nick's brisket as if fighting her instinct to begin hand feeding him, barbecue sauce and brisket all helter-skelter.

"Maybe so. And someone else disappeared yesterday too, right?"

Nick chewed her smoked sausage, deciding MaryLou's barbecue somehow had more flavor just by being near her.

"Yeah, a guy named Harlan, although I'm not sure if his disappearance is related or not."

"So you think it's just a coincidence he disappeared in the same woods?"

"I don't know what to think. In my experience there are no coincidences. I'm hoping whoever has our couple doesn't have his hands on Harlan."

Their barbecue completely consumed, they loitered over banana puddings, sharing stories about growing up in Texas. MaryLou sculpted whipped cream atop her pudding with a spoon.

"Why did you become a private investigator? Don't get me wrong, we need people like you in the world, but it always struck me as a very dangerous profession."

He slipped his spoon deep into his pudding. "I guess I've always had a strong sense of justice. Even when I was a kid, if there was a bully on our playground I felt like it was my job to keep the peace."

"How did that go?"

"Sometimes it worked out fine. But I definitely got my share of ass kickings. Anyway, after I got a history degree in college, a buddy of mine talked me into going to the police academy. Seemed like the thing to do."

He smiled, noticing how barbecue sauce had left MaryLou's lips looking full and blushed.

"How about you? I'd think a girl growing up in Austin would have ended up at UT?"

"Well, I actually didn't know what I was going to study. Then I met someone."

"A guy?" Nick couldn't believe he had actually infused those words with a hint of jealousy.

"Yes, a guy. We dated a bit. He had a whole Hemingway thing going. He drank too much and thought his opinion had to be more right than anyone else's. You know the type. So we didn't last long, but he did introduce me to writing. The next semester I went from undecided to Journalism and have been a writer ever since."

"Being a reporter, I suppose you've seen your share of tragedy."

"Yes, I suppose. Although I would think you've seen worse."

They sat silently, Nick wondering if like him, she was trying to keep the slide show of human depravity from running through her mind.

"Sometimes I wonder why I do this job, Nick."

"Me too."

"And then a story comes along. A really uplifting story speaking to the human spirit. In that moment I know why I'm doing this job. To help us all know we can make a difference. We all count."

Their conversation had begun to go into territory Nick preferred to leave alone. Then for some reason, MaryLou's openness, her beauty, the way she swept up whipped cream off her lips with a wisp of her tongue, for whatever reason, he heard himself say, "I think maybe I've lost my way, but I do know what you mean."

"You've lost your way? You seem like a pretty straight up guy to me."

"I try. But I've had my moments."

Fortunately, unlike the reporter she had been earlier on their date, MaryLou didn't pry into details of his failures. For a split second Nick noticed momentary sadness cross her face, belying some brokenness in her own past.

"I guess we've all lost our way at one time or another Nick."

He offered to take MaryLou home, but then she told him she had heard he lived in an Airstream trailer. On an impulse, Nick asked her if she'd like to see his 1962 Airstream Overlander. He couldn't believe his luck when she said yes.

~*~

"An honest to god Airstream. Wow. Nick, it's beautiful."

The polished surface of the aerodynamically shaped trailer reflected a soft glowing summer moon.

"Are you some kind of Airstream groupie, MaryLou? You found out about my trailer and have been stalking me, just to get a peak inside my little land yacht. Right?"

"When I was a girl my Mom used to take me to my grandparent's farmhouse in East Texas. I'd spend almost every summer there. There was an old Airstream sitting by the barn and we used to play in it constantly. Airstreams make great spaceships and post offices." The moon light left a soft glow on her face. "I guess an Airstream has a high nostalgia quotient for me. Can I see the inside?"

"Can the most beautiful woman in the world see the inside of my trailer, even if she's a stalker?" Nick paused, hoping he wasn't either laying it on too thick or coming across as too desperate. He felt the quickened pulse and shallow breath loneliness brings to sudden connection. "Of course you can."

He opened his door, helping MaryLou up the stairs, then followed her in. Pulling the door closed he turned back to her. MaryLou wrapped her arms around his neck, drawing him toward her. They stood kissing in darkness, taking in each other's heat, scent, and touch. He felt her warm, moist mouth open, her tongue exploring his own. She tasted earthy, her breast hot against his chest. He felt himself harden against her, his hands fumbling with buttons on her blouse as she released his belt, then moved her hands under his shirt, up his abdomen, her fingers combing through thick chest hair. He slipped her blouse off, pulling bra straps down, kissing her soft neck, a shoulder, then the top curve of her breasts. She shuddered to his touch, her bra falling away, his hands caressing her as he slid to his knees. MaryLou held his head in her hands, her jeans and panties falling to her ankles, Nick's tongue gently exploring her. He wanted this woman, he wanted all of her, mind, body and soul. If he could, he would have somehow devoured her, taking her completely within himself. He kissed his way back up her stomach, between her breasts, along her neck, then gently raked his teeth just behind her ear. MaryLou held Nick in her hand, feeling his hot power. He sensed her aching for him to be inside of her.

She kissed his ear, whispering, "Do you have a bed?"

"What?" Nick had to pull himself out of his lust to hear his lover's words.

"A bed. What I'm going to do to you requires padding."

What clothes remained fell to the floor almost on their own, Nick trying to navigate in darkness toward the only soft, flat surface large enough for their lovemaking in his trailer. Briefly he wished he had moved his dirty clothes off his bed, but as MaryLou pulled him inside of her, he only thought of her. She smelled of mesquite and honey, her body taking him in, enveloping him. Nick felt his self-imposed solitude dissolve into a deep intense desire, reason and civility giving way to a wild, physical rush of hot, sweaty, heaving merging bodies until for a moment, he turned inside out, exposing the innermost parts of himself. Both screamed out, a physical and emotional pleasure so intense, so intimate, he felt torn apart until his very essence lay exposed to the night air. A year of lonely nights had been broken by one glorious night of MaryLou.

They lay in a hot, sweaty entanglement of arms, legs, sheets, and pillows, suspending this moment, holding on to each other, willing the world to stay away. His hand followed the contour of her spine down to the small of her back. MaryLou's fingers found a necklace, its medallion lying off to one side of Nick's chest.

"What's this?"

"St. Sebastian. It belonged to a good friend of mine."

She turned the medallion over in her fingers, then held it in her hand as if weighing it's significance. "To remember?"

Nick wanted to tell her about Denny, about his failure to keep his friend alive, about the real Nick Sibelius, but he couldn't bring himself to say the words.

"Yeah, to remember."

She placed the necklace back on his chest, then ran her fingers through his chest hair, kissing his neck. "You'll have to tell me the story sometime."

Her head resting on his chest, Nick stroked her hair, surprised this serendipitous moment had broken into his world. "Where did you come from MaryLou?"

She held him more tightly. "Nick, there's something we should talk about."

"I'll talk with you about anything, anywhere, anytime."

"Nick."

He cocked his head to see her face. "Is everything okay? Did all of this happen too quickly?"

"No, no. Not at all. But Nick—"

Nick's cell phone ring tone interrupted.

"Maybe you better answer it."

"It'll wait."

MaryLou reached up to cradle Nick's face in her hands.

"The phone, Nick. Maybe you better answer."

"It's probably just some guy who thinks his girlfriend is lying to him."

"Or it could be about your missing couple."

Nick wondered how MaryLou could be worried about his phone when he was in the midst of sexual ecstasy, but he answered anyway.

"What's up, Alice? Yeah. I see. Okay, I'll be there in about twenty minutes. And Alice. I'm really sorry."

MaryLou watched Nick hang up his phone. "So?"

"Harlan."

"He's been found? Great."

"Not so great. He's dead."

21 DEATH COMES FLOATING

Nick wanted to drop MaryLou off at her hotel, but she insisted on riding along saying she wanted to know "what this private investigation thing is all about." She didn't have to do much to convince him, since he liked having her nearby. Yesterday, loneliness had defined him. Within twenty four hours he was making passionate love like none he had ever known to a reporter from Houston. For the first time in a long time he felt something in a way which didn't involve being alone. He liked the feeling. A lot.

As Nick turned into Junior's farm he could see a small crowd forming at one side of the road with an officer restricting traffic onto the farm itself. Nick drove past, parking on the grass a few hundred yards away.

"You should probably stay here, MaryLou. I'm not actually supposed to be walking around a crime scene."

"Right. If you think I'm sitting in this Cadillac while you investigate a murder, you're not the man I made love to."

Nick cradled her head in his hand, bringing her to him for a long kiss.

"Okay. But follow my lead."

Flashing red lights of a Fire Rescue truck and an ambulance created an eerie dance of shadows and light across the field and adjoining woods, as Nick and MaryLou made their way to the farmhouse. An EMS ambulance stood in the drive by Junior's house. One medic stood at the front of his truck, writing notes on a clipboard, while his partner sat inside the cab. Nick walked to the back of the ambulance where three teenaged girls huddled under emergency blankets. They apparently had been checked by EMS and were waiting for a police officer to interview them. He offered a warm reserved smile. "Quite a night."

All three girls stared at their feet, nodding in agreement. He figured these teenagers assumed he was a police officer, but he had no intention of revealing the truth of the matter unless asked directly.

Nick continued, "I know this whole episode has been very difficult on the three of you. I'm sure all you want to do right now is go home, forget this ever happened. But unfortunately, I need to ask all of you a few questions. Okay?"

The girls, avoiding direct eye contact with Nick, all mumbled assent to his request.

"What were you girls doing here so late at night like this?"

They looked at each other, attempting to communicate information with their eyes, until an athletic, sandy haired girl began talking.

"We just like to go out at night to look at the stars. You know, enjoy nature."

"And you are?"

"Christen."

"And how did the stargazing go for you tonight, Christen, that is before you found the body?"

"Fine, I guess."

"See some good constellations?"

"Yes, we're studying astronomy, so we get extra credit for observing the night sky."

"Saw some good constellations, did you? Given we've had almost a full moon tonight, I assume stargazing didn't work out quite so well." Nick looked directly at each girl. "Now ladies. This is a possible crime scene."

Megan, a blond, blue eyed cheerleader type blurted out, "He may have been murdered?"

"Oh my god." The third member of the group, with short brunette hair and a hint of fading freckles on her nose, spoke softly, almost to herself.

"Like I said," Christen spoke with conviction. "We were just out enjoying nature."

The brunette glared at Christen. "Didn't you hear what he said. That man could have been murdered. We've got to tell him the truth."

Christen angrily responded, "Pam, shut up."

"No, Pam's right, Christen." Megan looked to her two friends. "We've got to tell him everything.

"So girls, let's start again. Why were you out here?"

Megan spoke first. "Me and Pam and Christen came out to the pond to go skinny dipping. On a dare really. We just figured the pond would be a good place to go since it's surrounded by woods."

"I don't believe you're doing this. My Dad's going to kill me." Christen's eyes moistened with tears, anticipating what Nick imagined would be a very awkward conversation with her father.

"So you were skinny dipping in the pond, then what happened?"

Megan cried quietly.

Pam put a protective arm around her. "Megan found him. He had sunk to the bottom, but it's a pretty shallow pond. She felt something odd with her feet. Christen dove down to see what it was. When she realized it was a person she came to the surface screaming. Then we sat on the shore for a few minutes, trying to decide what to do."

"Whether to run or not?" Nick offered.

Pam continued, "Yeah. We put our clothes on, then we called for help."

"Did any of you notice anything else? Any unusual sounds? Anything at all out of the ordinary?"

The three sat silently for a moment, going through the night in their minds.

"Well," said Christen, "I don't know if this means anything, but the man? When I dove down to see what Megan was standing on, I couldn't see his body, but I felt it with my hands. We didn't see the man once the divers brought him up, but it felt like he was wearing clothes and I know he had at least one boot on. Why would you go swimming in a pond with your boots on?"

"Evening, Nick. What brings you out here to my crime scene?" Quentin's familiar voice broke into Nick's questioning.

"Hey there, Quentin. Just saw flashing lights. Thought I'd see what was going on."

Quentin put a hand on Nick's shoulder, guiding him away from his witnesses. "Oh, I see. A concerned citizen. So I suppose Alice monitoring the police band had nothing to do with you showing up?"

They stopped to face each other. "Okay, Quen. You've got me. But you have to admit a body being found on Junior's property within forty eight hours of my couple disappearing from the same area looks like more than a coincidence."

Quentin squinted, his jaw pulsing the way it always did every time Nick had seen his friend seriously pissed. Quentin let out a long breath. "Nick, you're not a cop anymore. The yellow tape, flashing lights, and those three witnesses over there? That's my crime scene. You can't just saunter up to witnesses and start interrogating them."

Nick knew he was in the wrong, but the wisdom of his old football coach who said the best defense was a strong offense formed words he failed to keep from passing his lips. "Maybe you need to protect your witnesses a little better."

Quentin's large frame visibly tensed. "Maybe you need to get the hell out of my sight before I take you in for interfering with an investigation."

"Interfering? I'm trying to find out what happened to Ayisha and Delton. Something, I've got to say, doesn't seem to be too damned high on your list."

"Turn around."

Quentin had a cuff on Nick's wrist, deftly twisting Nick's arm behind his back. Nick, resisted, spinning back to face his friend.

MaryLou stepped toward them, smiling. "Is this Quentin, Nick? I'm just so glad to meet you. Nick says all kinds of wonderful things about you." She extended her hand to him, the two men staring at this unexpected apparition. Quentin kept his left hand tight around Nick's wrist, shaking her hand with his right.

MaryLou glanced at Quentin's stainless steel cuff on Nicks wrist, the other cuff dangling from a chain, amusement sparkling in her eyes. "You boys playing a little game? Some kind of law enforcement arm wrestling match?"

Quentin released Nick's wrist. "No, just a little friendly misunderstanding. I believe Nick, you said you were in a hurry to leave?"

"Yeah." He raised his arm, a cuff hanging on his wrist. "Want your cuffs back?"

Quentin fished out a key, unlocking his cuff. "I'm glad we had this conversation. I wouldn't want there to be any misunderstanding."

Nick rubbed his wrist. "Right. I think we understand each other." He reached for MaryLou's hand. "Time to go, MaryLou. We don't want to get in the middle of Officer Matthews' crime scene."

Nick and MaryLou walked away.

"Thanks, MaryLou. I think Quentin was just about to run me in."

"I thought you two were friends."

"Yeah, we are. But I did crash his crime scene to talk to those witnesses. I'd probably do the same, if I were in his position."

They continued walking toward a cluster of tall grass. "We'll hide in this grass until everyone clears out. I'd like to get a look at the pond again. By the way, how did you know about Quentin? I don't recall telling you about him."

He could barely see her face in the dark, but he heard her voice, feeling her warmth next to him. "You must have said something to me. How else would I know?"

"Yeah, right. Anyway, thanks for jumping in. I have a feeling Quentin would have tossed me in jail tonight."

They waited for emergency vehicles, witnesses, and Quentin to leave. Alone, Nick and MaryLou walked back into the woods, making their way to where Ayisha and Delton had disappeared. They pushed through dense undergrowth to Carl's secret hiding place standing on hard ground.

"So this is where you think your couple disappeared? On Pendleton's farm?"

"Yeah, this is the place." Nick wasn't sure what he was looking for with a flashlight in the darkness. The pieces just didn't seem to quite fit together. Carl may have killed them, but someone like Carl overpowering a Marine seemed a bit of a stretch. And Carl, sitting in the town lock-up, had an alibi for Harlan's death. Junior could be responsible for all of this. Although Carl's recollection made it sound like the couple were suddenly taken up, rather than shot to death, which seemed to be Junior's preference. He also couldn't rule out Harlan simply drowning by accident.

MaryLou had wandered off to his left.

"What are we looking for Nick?"

"I'm not sure. Something's not right."

His thoughts were interrupted by a loud explosion in front of them, a fireball rising fifty feet in the air, followed by explosions on either side. The woods, as if a crop duster had dropped napalm from above, ignited into flames. A raging wall of fire rushed towards them, wind kicking up hot embers setting branches afire. The suddenness of this situation gave them pause, their minds racing to catch up, to respond.

"What the hell was that, Nick?"

"We've got to get out of here."

A fourth explosion rocked them. Only this time Nick watched Mary-Lou collapse, thick yellowish green smoke and fire threatening to consume her. He fought his way through heavy undergrowth to her, acrid fumes burning his eyes and lungs. He pulled out a handkerchief, covering his mouth, took in a breath, then holding her under the arms, dragged her further from the worst of the smoke. Her rising chest let him know she still lived, but he knew they had to get out of this death trap. Nick picked her up, cradling her in his arms, stumbling through brush and trees to find a path. The fire raced after them, trees, columns of flame crashing beside and behind them. Coming to the pond he thought about dashing along its shoreline, but the rapidly burning woods filled with dry kindling of undergrowth swept along both sides of the water. Surrounded by fire, their only path forward meant swimming the pond.

With MaryLou still in his arms, Nick ran into the cool, dark waters. Putting an arm around MaryLou's chest, his hip in her back to help her float, he swam for the opposite shore. By the time they reached the muddy bank, MaryLou coughed into consciousness. Laying her down on the shore, Nick could feel heat emanating from the blaze, millions of tiny red embers floating above them. MaryLou lifted herself up on her elbows.

Nick turned, relieved to see her moving. "Are you okay?"

"Yeah, I think. That's more than your usual fire, Nick."

"We need to go. Do you you think you can walk?"

MaryLou scanned the red and orange flames reflecting on the pond's surface. "Walk? I'm good with running."

They made their way up a bank where a dead Harlan had lain only a short time before, following a path away from the woods towards safety. Rushing out to an open field in front of the farmhouse, they turned to see the entire woods completely ablaze, the night sky lit up with a yellow red glow, county firetruck sirens wailing in the background.

Holding each other, they retraced their steps back to their car, coughing up smoke and taking in deep breaths of fresh, clean air.

MaryLou said, "That was one hell of a fire, Nick. I don't know what started it, but there's definitely something toxic in those woods."

"Yeah. Whatever it was knocked you out cold. You doing better?" Black soot streaked her face and her hazel eyes now floated in a sea of bloodshot red.

"I'll live. Thanks for getting me out of there."

Nick put his arms around her, stroking her hair. "I'm sorry, MaryLou. You shouldn't have been here."

She put her hands on his chest. "I wanted to come, remember? Like I said before, I know how to handle myself."

"Yeah, well, I should have told you what was going on. I put you in danger."

She rested her head on his chest. "What are you talking about? How are you supposed to know we'd find ourselves in the middle of a fire?"

"That fire wasn't' an accident. It was a trap. For me."

She pulled away to look into his eyes. "You think someone tried to kill you by burning down an entire stand of trees? Nick, that's crazy."

"You don't know the guy we're talking about."

"You don't mean Junior, do you? Because I find it hard to believe—"

"No, not Junior. A guy named Jayson Moore."

"Psycho drug dealer, Jayson Moore?"

"You've heard of him?"

"I'm a Houston Chronicle reporter, Nick. Of course I've heard of him. But why would he be after you? Why not just shoot you?"

"Long story, but he has his reasons. He tried to shoot me earlier today."

She pushed him away. "Earlier today? Don't you think you might have mentioned someone trying to kill you?"

"I didn't want you to worry. But you can see now why I shouldn't have brought you out here tonight. Jayson could be anywhere."

"I still would have come with you, Nick. I don't need you to take care of me, well, other than dragging me out of a firestorm. Like I said, I've been a reporter for a long time."

"So it's the story. You'd risk your life for a story."

MaryLou waved her hands, conjuring up a headline. "PI Hunted by Psychopathic Drug Dealer." She smiled, a tease in her reddened eyes. "I like it." Then she stepped toward him, kissing him on his cheek. "Actually, I'd risk my life for you."

He cradled her head in his hands, kissing her, then enveloped her in his arms. Nick knew he had found someone to love who he hoped could grow to love him. How this could be, so quick and intense? But he knew better than to question fate, when fate felt this good.

"I have something I want to give you, MaryLou." Nick unclasped Denny's St. Sebastian, then coming behind her, placed the necklace on her. She held the small medallion in her fingers, firelight dancing off an engraving of a man with an arrow in his neck.

"What's this?"

"St. Sebastian. It belonged to a very good friend of mine. St. Sebastian is the patron saint of protectors like police officers."

"Nick, it's beautiful. Where's your friend now?"

He wrapped his arms around her from behind, like a sailor in a storm holding tightly to a mast. "He died."

"I'm sorry. Are you sure you want me to have this, Nick?"

"Yes. Very sure. I know we just met, but for some reason I feel very good about you."

She reached behind her neck to unclasp the chain. "But Nick, this is too much. It was your friend's."

"I'll tell you what. Why don't you hold it for me. If you decide you've had enough of me, then give it back. Otherwise, hold it for me. How does that sound?"

MaryLou turned the silver medallion over in her fingers, feeling its shape and form. "Okay, Nick. Sure, I'll hold it for you."

He walked her around the car, opening the passenger side door.

"By the way, Nick, you were pretty good back there."

Nick said, "Just shear terror and adrenaline."

And love.

22 JUNIOR REVISITED

Driving back to MaryLou's motel, Nick watched her stare out of her window into the night. "Odd end to our first date, I suppose."

"What?" She turned to him. "Oh, visiting a crime scene and almost getting killed in a fire? Standard procedure for a journalist."

Nick smiled. He couldn't help but love a woman who let murder and mayhem roll off her back. Love. He knew the feeling and he couldn't deny what he felt around her.

"Well, I'm sorry the night went this way. I would have been quite happy to still be with you in my trailer."

She rested a hand on Nick's thigh. "Yeah, me too Nick."

They drove past housing developments, shopping centers and brightly lit billboards, back to the interstate and finally to her motel. Nick pulled beside her Prius. She leaned over, kissing him, her lips as soft as he remembered from earlier in the evening.

"Why don't you come in, stay the night?"

He wanted to follow her into Room 209, her soft, warm flesh against his own. But he also knew Jayson Moore lurked in the shadows, waiting for another opportunity to kill him. He was not about to share room on Jayson's bullseye with his fearless reporter turned lover.

"I need to go back to the Justice Center, look up Quentin. You know, make things right."

She put a hand on his cheek. Her perfume clouding his mind. "He must be a damned good friend, because I'm offering you a pretty good deal."

"Yeah. He's had my back more than once. But I'll see you tomorrow, right? Lunch at the Bluebonnet?"

They agreed on the Bluebonnet, then Nick drove directly back to Junior's farm. He waited for the last fire truck to leave, then left his Cadillac down by the main road. Walking up to the farmhouse burnt wood and smoke from embers thickened the air. To his surprise, Junior sat on a porch swing, a beer in hand. Stepping up onto his wood porch, boards creaked, startling Junior. He reached for a rifle leaning against the wall.

"Touch that gun and I'll shoot you dead, Junior."

Junior's hand hesitated over his weapon, a 30.06.

"Okay. Okay. I'm not touching it. You *federale* types are kind of trigger happy, aren't you?"

Nick stepped past Junior, grabbing his rifle, then tossing it into the yard.

"Now goddamn! Why you keep tossing my perfectly good guns across my property?"

"Because I don't trust you around guns, Junior. Too many people seem to get hurt when you have one in your hands."

Junior stayed seated in his swing, Nick standing over him. "You've got nothing to hold me on, so you might as well go home."

"I'm a private investigator, Junior. I can't hold you on anything."

"Yeah, whatever." Junior pushed his swing into a rocking motion with his legs.

Nick asked, "Where were you late Thursday night?"

"I told you when you asked me before. I was at home and there ain't no witnesses."

Nick grabbed the chain suspending Junior's swing to stop its rocking. "That's too bad. An alibi would be helpful to you about now. What about Saturday morning between nine and eleven?"

"Working on my tractor. Again, no witnesses. I'm a farmer. I don't go walking around all day with a posse like some movie star."

"Did you see Harlan Jones anytime Friday or Saturday?"

"No. I didn't see him."

"How do you think the fire got started?"

Junior rose from his swing, ducking past Nick to the other side of his porch. "You trying to pin that on me too? Why in the hell would I burn down my own property?"

Nick followed him like a wrestler tracking his opponent in a ring. "Maybe you found a young couple in your woods and you didn't like that. You got your shotgun, scared Carl off and then killed them both."

Junior pinned against the railing, said, "That's crazy. You got nothing on me."

"And Harlan, he stumbled upon something. Maybe bodies. So you had to get rid of him, too. But now you've got a problem. Three bodies and evidence all over those woods. What better way to clean up your mess than by burning them down."

"Bullshit!" Junior squirmed away.

"Sit down, Junior. Now!"

Junior slide back onto his porch swing, mumbling. "That's bullshit."

"Really? This is a farm. I'll bet you've got lots of ways to start a fire. Gasoline, ammonium nitrate."

"Ammonium nitrate? Do I look like a damn chemistry teacher to you?"

"Fertilizer, Junior. Fertilizer. You keep telling me you're a farmer. Don't you use fertilizer?"

"Sure I do. Oh, okay. Yeah, ammonium nitrate. Fertilizer. Sure. I've got it stored in a shed, but that don't mean I'm setting my own farm on fire."

Well somebody started the fire, Junior. Maybe Jayson Moore? What do you know about him?"

"Jayson Moore? Lemme think. I heard of him somewhere. Wait, ain't he that cop killer who was all over the news a few months ago? You think he's in my woods?" Junior looked toward his fields as if Jayson Moore might step out at any moment.

"Very good question, Junior. Why would Jayson Moore be on your property?"

"I ain't said he was. Whoever did this is crazy though. Somebody could have been killed. Hell, I guess you're lucky to have made it out alive. It sure burned the hell out of my woods. My Daddy, God rest his soul, would be so deeply saddened to see his woods burned down, being a nature lover and all." Junior stared at his hands for a time, as if honoring the memory of his dear departed daddy. Then he raised his eyes to meet Nick's, a crooked smile and renewed confidence guiding his voice.

"You don't have shit, Mr. Private Investigator. Oh, you've got your theories, but it sounds to me like you've got nothing to back up anything you're saying. Seems to me your couple just ran off to get some distance from the girl's crazy preacher daddy. They're probably banging away in some motel room as we speak. And Harlan, he just tried to swim my pond and drowned. It happens. As for the fire, well they sell those damn fireworks to anybody. We are in the middle of a drought, you know. Seems to me you've got all the evidence you need and not one damned bit of it has anything to do with me. In fact, I'm the damned victim here! My property has been destroyed, my good name is being dragged through the mud, all because you want to prove something. You know, the story I heard was you let that Jayson fellow kill your partner right in front of you and you didn't lift a damned finger. So don't come up to me being all righteous and shit."

Nick picked Junior up by two fistfuls of shirt, ready to drive him right through the wall of his house. Junior glared defiant, almost willing Nick to act. Nick shoved him back into the swing.

"If I find out you have anything to do with Ayisha, Delton, or Harlan, I will come back Junior. And when I'm done with you, you'll be eating from a tube."

Junior opened his mouth to speak, but stayed silent. Nick stepped off the porch, picking up Junior's rifle on the way to his car. His back still turned, he raised Junior's gun up in the air. "You can buy this one back on eBay too, Junior."

Walking away Nick heard Junior's cursing all the way down his drive to the main road.

23 HANDSHAKE

When Nick got to his car he found Quentin sitting on his front fender waiting for him. "Am I under arrest again?"

"Sorry buddy," Quentin said, laughing, "but you've got to admit you were out of line."

"Yeah, maybe. So, what do I owe the pleasure of your company?"

Quentin rose from the fender, breathing in damp, burnt air. "Before you prevaricate about being here during the fire, I've got witnesses who saw you drive away in this very vehicle."

"You're not accusing me of starting a fire?'

"Nick, what's going on?"

"I told you, I'm checking into this missing couple. The girl's dad thinks she might be shacked up with the boy."

"Let me rephrase my question. In order to give me a reason not to arrest you, then hold you in lock up for suspicion of arson, what's going on?"

Quentin didn't have the look of someone making a practical joke, but rather the stern fixed jaw of a man who has had enough. Nick had wanted to avoid getting Quentin involved simply because he wanted, no, he needed to deal with Jayson Moore on his own. He owed Denny and he had no intention of letting another friend take a bullet for him. However, he also knew Quentin would not step aside easily.

"Okay friend, you win. At first I thought the father had it right about his daughter simply running away with her young man. But when I spoke to Junior and then to Carl, I knew something else had to be going down. And I don't think the dead body in the pond was an accident."

"The man drowned, Nick. The coroner said there was no sign of foul play, no marks, no sign of a struggle. Just a fully clothed guy drowning in a pond."

"We're talking about Junior's pond, Quentin. You can't tell me you don't think Junior had something to do with it."

"Sure, I do. But I have to work with the evidence and all I've got is a drowning victim." Quentin tipped his hat brim up with a finger, leaning back against the Cadillac again. "What do you make of this fire?"

"Junior might have started it in a crazy plan to destroy all of the evidence."

"But?"

Nick let out a sigh. "I think whoever set off the explosion which caused the fire was also the one who tried to shoot me yesterday."

"Jayson Moore?"

"How would you know about Moore?"

"I put it together like I imagine you did, my friend. Who else would go to the trouble to kill a sorry ass private investigator? And then the answer came to me. Only someone who doesn't want you around to testify against him. Which leaves Jayson Moore."

Nick leaned against the fender with Quentin. Rasping cicadas and an occasional barn owl hoot filled the night air. "I saw him at the overpass, Quen. Sorry I didn't tell you. I guess I just didn't want you to get hurt."

"Nick, not only am I your friend, but like you, I do this for a living. What happened to Denny could happen to any of us. He knew what he had signed on for."

"I know, I just, I…"

"You feel responsible. I get it. But you need to honor the man's commitment. He stood in front of a psychopath because he wanted to be there. Don't take it away from him."

Nick's head told him Quentin was right. Denny died because Jayson Moore killed him, not for anything he either did or didn't do for his partner. However, Nick's heart told him he'd find the sick bastard and make him pay.

"Look Nick, I know you want Moore. Hell, I'd love for you to have a shot at him, but you've got to do this the right way. If you're going to take him down, it needs to be legit. I have no intention of visiting you in prison for the next twenty years."

"So what do you have in mind?"

"Just keep me in the loop. Don't go after this guy by yourself. We've always had each other's backs, so let's keep it that way. I'll help you find Moore and if opportunity allows, I might accidentally leave you alone with him. Then we'll put the bruised and battered bastard away, by the book, for good."

Quentin offered his hand, which Nick took in his own. Both of them knew their handshake, born out of a foundation of trust, had very real consequences. Quentin, whether Nick had second thoughts or not, was now officially in the loop. They sat on the fender for a time, an occasional shooting star streaking across the sky.

"So tell me about this new girlfriend of yours. Nice looking lady."

"MaryLou? Yeah, I just met her today, but I've got to admit I'm a bit smitten."

"Having met her, I can definitely see how you might be, my friend. She from around here?"

"Well, that's the downside. She's a reporter from Houston."

"I'm just glad to see you back in the saddle. For awhile I was beginning to think you had taken a vow of celibacy."

"Yeah, me too."

Quentin stood, his hands on his hips. "I'm going to be on my way. We'll be in touch."

As the red taillights of Quentin's patrol car disappeared over a hill, Nick opened the creaky door of his Rent-a-Wreck. He needed something to go on — some clue leading him to the couple, to Harlan's killer, or Jayson Moore's hiding place. Something had to break loose and soon.

24 FREE AND CLEAR

Junior's world seemed to get more complicated with each wheezing breath. He had watched his friend Harlan drown right in front of him, followed by a visit from the damned police because Harlan had done a floater and some nosey naked teenaged girls discovered the body. He wondered what kind of parents let their girls go skinny dipping looking for dead bodies. And the whole time he talked to the cops he kept wondering if he had removed all traces of those two agents from his barn. *Thank the Lord the whole damn circus finally packed it in.*

When Nick took a walk in the woods, Junior realized he had been presented with an opportunity to remove at least one of the monkeys off his back. A couple of months ago, he followed through on a brilliant plan to protect his toxic waste dumping sites from prying eyes. He had seen a show on television where a bad guy had a burn room where he kept all his stuff. When the good guys showed up, his burn room went up in flames, all the evidence turning to ash. Junior figured he'd turn his farm into a "burn farm", so if the cops got too close he could flip a switch, walking away a free man. He made up gasoline bombs using some instructions he got off the internet, then placed them strategically around his toxic dumping sites. Now, with Nick Sibelius walking right into the middle of his burn farm, he wished he had lit a few of those bombs up. He figured a few fiery explosions and Mr. Private Investigator would be so terrified, he'd never come back.

To his astonishment, his handiwork exploded without his help, although for a moment he wondered if he had somehow ignited the bombs with the power of his mind. Seeing explosions in his woods, he decided to stay in the farmhouse, wanting to look as innocent as possible. He stood in his bedroom peering out his window. To his horror, his bombs proved way more effective than planned, as a raging fire swept up not only the woods, but the surrounding corn and cotton fields, including his hidden patch of marijuana, not to mention a few miscellaneous barrels of environmental resource. Then he saw Sibelius and some woman run out of the woods. Didn't anyone respect private property anymore?

Junior had gone out on his porch expecting Sibelius to come for him, but to his relief, his plan had worked and mister investigator slash pain in the ass must have been too shaken up to come after him. So he kept a watchful eye on some county fire department boys putting out the blaze, ready to run if some wise ass fireman decided to start identifying narcotic plants in the middle of extinguishing a grass fire. With only embers left smoldering and the county trucks driving off, Junior took a long pull from his beer. Things were starting to turn in his favor. Finally able to relax, he leaned his head back, drifting towards sleep. Then Sibelius showed up out of nowhere, spiraling things down the toilet bowl of his life, once again.

~*~

He had spent all morning, after Nick's late visit, trying to work through how he got himself in this mess and how he could possibly get out of it. Junior, at wits end, sat in his pickup in the Justice Center parking lot with an overpowering desire to vomit, crap his pants, and drink himself into unconsciousness. However, the penalty for not showing up at Barry's frightened him too much to give in to his body's desires.

He didn't want the couple snooping around his farm anymore, but he didn't want to kill them just because Barry was one paranoid son of a bitch. Taking them to Barry's place had seemed like a good option, but he hadn't really thought through what Barry would do with them. Thank you Jayson fucking Moore. Given Barry seemed even more hyped up than usual, Junior had a bad feeling about where all of this might be going. Maybe getting Carl out of the town lock up and therefore, not rambling on and on about their illegal operations, would soften Barry up a bit.

He also had second thoughts about his shotgun, especially after the private dickhead took his rifle too. Sibelius acted all law and order, but Junior figured he just wanted those guns for himself. He considered reporting the theft of his cherished twelve gauge, but reconsidered as he sat in the Justice Center parking lot. The more time he spent around police types, the more the odds went against him and he'd be having to call his attorney again. How Sibelius stole his guns still pissed him off. They must teach them some crazy *ju jtzu* at wherever investigator's learn their stuff. Having riled himself up, he re-considered claiming both of his guns. However, Barry told him to get Carl, and get Carl was exactly what he was going to do. So he walked down the hallway to be greeted by a pretty young woman in a police uniform at the front desk.

"How can I help, Mr. Pendleton?"

"Oh, you know who I am." Junior liked the idea this pretty little thing knew him by name.

"Well, sure. You've lived here all your life. I used to go swimming in your Daddy's pond."

Junior paused imagining this young woman sitting behind the counter swimming naked in his pond. She sat back, lifting a file to chest height, which made checking out her titties pretty much impossible.

Junior said, "I am heartily sorry I missed your outdoor recreational activities."

"Yes, I'm sure you are. Must be odd knowing *you're* old man Pendleton now."

Junior, actively sowing his oats as it were, physically felt the sudden impact of her words, tone, and body language leaving him with the feeling of having the sexual attraction equivalent to a chunk of discarded concrete. One moment, in his mind, he was a vibrant sexual alpha male teasing a hot, young woman into bed and the next moment he was a decrepit old man saying creepy things to a girl who could be his daughter.

She looked at him with what he perceived to be disdain or worse, judgement, saying, "Now, how can I help you?"

Junior felt so deflated his words mumbled out. "I need to bail out my nephew."

"Carl?"

"Yeah, that's him."

Junior noticed Officer Matthews, the same cop who came to his door the night before, eyeing him from a distance. He got up from his desk, walking over to the counter.

"Is this gentleman causing you any trouble?"

Junior's confidence dissolved further under her gaze and now with this other cop eying him, a slight panic crawled around his stomach.

"No problem. He's just here to pick up his nephew."

Matthews rested one hand casually on his sidearm, the other on the countertop. "If I were you I'd keep an eye on that nephew of yours. Do you know he's been peeing all over people?"

Junior stepped back, taking a moment to comprehend the officer's words. "Uh no, I don't keep up with where he pees. I'll definitely have a word with him, officer."

"You do that. I don't want to see him in here again. Okay?"

~*~

As soon as Junior signed all the papers, he gathered Carl up, walking quickly out of the police station toward his pickup.

"Thanks, Uncle Junior."

"Shut up."

They drove in silence back to the farmhouse until Junior could no longer keep from speaking.

"What in hell's name were you doing, Carl? I mean, I get you jacking off in the woods, but standing on a table and pissing all over a family?"

Carl stared out his window wishing he lived in one of those nice suburban houses in subdivisions with names like Heatherwilde and Falcon Point. Anywhere but with his uncle. He'd mow his lawn and have a dog named Hank. "I was a bit drunk, Uncle."

"So what did you see in the woods, Carl?"

Junior's question pulled him off his manicured lawn and into the dark woods several nights ago. "Nothing. Just a couple."

"So what the hell were they doing in my woods? Did you see 'em snooping around, like they were looking for somethin'?"

Carl looked over at Junior, a smile crossing his face. "They were lookin' for somethin' alright."

Junior banged his open palm on the steering wheel. "I knew it!"

"They were looking to fuck their brains out. Man, you should have seen 'em."

Junior grabbed the wheel with both hands to steady himself. "What? What are you saying? You saying they were just fuckin' in the woods? That's it? Damn it, boy."

"What?"

"Nothin' Carl. Nothin'."

Carl thought watching two people do it in the woods was a pretty good story, but Junior didn't seem impressed at all. They passed a gas station offering a free liter of soda with a fill up, a storage lot with a couple of bass boats on trailers behind a fence, and then left the suburbs down a two lane road leading to their farm. Junior turned up a dirt road stopping by the front porch.

"Carl, I want you to stay here until I come get you. Understand?"

"Yessir."

"And whatever you do, you stay clear of a guy named Barry Swenson. I mean it now, Carl. Don't mess with Barry. He looks harmless, but he's one crazy sonvabitch. I have a feeling he's going to be a bit moody for the next few days. Can you do that for me?"

"Yessir. Stay clear of Barry Swenson."

"And Carl?"

"Yessir?"

"How 'bout if you keep your prick to yourself for awhile. That's not too much to ask, is it?"

"No. No sir. I'll keep it to myself."

"Good."

~*~

Junior eased his truck out onto the main road. Given Carl hadn't seen much of anything and now he knew his couple were not federal agents, he had decided to keep Carl away from Barry for the time being. He felt apprehensive about going back to meet with Barry, but he figured the man had to chew his ass at least a little, just to let his other guys know he was in charge. The talk about killing those two people was just that—talk. He knew some things hadn't worked out quite the way they were planned, but he also knew from years of experience shit happens. At least shit always seemed to happen to him.

Arriving at Barry's compound, Junior stepped out of his truck to see Barry leaning against the front of a nearby van, not saying a word, staring at Junior with those cold blue beady eyes. Junior tried to hold his gaze, but as moments passed he felt increasingly uncomfortable and exposed until he couldn't keep silent any longer.

"Helluva time, eh Barry? Helluva time. I thought those two were *federales* or some such, but you know what I found out?"

Barry continued to glare at him.

"They're not agents at all, Barry. Hell, they were just fuckin' in the woods. Imagine. Mosquitoes must have been having a field day."

Junior could swear Barry's eyes were burning holes in his flesh.

"But of course, we definitely need to do something. Can't let them get in the way of commerce. No sir. One accidental slip from them and I'd have the USDA or the EPA or some such federal agency right up my ass. Yessir. That's no way to run a legitimate toxic waste disposal business. No way at all."

Barry stared blankly, his face not giving any hint of his thoughts. Junior found himself talking just to fill space.

"The girl's pretty cute though. I'm thinking maybe, instead of killing her, we might as well have a little fun with her. Maybe beat the shit out of her Marine. Put the fear of God into both of 'em, then send 'em on their way. That'd do the trick. Absofuckinlutely."

Junior looked to Barry for some sign of agreement. Getting none, he plunged forward with his argument.

"I mean, being an entra-manure can be lonely work, if you know what I mean. I'm just saying it would be a bit of a waste if we didn't...well, you know what I mean. What's going on, Barry? You're making me a bit nervous just staring like that."

Barry squinted his beady eyes. "I'm making you nervous? My apologies. I guess I was just listening to you drivel on about the girl, when I really want to know why you seem intent on sabotaging our entire operation."

"Sabotage? What do you mean sabotage?"

"Where to start?" Barry cocked his head, hands on his high waistband. "Let's see. You told Jayson you needed some help, which he apparently was happy to do for an old friend. I imagine he assumed you wanted help offing those two and burying them on your property somewhere. Instead, you bring them to *my* compound, compromising *my* operation because some couple was fornicating in your woods. Now you've got a private investigator and a journalist sniffing around, Carl's talking to the law—"

"I just picked him up. He didn't say a word, Barry."

"Shut up, Junior. We've got your idiot nephew talking to cops and now I understand the law found that Harlan fellow you killed in your pond. Are you trying to get every law enforcement organization in the country after us?"

"But I handled it, Barry. Its all taken care of. When Harlan wandered into my property the idiot drowned hisself."

"You told me you killed him."

"In a manner of speaking." Junior flashed a knowing smile as if speaking to a co-conspirator. "That's the beauty of it. He tried to get away from me by swimming across my pond and he didn't make it. Get it? He's just another drowning victim. And just to be sure our tracks were covered, I set the woods on fire. Burned the whole damned thing down." Junior made a sweeping motion with his arms to emphasize the grandeur of his plan. "Used some gasoline bombs I made. Man, that stuff really packs a punch. Ka-Blam!" He waved his arms for effect. "Those woods were afire like Satan lit a match. So there's no evidence for the cops to find. We're free and clear, Barry. I'll bet you don't have anybody else around here willing to burn down their entire farm for the cause. No sir. And Carl, well I agree, he's an idiot. But his lack of mental capacity works in our favor. Look, if the police had anything on Carl they wouldn't have let him walk. We're clear, man."

Barry reached behind his back. Retrieving a gun from his waistband with his right hand, he racked the slide of his .45 with the other. Slamming Junior up against the van, Barry pressed his gun's cold, steel muzzle so hard against Junior's temple his vision blurred.

"I want to just outright shoot you, but our history together leads me to hesitate."

"Barry, please—"

"Shut up, you imbecile. Did you ever think maybe Jayson set off those explosions to kill Sibelius and destroy the evidence of your stupidity?"

With a gun to his head, Junior realized thinking he had exploded those bombs with his mind might have been a bit hopeful. "What? Well, yes, but—"

"I'm not asking you a question you lying moron. Until you prove otherwise, you don't deserve to talk to me. I don't want to hear you. I don't even want to see you. I know we were classmates as children, Junior, but one more fuck up, one more, and you're dead. Do you understand me?"

Junior shook uncontrollably.

Barry shouted, "Do you understand me?"

"Yes. Yes, I understand. I'm sorry. I'm sorry."

Barry grabbed Junior by his collar, throwing him to the ground.

"Now take the Marine and his girlfriend to the back pasture and deal with them. And be sure their bodies won't be found. Do you think you can accomplish this one simple task? Because I swear to God, if you screw this up, I will personally strap you to my dental chair, shove my gun up your ass and pull the trigger."

Junior crawled away from his tormentor. "Yes sir. I've got this. Definitely. Thank you, sir."

With a swift kick to Junior's retreating rear end, Barry yelled, "Stand up and walk like a man. Jesus!"

~*~

Junior walked back into the barn sweaty with fear, covered in dirt, the left side of his face bruised and swollen. Pulling himself together, he ordered one of the guards in a still quavering voice, to untie his prisoners, except for ties binding their hands. Junior, led Ayisha and Delton away at gun point. After getting some distance from the barn, he took off their hoods so they could navigate their way to the killing field. He walked them through several pastures, finally coming to a pasture surrounded by trees, about a mile from Barry's barn.

"Okay, this is far enough. You two stop."

Delton said, "Look, you don't want to do this, man. Just let us go. We'll keep quiet."

"I don't think Barry's the type to let you live. You two seem alright, but this is about protecting my business interests."

"Business interests? We were just walking through your woods. Let us go. We won't tell anyone about you guys."

Junior shrugged. "I can't help it if George Washington screwed things up. If it wasn't for him, we wouldn't be having this conversation."

Delton looked to Ayisha and then back to Junior. "What does George Washington have to do with anything?"

Junior didn't feel like killing anyone, even if they didn't have a complete grasp of American history, but then again, he really didn't like the idea of Barry killing *him*. The shame of being thrown in the dirt with that fat bastard screaming at him in front of everyone left Junior desperate to have some power, some control. He'd kill them alright, he had to. But on his own terms.

"How about this. How about if we do a little trade. I get a little quality time with your girlfriend here, then you two can walk free."

"Leave her out of this."

"You're telling me what to do? You're really not in much of a bargaining position, now are you?"

"Leave her alone, you son of a bitch!"

"I don't think I like your attitude." With his hands tied behind his back Delton couldn't block the backhanded blow of Junior's gun against his head, knocking him to the ground. Junior felt a rush of adrenalin and the control he felt with a gun in his hand. He turned to Ayisha.

"Look, I'm not going to do nothin'."

Ayisha stood trembling, an overwhelming fear and dread taking hold of her. "Delton..."

Junior stroked her face with his pistol. "This is harder on me than on you. I'm the one who's got to bury you both. Do you have any idea how long it's goin' to take digging in this hard dirt? So stop your whining. I told you, I'm not goin' to do nothing. Well, except shoot you, of course. Move over by the fence."

Ayisha stood frozen, terrified, alone.

"Move! Or I'll put a bullet in your boyfriend right now."

This was working out far better than Junior had imagined. He had his Marine face down unconscious in the dirt and he figured the girl would go down with one shot. He hoped so. He didn't want to kill her, but this was one of those "you or me" moments and Junior definitely felt in the "me" camp. Yeah, he'd kill these two and bury their bodies. That damn Barry didn't know who he was dealing with. No sir.

Junior, lost in visualizing the murder and burial of his victims, barely had time to consciously register a quick movement at his feet. Delton, breaking free from his bindings, had hammered Junior's knee with a powerfully placed kick. Crashing to the dirt, Junior's gun slipped out of his hand, as excruciating pain seared up his leg. He looked up toward an azure Texas sky just as Delton's boot impacted his face and all went black.

~*~

Delton used Junior's knife to cut Ayisha's bindings, then held her shuddering body, stroking her head, kissing tears from her cheeks.

"I'm so sorry, Ayisha. I'm so sorry."

"Not your fault." She wiped a final tear away, her voice strengthening. "Let's just get out of here."

Delton looked over at Junior lying unconscious, his leg twisted awkwardly. "I should kill the son of a bitch."

"Let's tie him up and get out of here. Killing him won't change anything."

If he had been alone, Delton knew he would have broken Junior's neck. But he wanted to be more, better, for Ayisha. For her, he would walk away. Delton used Junior's belt to hog tie him knowing once he came to, the awkward position would maximize his pain. He then took Ayisha's hand and they ran away from the farm, away from their nightmare, and toward freedom.

25 LOST AND FOUND

Walking for about an hour, Delton and Ayisha shared silence, only communicating through a firm grip of each other's hand. Hearing the rumble of traffic, they crested a hill to see a four lane highway. The two walked the shoulder, hoping to hitch a ride, but a bloodied, battered black couple on a lone highway did not seem to attract any takers. Then a black pickup slowed down, pulling off the road just behind them.

Delton glanced back at the truck. "Great. That's all we need."

"What do you mean? This is good. Maybe he'll help us."

"I don't know where you're from Ayisha, but in my world a big pickup coming to a stop behind you usually doesn't have a happy ending."

A large white man with shoulder length blond hair climbed out of his truck.

Ayisha squeezed Delton's hand. "Delton, we were kidnapped. Of course he'll help us."

Delton looked at his beautiful Ayisha, dirty, bruised and disheveled. He figured he looked even worse. No, even if this guy wanted to help, one look at them and he'd have a cop put them in handcuffs in the back of a squad car before you could say "racial profiling." However, given there could be several angry, radical right white guys with guns chasing them, the back of a patrol car just might be their best refuge.

~*~

When Junior hadn't returned from his killing duties, Barry had sent Jayson Moore down the road to be sure the Marine and his girlfriend weren't getting away. Only a few miles into his search he came across them walking beside the road. The man didn't wear a shirt, so if he had a gun somewhere, by the time he reached in to get it, Jayson knew he'd have the drop on him. Getting out of his truck, he scanned for weapons or odd movements, while he started a casual conversation.

"Afternoon. How are you folks doing today?"

The man looked guarded, almost trapped. The girl, however, looked relieved.

"Thank you for stopping, mister. We were kidnapped. You've got to help us. They may be chasing after us."

"Kidnapped you say. What's your name?"

"Ayisha."

"And you are?" he asked the shirtless man.

"Delton. Look, if you don't believe us—"

"Whoa there, who said I didn't believe you. If you're Delton Jessup, then you must be Ayisha Anderson. There's a lot of people worried about you two. Why don't you hop in my truck and I'll give you nice folks a ride to the police station."

They moved toward his truck when Delton held Ayisha's arm to stop. "How do you know our last names?"

"Like I said, everyone in town's looking for you two. Come on, I've got some bottled water in my truck."

Ayisha turned to Delton. "It's okay, Delton. He's here to help us."

"I don't know, Ayisha. Something doesn't feel right. His voice, it sounds familiar."

Jayson asked, "Are you two coming or would you prefer to just keep walking down the highway until your kidnappers catch up to you again?"

Delton still hesitated, but Ayisha pulled on his arm. "Come on Delton. He's going to help us."

He lifted Ayisha into the truck, not seeing Jayson come up behind him. The big man slammed a crushing blow with the butt of a handgun across Delton's skull. The Marine crumpled to the ground. Ayisha, screaming, lunged for Jayson, but the big man blocked her attack as if playing with a toddler. Grabbing her hair he yanked her out of his truck to the hard dirt. As blood pooled by Delton's head, Jayson kept his attention on the girl. Raising his gun, he increased pressure on the trigger. Ayisha crawled away on all fours, rocks strewn across the shoulder cutting into her legs. Before he could fire, a rig hauling a back hoe came to a stop behind them. Jayson stepped over, grabbing the girl by the waist of her shorts. Lifting her like a grocery bag, he slammed her to unconsciousness against his pickup, then tossed her into the truck bed. He fired at the two men getting out of their big rig's cab, missing in his haste, but keeping them at bay long enough to make his way back inside his pickup. He shoved the truck into drive, the rear end fishtailing, kicking up rock and dirt, then speeding away, the dead Marine all the while getting smaller in his rear view mirror.

26 ICU

When MaryLou and Nick parted the previous evening, they had agreed to meet at the Bluebonnet for a late breakfast the next day. After a busy night, the idea of breakfast with MaryLou felt grounding to Nick. His only hesitancy being some questions he knew he needed to ask. Something about the previous night, how she had insisted he take his phone call, nagged at him. Lying in bed, naked and spent after making love, and she had wanted him to answer his phone. She may have been insistent out of concern for the missing couple, but something didn't feel right. Of course, imagining darkness on a bright, sunny day had been one of the things his ex had teased, then later in their relationship, accused him of doing. However, Nick knew his intuition had saved him more often than not.

As MaryLou walked at his side toward the cafe, he noticed a confidence and maturity she carried, her beauty deeper than the usual external markers of looks and fashion. Now sitting across from each other in a booth, bacon grease, sweet maple syrup, and coffee permeated the place, small talk providing background noise to their conversation.

Nick took a sip of coffee, then sat back resting from a long night. His nature required him to tie up loose ends, but he wasn't looking forward to tying up a loose end called MaryLou.

"Quite a night."

She smiled, looking into her coffee cup, then up to Nick. "I suppose getting shot at by an armed redneck, then running for your life from a fire does qualify as quite a night."

Nick took in MaryLou, her eyes penetrating several layers below his surface. He didn't want to ask his question, some part of himself knowing the truth might break the bond they felt for each other. However, he had a missing couple and a dead fisherman.

"MaryLou, what's a Houston Chronicle reporter doing in Pflugerville, Texas anyway?"

MaryLou put her coffee cup down, pausing to speak. Nick noticed her unconsciously biting her lower lip, then exhaling deeply. There was something she was not telling him. A sense of dread and impending loss came over him. Did he love her? His failed marriage had taught him opening his heart to someone could result in pain. But he had been captivated by this smart, fun woman and he needed to be touched. He needed the physical release of making love. He kept thinking about MaryLou, remembering her touch, the earthy smell of her body. In quiet moments he found himself wondering what she was doing, how she was doing. And yet, his intuition kept telling him something about MaryLou didn't quite add up. But what?

"MaryLou. I wanted to say this to you under other circumstances, but before you speak, you need to know. I care about you. A lot. I have a sense you're feeling the same way about me. So before you speak, think about us. We've got to be able to trust each other."

She smiled, reaching across the table to hold his hand. "I'm pretty fond of you, Nick. And to answer your question, I'm just a journalist."

Nick heard her words, but his inner voice continued to harass him, coloring his voice with disbelief. "You are."

"Yes." She said the word with some insistence, as if she could sense his doubt. "Initially I was going to do a story about cycling east of Pflugerville."

"Cycling, like bicycles?"

"Yeah. I write for the travel section. Austin is a cycling town, you know. But then a great story dropped in my lap, so I decided to stick around."

"The disappearance."

MaryLou smiled, her eyes mischievous. "And a dead handsome private investigator working the case."

Nick looked at her, wondering if his lingering feeling MaryLou had something to hide had more to do with being a burned out cop from Houston than some secret harbored by this beautiful woman sitting in front of him.

"So how's your story going so far?"

"You're going to have to work your way through the *Kama Sutra* with me first before I start giving up my sources."

Nick pulled out his cell phone, busily tapping the screen.

MaryLou leaned in. "What are you doing?"

"Downloading a digital version of the *Kama Sutra*. I learned long ago if I'm going to be an effective PI, I have to be thorough in my investigations."

He held her gaze, a combination of love and something else. Something disturbing he couldn't quite put his finger on.

She glanced away first. "Nick, I wanted to talk to you about this last night and well, we didn't get a chance. I—"

Quentin's photo came up with a tone on Nick's phone. He put the phone to his ear. "I better take this." He mouthed the word, 'Sorry', turning his attention to Quentin's voice.

"I've got some news for you here buddy." Quentin sounded solemn. Nick wondered if his friend still harbored some hurt feelings from their altercation the night before.

"You've decided to finally pay me back for the Cowboys game?"

"You never give up, do you Nick. But listen. An ambulance brought Delton Jessup in an hour ago."

"An ambulance? How is he?"

"Not so good. The docs here tell me it looks pretty bad."

"Have you spoken to him?"

"Not yet, but I'm hoping to. You can join me if you want."

"Absolutely. I'll head right over." He ended the call with a glance toward MaryLou.

"Did he find the couple, Nick?"

"Only Delton, and he's in pretty bad shape. I'm going to go over to the hospital in a few minutes."

"You mind of if join you?"

Nick began to get up from the booth. "I don't know, MaryLou. I probably should do this on my own."

"I'll stay out of your way. It's just, since I met you, I feel invested in this couple. Please?"

MaryLou's sincere, pleading eyes convinced him against his better judgement to concede to her request. They left two cups of coffee steaming at their booth, Nick dropping enough money for coffee and a tip on their table.

Nick's Rent-a-Wreck proved a fiery furnace in the summer heat, carrying them to a hospital on I35, where Nick parked by the ER. Quentin walked through sliding glass doors as they approached the emergency room entrance. He briefed Nick while they made their way to the ICU. Delton lay on a bed surrounded by myriad drawers and cabinets labeled for a variety of urgent care pads, tubes, bandages, and other tools of the trade. Overhead fluorescent lighting flooded his room with harsh light, which along with the cold temperature and his wounds, gave Delton a sickly pall. His eyes were open, but they stared unfocused at the cabinets.

Quentin leaned over Delton. "I know you've been through a great deal, but I do need to ask you a few questions. Delton, is there anyone you'd like us to contact?"

Delton spoke in a whisper, "No, I'm good."

"Can you tell me about what happened to you."

"Kidnapped. We got away, but then...Ayisha."

Delton tried to move, but Quentin laid a hand on his shoulder to encourage him to stay down. "We're looking for her, Delton. Can you tell me who did this to you?"

"Big, blonde, white. Black pickup."

Nick, standing behind Quentin, said, "Jayson."

Quentin continued, "This big, blonde white guy kidnapped you?"

"No. Pendleton. Junior. Barry Swenson." Delton reached up, tubes running from his arm, grabbing Quentin's sleeve. "Ayisha. Find her. Stop..." His voice trailed off, losing consciousness again. Throughout their interview Nick's focus had been on Quentin and Delton. Now he turned to look at MaryLou, noticing the color had completely left her face.

"Are you okay, MaryLou?"

"I, I think I must have eaten something a bit off. If you don't mind, I better go on back to my motel."

Quentin gave Nick a nod. "We're almost done here, Nick, if you want to go.

MaryLou offered a faint smile. "Don't be silly. You do what you need to do with Quentin. I'll be fine. I imagine I just need to go lie down for awhile, then I'll be as good as gold."

Nick locked eyes with her, the same inner voice still sounding off, but he needed to focus on Delton. "Well, call me if you need anything."

"You're a sweet man. But when I don't feel well I usually just lock the door and turn out the lights. Don't worry. I'll be fine."

27 HAPPY REUNION

Junior came to, face down in the dirt, hog tied with his own belt. The tension of leather pulling at his aching knee hurt badly enough for him to thoughtlessly scream out for help. As soon as the cry left his lips he wished he could take it back. If Barry discovered he had let the couple escape, he would be dead. He writhed on the ground, trying to swallow his cries, sobbing as he struggled to free himself. Hours passed and the knowledge he might die hog tied out in this field, fire ants feeding on his carcass, crept into his thoughts. Then he heard voices. He wanted to shout out, but what if it was Barry? He had to risk it. Even if Barry found him, maybe he'd understand. The black guy had been a Marine after all.

"Here. Over here!"

Grass rustled with the movement of several people. Junior rolled on his other side. Seeing his four rescuers armed to the hilt with Barry in front almost made him pass out. Barry stood about ten feet away. His bulbous shape and white skin reminded Junior of the giant Yeti guy he saw on the Discovery Channel a couple of weeks ago. He wished he could remember if Yetis were cannibals or not, although he wasn't altogether certain being eaten by Barry would be better or worse than being devoured by a swarm of fire ants.

While Junior's instincts told him to scream, begging for mercy, he decided to see what being grateful would do for him. "God, I'm so glad you're here, Barry. Damn Marine. He got the drop on me. Knocked me clean out. I didn't have a chance. Thank God you're here ol' buddy. Man, I'm glad to see you."

Barry pulled out a long hunting knife from its sheath on his belt, its honed blade flashing in bright sunlight. Junior panicked, but before he could protest, Barry slit the belt, freeing him. Junior rolled over on his back, favoring his knee and lifted himself up on an elbow.

"Thanks, Barry. That damn Marine got the jump on me. Sonvabitch." He intoned his words with as much disgust and disdain as he could muster.

Barry said, "Yea, those Marines can be tricky bastards, Junior. If only he had been tied up and I don't know...maybe you had a gun in your hand."

Junior hesitated, not sure if Barry had just agreed with him or not. "Right. Tricky. But, well, he *was* tied up, but somehow he managed to get untied. Damnedest thing I ever saw. A fucking Houdini."

Barry chuckled, turning to his heavily armed confederates. "A fucking Houdini. Yeah, Junior, that's a good one." The others nervously laughed in unison with Barry, like a pack of hyenas anxiously awaiting the moment when their alpha leader allows them to rip the carcass of their prey into little bite sized pieces. Junior had seen that on cable too.

Junior stopped laughing as Barry turned, the man's stare fixed with a crazy anger which made Barry's right eye twitch repeatedly. He decided maybe begging would be a better strategy. "You don't have to do this Barry. I know I've screwed up, but it's not all my fault. I can make up for it. Yeah. I can. You don't have to do this."

"What do you think I'm going to do, Junior?"

Junior turned his eyes away to avoid seeing Barry's long knife blade, like a patient avoids a needle. "I, I don't know."

Without speaking Barry raised his knife to strike, when a woman's voice, a familiar voice, interrupted him.

"Make a move and you'll be dead before your head hits the ground, Barry."

Barry froze, his blade in mid-air. "MaryLou? Is that you?"

"As a matter of fact, yes, it is."

Junior, the sound of potential salvation eclipsing his fear of death, cried out, "Lou Lou, thank God, darling, I thought I was a goner."

MaryLou, broke through the undergrowth in jeans and a tee shirt, holding a very large Glock handgun. "Shut up, Junior. I don't know why you got this fat asshole about to put a knife in you, but I'm sure he's got his reasons."

Barry, still holding his knife in mid-air, said, "Yes I do, MaryLou. God, its good to see you. Been a long time."

A moment passed where MaryLou recalled a summer after high school when she met Barry Swenson. The summer had started out a dream come true, but then turned into the worst damned nightmare of her life. The source of her torment was Barry.

Barry said, "You know, MaryLou, I've always been sorry you and I didn't have a chance to make a life together. My brains and your beauty, well, our babies would have been something else. Of course," Barry winked at her, his hunting knife still poised above Junior's chest, "there's still time."

In spite of everything, MaryLou couldn't believe Barry had finished dental school without doing any prison time. Nothing worse than an educated red neck aryan asshole.

"You think so, Barry? Only a real man would do what you did, then run away, you piece of shit."

"Now, MaryLou. I know having me leave to serve my community inconvenienced you..."

"Inconvenienced? You pathetic..." MaryLou's 9mm exploded, ripping Barry's knife painfully out of his hand. Barry's men pointed their guns her way, but the authority of her perfectly placed shot stayed their trigger fingers.

"Son of a bitch! Goddamn it, MaryLou! What are you trying to do? Kill me?"

"Don't give me an excuse, you shit."

Barry rubbed his previously knife wielding hand, flexing his fingers. "Okay, okay. Let's turn this down a few notches. I was just having a conversation with your brother here about a business situation."

"You hog tie and cut your business partners with a big ass knife as a regular practice?"

"Cut? No, no. You've got it wrong. I'd never hurt your brother. Hell, we're old buddies. Aren't we, Junior?"

"I don't know, Barry." Junior had rolled on his side to a position where his leg hurt less. "You sure looked like you were about to stick me with that knife of yours."

Barry urged, "Junior. Don't exaggerate."

MaryLou took a step toward Barry, "Shut up, you piece of shit."

"MaryLou, can't you use my name? Calling me shit, especially in front of my guys here, well it's just hurtful."

MaryLou kept Barry in her gaze. "Well I certainly wouldn't want to be hurtful, Barry, you pathetic piece of shit." She checked her perimeter, noting the position of Barry's three minions. If necessary she could take them all out. "Now boys, I want you to throw your weapons over by the tree, then lie down on your stomachs with your hands behind your heads. If you hesitate, I'll start putting strategically placed bullets in your boss here."

Barry, moved quickly to lie down in the dirt. "Do as she says. I've seen this girl hunt. She can take down a squirrel at a hundred yards. So just do as she says."

With their guns piled by the tree and Barry and his boys lying prone on the ground, MaryLou untied Junior.

"Junior, what the hell is going on? I find out Barry fucking Swenson is holed up outside of Pflugerville, then when I get here, I discover you're working with the bastard."

"I can explain."

Barry said, "MaryLou." Before he could say another word she was on top of him, her gun's muzzle pressed hard against his forehead causing a trickle of blood to dribble down his face.

"Give me a reason, Barry! Give me a goddamn reason."

Barry lay still.

Junior said, "I can explain, LouLou."

MaryLou asked, "Working for this piece of shit, Junior, after what he did to me? Then I hear a young man in a hospital bed fighting for his life say you kidnapped him and his girlfriend? What the hell are you doing?"

"Lou Lou. It sure is good to see you. How long has it been?"

"Cut the crap, Junior."

"How did you find me?"

"The guy you kidnapped told the police all about you and also mentioned Barry fucking Swenson."

Barry said, "How'd he know my name? Do I have to do every damn thing myself?"

MaryLou heeled Barry hard in his side.

"Did I not tell you to shut the fuck up?"

She turned her attention back to Junior.

"So I found out Barry had this place and decided to do a little walk about. See if I could figure out what kind of a mess you had gotten yourself into this time. What have you been up to, Junior? Did you really kidnap and try to kill those kids? And Harlan? You killed your friend, Harlan? You know Nick Sibelius and probably the police are onto you, right?"

"Nick? You're on a first name basis with that private investigator?" Junior forced a smile through his grimace. "You are a bad little girl, Lou Lou."

"It's none of your damned business. Just tell me why you're doing this. Why do you have the cops and Barry fucking Swenson after your ass."

"Its not my fault, Lou Lou. Really." Junior grimaced with pain. "Can't we do this another time. My leg is killin' me, Lou Lou."

"If you don't come clean it will be more than your leg killing you, Junior."

"Okay, okay. Well, Barry, he's a bona fide dentist."

"What does Barry being a dentist have to do with anything, Junior?"

Barry said, "Maybe I should explain."

MaryLou's 9mm exploded again, her bullet impacting the ground between Barry's legs. Barry stopped talking.

Junior said, "No need for that LouLou. I'm talking. His practice in Austin ran into some problems due to a couple of lawsuits and I think he was doing his receptionist. He's innocent of course."

"Of course. I still don't see what Barry has to do with you kidnapping and killing people and being hog tied out in the middle of a field."

"Things didn't go well in court and he ended up losing his license. Right Barry?" He eyed MaryLou's gun. "Better not say nothing there, Barry. So when his practice tanked he started a toxic waste disposal company."

MaryLou interrupted, "Junior, I don't want a damned Powerpoint presentation. Get to the point."

"I'm getting there. See, he needed a place to dump his waste. One day he dropped by my farm, well it was Daddy's farm at the time, and we struck up a business arrangement where he could dump his waste and I could make a nice profit."

"You're dumping toxic waste on your farm?"

"I'm what you call a resource management professional."

In her peripheral vision, MaryLou caught one of Barry's men inching his hand toward his ankle and probably his backup gun. She fired once, the bullet ripping his index finger off. He curled up in a fetal position. screaming in pain. The others tensed, but did not move.

"How many times do I need to tell you boys to stay put. Sorry about your hand, but you can't say I didn't warn you."

The wounded man took in big gulps of air, staving the flow of blood from the stub of his index finger with his other hand.

MaryLou returned her attention to Junior. "And how does Jayson Moore fit into this?"

"I didn't know it at the time, but Jayson works for Barry. Apparently Barry has a little meth business. When Jayson showed up running from the law, Barry figured he'd give him a place to hide and also expand his meth business."

"Junior, it's not a business, it's a crime. And what does the couple have to do with this?"

Junior shifted position, propping himself up with his arms. "That's when things sort of went pear shaped, Lou Lou. You see, I caught those two in my woods by the pond. Well, the girl was screaming and the guy had knocked himself unconscious somehow."

"Why was the girl screaming?"

"I'm not sure, but I think it has something to do with Carl. Idiot."

"Your dead brother's kid? So what happened, Junior?"

"I couldn't let them go, could I?"

"Why the hell not? It's not like they knew about your little deal with Barry."

Junior's eyes wandered, the validity of MaryLou's observation sinking in.

"Well, in the heat of the moment, I guess I got a little paranoid."

"Ya think?"

Junior ignored MaryLou's taunt, plunging forward with his story.

"So I tied them both up in my barn until I could figure out what to do. Then your boyfriend Sibelius showed up. I thought for sure he was going to look in the barn, but he didn't. Soon as he left, I got ahold of Jayson for some help. That's when we decided to take them to Barry's place."

"You took the advice of a cop killing drug dealing waste of space to give those two kids to Aryan Barry, Leader of the Master Race? Junior, when are you going to learn?"

"See, Barry's my business associate, LouLou. I figured we'd sort it all out together."

Barry said, "I told you, Junior and I are associates, MaryLou."

MaryLou moved swiftly, planting the pointy tip of her cowboy boots into Barry's ribs with such force his body lifted off the ground. He opened his mouth, probably to curse MaryLou to hell and back, but sucking sounds hinted that his desperate need for oxygen seemed to have become his primary concern.

MaryLou leaned over Barry. "I'm only going to say this one last time. Shut. Up. You. Piece. Of. Shit."

She turned back to Junior who lay curled up on the grass, trying not to move in order to avoid the worst of his pain.

MaryLou asked, "So you took the couple to shit head and then what?"

Barry once again spoke up, "MaryLou, I told you such language hurts my..."

Her 9mm exploded again, the bullet impacting the ground right by Barry's head. Stones splintered, spraying across and bloodying his face.

"Shit! You could have killed me, MaryLou."

"My bad. My aim must be slightly off today. Now shut up." The gun blast had startled Junior who now whimpered on the ground. "Junior? We're not going anywhere until I know what's going on. So you better keep talking."

"Damn, Lou Lou. Shit. Jesus, this hurts. Okay. Well, before I could get them out of the barn I find Harlan wandering around."

"So you really did kill Harlan?"

"Not my fault, Lou Lou. I just scared him away for his own safety. You know, toxic waste and all. But for some reason he decided to swim the pond and drowned on the way."

"And so in mourning for Harlan you came back here to murder a young girl with her boyfriend?"

"I got confused, Lou Lou."

"Confused. Confused is not knowing where you parked your car, Junior."

"I know. I just... Things got a bit out of control. I don't know. I guess I was trying to be a player like Barry."

"A player. Like shit for brains Barry. Jesus Christ, Junior." MaryLou lowered her gun, overcome by the incredible stupidity of her half brother. How could she be related by blood to such an idiot?

"Junior...my God. What have you done?"

"I didn't do nothin' Lou Lou. You know I wasn't really goin' to do nothin' to the girl. Her Marine beat the crap out of me before I could anyway. And like I said, Harlan drowned hisself."

"The Marine is lying in an ICU, Junior. Where's the girl?"

Barry said, "Jayson must have her. Probably wants to have a little fun with her first. "

MaryLou pressed her gun against Barry's face. "Where is the girl, Barry?"

"I don't know. Okay? He was supposed to clean up after Junior. Something which seems to be happening a lot lately. We haven't heard from him."

"I'm going to check the barn and the house before I leave here Barry. God help you if I find out you're lying to me."

She turned her attention back to Junior. "What about the fire, Junior, did you set the fire too?"

"I had nothing to do with that Lou Lou."

"Right. You realize, you almost killed Nick and me in the process."

"It wasn't me. I think Jayson may harbor some resentment toward your man there, Lou Lou. So what's the story with you and Sibelius? I mean are you doing him, Lou Lou? Don't get me wrong. If you are, that's a good thing. We can use it to our advantage."

"There is no 'we', Junior. There's me and there's a stupid idiot of a half brother who has made a complete pigs breakfast out of everything."

For a moment no one spoke. Barry and his comrades lay silently on the ground, Junior sullen and MaryLou wondering how a homeland security assignment had gone to aiding and abetting her stupid half brother in god knows what felonies and misdemeanors.

Junior asked, "What do we do now, Lou Lou?"

MaryLou recalled the last time she risked her job with Homeland Security to help Junior get rid of a stolen car with a trunk full of weed. She didn't want to get involved and she certainly could have lost her job. She definitely tossed her integrity over the side. But he did, after all, help her with The Situation when no one else was willing to help. Over the years Junior kept getting into trouble. And each time she felt compelled to save him having convinced herself Junior was family—blood is thicker than water and all that crap—until she just got involved out of habit.

"I'll clean up your damn mess, Junior. Just like I always do. God, this is the very reason I moved the hell away from here. And damned if I'm not in Pflugerville for twenty-four hours and I'm neck deep in your bull-shit."

"Sorry, Lou Lou."

"Save it, Junior. If I had a dollar for every time you apologized to me for doing something stupid, I'd be a damn millionaire. I'm going to get you out of here and then figure out how to get you some medical care."

Barry spoke, "If I may, MaryLou—"

"I thought I told you to be quiet, Barry."

"That's nice. You used my name. Thank you. Anyhow, I might be able to help with your brother's current medical needs."

"He doesn't need a root canal, Barry."

"As much as I'd like to cut Junior's nerve endings out of his jaw, I'm speaking of medical, not dental care. An operation like mine has to have medical resources at hand for when the war begins."

"I'll just skip past your war nonsense and ask you to get to the point. What medical resources?"

"Dr. Jenkins. He works on kids, but he's got the skills and is a proud member of my militia."

"You've got to be joking. A Nazi pediatrician?" Barry's serious expression clearly communicated he was not joking. "Can you get Dr. Death to patch up Junior here?"

Barry lifted himself up on one elbow. "On one condition."

"I don't think you're in much of a position to make conditions you pathetic piece—"

"Now, now. I have only one simple request."

"Yes. I'm listening."

"Stop using such hurtful, derogatory language when referring to me and instead use my God given name."

"Fucking Asshole?"

"Now, MaryLou, you know my God given name is Barry...Barry Swenson. All I'm asking in return for bringing the healing power of med-icine to your brother over there is that you call me Barry."

"Okay. Bernard." She thought she heard one of Barry's minions snicker. "Now, you're going to tell me where to find the nazi pediatri-cian."

Junior asked, "And then what, Lou Lou?"

"Then I have to come up with a plan to get you out of the mess you've made, Junior."

28 SANDS MOTEL

Barry pushed the "end" button on his cell phone, having talked to Dr. Jenkins about taking a look at Junior's knee and stitching up his now nine fingered henchman. Junior, his back propped against a tree, rested in the shade, while Barry and his "boys" sat under a hot sun, following MaryLou's warning to keep their hands visible. Barry stuffed his phone back in his pocket.

"The doc may not be available today, MaryLou."

"Out of town?"

"Had a little bout with his emphysema. His daughter just took him to a hospital. He is in his eighties, after all."

MaryLou felt a bit perturbed by Barry's words. His Nazi pediatrician sounded too decrepit to be useful to Junior. "Maybe we need to think of another option."

Junior said, "Lou Lou, I'm okay. My knee's a bit swollen, but I can get around on it."

She knew she couldn't leave Junior with Barry without one of them dying in the process and she certainly couldn't trust Barry or one of his associates to leave and return with a doctor. So she had Barry tie up all of his thugs, then encouraged him at gun point to help Junior out to his pickup.

After installing Junior in the passenger seat, Barry turned to face MaryLou. "MaryLou, I really don't think it's such a good idea for you to be driving around with a known felon."

"I'm touched you suddenly give a damn about my welfare, Barry."

"I just fear for your safety, MaryLou. It's a dangerous world out there."

"I fear for your safety too, Barry. So I think you better lie face down in the dirt with your hands behind your head. If I see you in my rear view mirror even think about moving I will run you down, then shoot you."

Barry frowned with a shake of his head. "You're mighty harsh, Mary-Lou."

"Well, Barry, I think I've got a right to be harsh. I came here with the intention to nail your ass."

"But you've decided to let bygones be bygones?"

Bygones. She wanted to blow his brains out right then and there if it wasn't for the fact she'd have several witnesses. Dying would be too much of any easy out for Barry Swenson.

"Bygones? For now I've got to get Junior out of this mess. But be assured, Barry, I will be back. And the next time you see me, your ass is mine. Now down on the ground."

She pulled away from the compound, checking her rear view mirror for movement. Once out of sight, they drove back to her car, leaving Junior's truck by the road.

"I can't just leave my truck here, Lou Lou."

"Junior, think. The police are looking for you and the truck is registered in your name. If you drive down the road in that thing you might as well have a sign painted across the side in big letters, "I'm the idiot felon from Pflugerville." Now get out so we can put some distance between us and the Nazi Amateur Hour."

Grudgingly Junior eased himself out of the passenger side of his pickup, hopping on his good leg over to her rental Prius. Back on the road they drove in silence past grazing land dotted with cattle and lone water towers for about ten miles, MaryLou wondering how she would ever get out of this mess Junior had created.

"You need to disappear for a time, Junior."

"You'd like that, wouldn't you?"

She kept her eyes on the road ahead. "What are you talking about?"

"What am I talking about? Well let me see here, Sis. You get me out of the picture, then you just happen to steal my farm right out from under me."

"You've got to be kidding me. Don't be an idiot, Junior." She took a quick glance at her crazy brother. "Wait. I mean, don't be more of an idiot."

"Yeah, real funny. Well, I'm no idiot, Lou Lou. Even I know if you get me out of the picture, then you can use your girly tricks to take what's mine."

Junior had clearly become more paranoid and downright weird than the last time MaryLou had seen him a couple of years ago. "My girly tricks? Junior, I know this will be difficult, but try to think clearly for a moment. If I wanted you out of the way, I would have let Barry filet you in his pasture. Right?"

He nodded his head back and forth as if weighing probabilities. "Yeah, I guess."

"But I didn't let him kill you, did I. Why? Because even though you're a complete idiot and apparently a felon several times over, you're still my half brother. We're family, Junior."

"Family, huh?" A grin spread across his face. "So I guess this means we're kinda like Bonnie and Clyde or Michael and Janet."

She hadn't seen that one coming. "Michael and Janet?"

"You know, Jackson."

MaryLou rolled her eyes with a sigh. "First of all, the Jackson's weren't running from the police, and second, Bonnie and Clyde... Never mind. Junior, just shut up and listen. Nick knows you're responsible for kidnapping those kids and he has some strong suspicions about the guy at the lake."

"Harlan."

"What?"

"The guy at the lake. Harlan. We grew up together." Junior's voice cracked, tears filling his eyes. "I didn't mean for that fool to go drown hisself. Shit. How do you fish and not know how to swim?"

"Maybe it was an accident, Junior. But you have to understand Nick will probably not be thinking about it that way. He's after Junior the kidnapper, the guy who shoots at transients and hot air balloons. Junior the felon. So until we get things sorted, and honest to God I have no idea how we're going to do it, you need to disappear.

"Like to Mexico or somethin'?"

"In the short term, just away from Pflugerville, until I can talk to Nick."

"Nick? Aw, come on, Lou Lou. Nick is all buddy buddy with a Pflugerville cop. You talk to him, you might as well just put me in prison."

"If you want to stay alive, there is no scenario where you don't go to prison. It's more a matter of how much time you'll spend there."

Junior noticed a yellow biplane pop up over a line of trees, crossing about a half mile ahead of them, then flying low over a cotton field. "Look at that. You see that plane? Man, I'd love to be able to fly one of those things. I'd just fly away. You know what I mean, Lou Lou?"

"Junior, will you focus? If you run, you'll be caught either by Barry or by the police. You and I know you're not the type to be able to keep away from trouble for long. So your best option here is to surrender to someone you can trust and end this comedy of errors."

"I don't know what you mean by comedy of errors. I'm sure not laughin'. And for the record, none of this has been my fault. I'm what they call a victim of circumstance. Just like you were a victim of circumstance back when, well, you know. When you got pregnant."

MaryLou gripped the steering wheel, staring straight ahead. "Well, Junior, this is a bit different."

"Don't see how."

"Unless I'm mistaken, they don't tie you down to a gurney and give you a lethal injection for being pregnant."

Junior squirmed in his seat to stare out his window, then turned back to MaryLou. "You gotta point there, Lou Lou."

She glared at her half brother, her eyes burning with rage. "And I didn't just get pregnant."

"I know, Lou Lou. I guess I don't know how to talk about it sometimes."

Junior stared out the window at passing rolling fields browned off from summer heat. Stuck behind an eighteen wheeler in a no pass lane, MaryLou began running a hypothetical conversation with Nick in her mind.

"Nick, there's something I need to tell you."

"Sure, what is it?"

"First of all, I'm not really a reporter. I'm actually a special ops agent for Homeland Security."

"Makes perfect sense to me, MaryLou."

"I knew you would completely..."

Wait. What total bullshit. You don't tell a man you love and have slept with, for Chrissake, you've been lying to him and he just says, "Makes perfect sense." Okay. Try again.

"You did what? You're a Homeland Security agent? What else are you keeping from me?"

Yeah, that's more like it.

"Well Nick, I didn't mean to keep this from you. In fact, I had no idea how crazy things were going to be here. You see, Junior is my half brother."

"You're saying I've been sleeping with the half sister of a murdering felon? Let me guess. You're wanted by the FBI for bank robbery and assault. Are you trying to destroy my business and break my heart at the same time?"

"Don't be stupid, Nick! I'm a covert agent. I'm here because Barry Swenson has become a national security risk. And doesn't Junior get his day in court by the way, you right wing fascist pig!"

Okay, that's not quite the direction I want to go with this.

"Nick, Junior's an idiot. I've stashed him at the Dunes Motel in Hearne. How about if you forget all about Junior?"

"I don't know MaryLou. Junior has committed kidnapping and possibly murder."

"Maybe we can stop over at your trailer on the way, Nick. I can make it worth your while to forget about him."

MaryLou slammed her hands on the steering wheel. "That's disgusting."

Junior yelled, "Get outta my head!"

"What?"

Junior glanced at MaryLou, then down at his lap. "You're not talking about me, are you. So what are you talking about?"

"Nothing, just thinking about what Barry was about to do to you."

"He was a bit pissed. How'd you find me anyway?"

"When Delton mentioned Barry Swenson, I figured he had kept the family property. So I came out there assuming you were probably with him."

"Delton knew my name? Damn." Junior's brow furrowed in thought at this turn of events. "By the way, I figured you'd kill Barry if you had the chance. What happened?"

"Too many witnesses." She stared straight ahead.

"Really? Damn. So you would've."

"No, Junior, I work for Homeland Security, not the Mafia."

Junior looked out his window in thought for several minutes. "So MaryLou, do you really think, given I'm a real felon now, going to the police is in my best interest?"

"If you have a desire to live, yes."

"I do have a desire to live, but I also don't want to be some big, nasty gang member's prison bitch. Besides, I have business interests I can't run from prison."

"You have business interests? Come on Junior. It's me, Lou Lou, you're talking to here."

"I can't go to prison, period."

"Junior, you do understand Barry wants you dead?"

"Oh, you don't need to worry about Barry. I can handle him."

"He was about to shove a very large knife into your chest, Junior."

"Well, yeah. Heat of the moment. Now that he's had time to ponder his actions I know he won't be tryin' to kill me."

"Junior, I cannot stand by and let you be killed."

"I can't go to prison, Lou Lou. If I go to prison, I'm as good as dead. You gotta help me, Sis. You gotta."

MaryLou looked at Junior's pleading face, the face of a man with a good heart who just kept making really bad decisions. She wished she could just kill him and dump his body on a back road, but Junior had been good to her and in spite of herself, she did love her half brother.

"When Nick finds out I'm your half sister—"

"He's goin' to dump you like a big ol' sack of manure. Trust me. No private investigator can be connected to some babe he's been doin' who also happens to be aidin' n' baitin' a felon."

"Aiding and abetting, Junior."

"Right. Aidin' n' baitin'. Nope. He'll dump you like a farmer dumpin' a hay bail in a pasture, like Lance Armstrong's fans dumped his doped up bike butt, like Becky Nelson dumped my ass when she saw that rash—"

"Enough, Junior."

"You know I'm right, Lou Lou. Tell him who you really are and it's over."

"Shut up, Junior."

They drove the remaining sixty miles east in silence. MaryLou stopped once to buy a knee brace and ibuprofin for Junior at a drug store, then continued until she pulled into a Sands Motel just outside of Hearne on the highway to Bryan-College Station. The motel, built in the late 50's had been painted an aqua blue MaryLou assumed had to be the result of either color blindness or just bad taste on the part of its owner. She gave Junior two hundred dollars in cash, not knowing how many pizzas he'd have to order before she returned, telling him to stay in his room until she figured out what to do. Then she turned her car around, heading back to Pflugerville, to Nick, and she hoped, the end of this little drama.

29 BEER AND PEANUT BUTTER

Leaving the hospital, Nick drove out to Alamo Inn to check on Mary-Lou. When she didn't answer her door, he scanned the parking lot for her rental Prius and seeing it was missing, assumed she must have gone to find a drug store or a drink. Quentin had invited him to ride along out to Junior's place, so he went over to the Justice Center to meet his friend. Neither of them figured Junior would be around, but they were hoping to get a clue about where he might have run.

Quentin pulled up to the house, Junior's cow dogs running up to greet them. Without their alpha leader they seemed more curious than territorial. Nick and Quentin made friends with the dogs, then walked over to the barn where, according to Junior, he spent most of his time fixing a broken tractor. Light scattered across an open interior space through slits between wall boards. Decaying wood, cow manure and hay combined into a sweet and sour mustiness. A rusting blue Ford tractor with a pan underneath partially filled with oil sat to one side. Nick kicked one of its large back tires.

"Maybe Junior actually told the truth about working on this machine."

Quentin, walking to the back of the tractor, whistled as he looked over an unshielded splined power take-off shaft.

"Hard to imagine a man caught up in one those, Nick, just flopping around at the mercy of the thing."

"Yeah, definitely not my first choice of ways to die."

"I read the report about Earl Sr. getting caught up in this machinery, Nick. Junior had been in the barn at the time. He said Sr. must have lost focus for a moment, backing into it. Junior also implied his Dad had been slowing down mentally prior to the accident, maybe the beginnings of Alzheimer's. However, other people who knew Earl Sr. well, reported he had been sharp as a tack up to his untimely death. There were some suspicions Junior may have decided to whack his daddy in order to inherit the farm, but with little in the way of evidence, we had to drop it..”

Nick opened a warped door to a storage area filled with pick axes, sledge hammers, shovels, and he imagined the odd snake or two. “Did Earl Sr. have a will?”

“Yeah. If I recall he left the farm to Junior and to a daughter, Mary, I think.”

“Given that people seemed to die when they’re in the vicinity of Junior, we better find this Mary before Junior has a chance to be Earl Sr.’s sole heir.”

Stepping out of the barn, Nick caught a brief glimpse of someone in a second story bedroom window of the house.

“Don’t look, but did you see something move up there, Quentin?”

“A guy in the window? Yeah, I saw him.”

Nick couldn’t believe Junior would be so thick as to come back to his house when he had to know he was wanted for kidnapping, manslaughter, and attempted murder. Whoever peered out the window had quickly ducked away in an attempt to not be seen. Nick and Quentin walked casually across the yard hoping to give an impression they had not noticed, then moved down the side of the house, stepping onto the back porch. The back door stood open.

“Nick, I’ll take the front. Wait for me.”

After giving Quentin sufficient time to get around front, Nick drew his weapon, stepping through the doorway, then quietly creeping into the kitchen. Bread and an open jar of peanut butter sat on a formica counter. A Shiner Bock, ice cold from the fridge, sat sweating with condensation. Nick wondered why anyone would combine beer and peanut butter, pondering briefly if eating a peanut butter sandwich with a beer should be a criminal offense. He stepped through a passageway to the dining room. Turning the corner he saw a man of average height and weight peering through blinds to the front yard, obviously looking at Quentin. Taking a few more steps he had the answer to his peanut butter and beer riddle. Carl.

“How you doing, Carl?”

Carl jumped, turning toward Nick’s voice, then crashed backwards into venetian blinds.

“Jesus! You scared the crap out of me.”

Quentin rushed through the front entrance, the door slamming with a bang against a wall.

“Just Carl here, Quentin. You alone, Carl?”

“Yeah. Uncle Junior told me to stay right here.”

Quentin moved to the stairs, peering up to a landing above, then cautiously took the steps one at a time.

Nick asked, “Where’s Junior, Carl?”

"I don't know."

Nick, holstered his gun, looking around the living room.

"You don't know or won't tell us."

Carl paused to think it through. "I won't tell you, cause I don't know."

"When did he drop you off?"

"Who?"

"Are you trying to be funny, Carl? Because if its comedy you're after, I'm sure Officer Matthews will put some cuffs on you and take you down to the town lock up where you can be funny all night long."

Carl hugged himself. "I just got outta there. Look, I really don't know where he is. He didn't say. All he said was..." Carl stopped himself in mid-sentence.

"All he said was what, Carl?"

"I didn't mean to say that."

"Well, since you started, you might as well finish. What did he say, Carl?"

Carl brushed a hand through his hair. "He dropped me off here and told me to stay put until he got done with Barry."

"Who's Barry?"

Quentin came back down the stairs, his weapon holstered. "Answer the man, Carl."

"Come on. I'm pretty sure Junior doesn't want me talking about all this."

Quentin came alongside Nick. "Carl, you can either have a problem with Junior, which I assume involves some shouting followed by you having to shovel shit or some other nasty chore, or you can have a problem with me, which means I'll drag your sorry ass back to jail, then Junior and this Barry fellow will know you've been talking to me."

"That's not fair!"

"Life isn't fair, Carl."

He sighed, nodding his head. "No shit."

Quentin reached for his handcuffs.

"Alright. I suppose it can't do no harm. Barry's a friend of Junior's. Used to live around here when they were kids."

Nick asked, "Barry lived around here?"

"Still does. He's got a place out near Thrall."

"You ever been there?"

"Yeah, once or twice."

"Good. Let's go."

"What? Junior wanted me to stay here."

"And I want you to show us where Barry lives."

"Can I grab a beer and a jar of peanut butter for the road. I'm really hungry."

Quentin said, "You want to get beer and peanut butter on my uphol-stery? Not a chance, Carl."

"You like peanut butter and beer too? You know I invented the com-bination. Yessir. You must have seen my YouTube video. I'm goin' to be famous."

30 WOULDN'T WANT TO BE YOU

Barry waited for the creaking suspension of Junior's pickup to fade before struggling to his feet. He wasted no time untying his men and putting a plan he had worked out while on the ground into action. He had to get rid of the girl, Ayisha, the private investigator, Junior, and Mary-Lou. The more he thought about it, Jayson needed to go too, in spite of his utility as an above average thug. He had enjoyed employing a man known for killing cops, but in hindsight he realized Jayson's presence had turned the heat up on his entire drug and toxic waste empire. Without money generated from his many operations, he'd never be able to fully fund his militia which would stop the current sorry decline of America.

As he directed his men to pile weapons and ammunition into his black Hummer, a police car approached. Barry ideally he would have liked to take on law enforcement at a time and place of his choosing, however, he realized these cops were actually helping him out. Now he could kill them, then use their patrol car to covertly go after his other targets.

~*~

Following Carl's directions, Nick and Quentin turned down a dirt track approaching a farmhouse with an adjacent barn. Scanning the scene Nick picked up three armed men in addition to a large guy with shoulder length blond hair, who he guessed had to be Jayson, and a smaller man with red hair in the passenger seat of a Hummer.

Quentin said, "Nick, this is going to get messy. Stay behind cover and don't try to be a hero. Okay? You still owe me for the Cowboys game."

"What kind of a man bets against the Cowboys anyway?"

Quentin shook his head. "Here we go."

"What do you mean 'here we go.' You and I both know the only reason the Packers scored was because of a bad call."

"Nick, can we do this another time? Okay?'

"Yeah, sure. But it was a bad call." Nick glanced to the back seat. "Carl, stay out of sight until we tell you otherwise."

"And if you don't come back?"

"Run."

Nick and Quentin opened their doors, being careful to stay behind them for what minimal protection they offered. Jayson, standing behind the Hummer's driver's side door with one foot in the vehicle, spoke to Quentin.

"How can I help you officer?"

"We're looking for Earl Pendleton Jr. Goes by Junior. Have you seen him?"

"Junior? No, can't say I have."

Nick noticed a gunmen had taken a position on the porch to his left, one on the roof and a third by a split rail fence to his right.

Nick said, "That's a bit odd, Jayson."

The large man's mouth formed a slight smile at the sound of his name. "How so?"

"I understand Junior was heading up to visit Barry today."

"I don't know who you get your information from but—"

"Are you calling me a liar?"

Jayson frowned, crossing his arms. "I'm not calling you a liar. I'm just saying you've been misinformed."

Nick moved toward Jayson with purpose. The man who had tried to kill him from an overpass. The bastard who murdered Denny. Jayson Moore. He struggled to maintain an alert awareness of his surroundings while his mind screamed to simply attack.

Jayson said, "I think you need to stop right there."

"Tell your boys to put their guns down. No one needs to die today."

"Well, I don't know, Sibelius. Maybe one of us needs to die today."

Jayson gave a nod to the others. Having moved close enough to the Hummer to block the porch shooter, Nick dove for the ground, firing his weapon at a gunman on the roof who fell, crashing onto the porch below. Jayson had jumped into the Hummer, slamming his door shut. Quentin hunkered down at the sound of shots from the fence, a rain of bullets slamming into the door. He turned, putting his years as the department's sharpshooting champion to work and with a single shot, hitting the gunman directly in his chest. Nick rolled to stay hidden behind the Hummer as the porch gunman tried to make a shot. Jayson gunned his engine, its big off road tires kicking up a cloud of dust. He aimed the behemoth directly for Nick, who rolled away, leaving him exposed to the porch gunman. Nick could see the man aim an assault rifle directly at him, knowing in an instant he would not be able to bring his weapon around fast enough to stop him before the gunman fatally pulled his trigger. Time slowed. He thought of MaryLou. He didn't hear Quentin's shot propelling a projectile faster than the speed of sound, slamming with ferocious inertia into the gunman's skull just above his right eye and, as the slug deformed, ripping the back side of his head away.

In his peripheral vision Jayson's Hummer smashed the patrol car's front fender, tearing a door away, as it swept by. Nick continued firing, but his shots fell impotent against the Hummer's armor and bullet proof windows. He scanned for more shooters, then ran over to Quentin's partially crushed squad car, expecting to see the worst. Instead, Quentin crawled out of a deformed and now doorless front seat.

"You think maybe next time you might give me a little more warning before you do your Rambo thing?" Quentin peered over the remnants of his car, shaking his head. "Damn, I just got this cruiser, Nick."

"What's important is we're both alive, right?"

Quentin looked at Nick, shaking his head in resignation. "You obviously don't know our mayor. Her ass is so tight if she whistled Dixie with it only dogs would be able to hear."

Nick remembered their passenger. "Carl? You okay back there?"

Carl raised his head up from the back seat. "I'm good. Thought we were all going to die there for a second."

Quentin cocked his hat back. "You'll live to pee another day Carl." He looked to Nick. "I'll check the guy by the fence and then call this in. Why don't you take the one on the ground over there."

Nick walked over to a man lying on the dirt where a Hummer had been only moments before. Twenty something with close cropped hair, blue jeans and a drab green Army issue tee shirt, he held his leg, blood oozing out between his fingers, his eyes looking toward an assault rifle several feet away.

Nick kept his weapon aimed at him.

"Don't you think you've had a bad enough day?"

He looked at Nick, back at his rifle, then closed his eyes, grimacing against the pain. Nick kicked the rifle further away.

"Normally the officer over there would cuff you, but it looks to me it's in your interest to keep pressure on your wound. Wouldn't want you to bleed out before we can get you some medical attention."

"I'm a prisoner of war. You gotta treat me right."

"Yeah, yeah."

The man raised himself up on an elbow, momentarily easing pressure off his calf, blood pouring from the wound. Nick tore a piece of the man's tee shirt away.

"Which is why I'm providing some first aid coaching. Here, take this and keep pressure on it."

The man fell back to the ground, curling up sufficiently to keep pressure on his left calf.

"You're a bit over your head here, aren't you? I mean conspiracy, kidnapping, murder, assaulting a law enforcement officer with intent to kill. That's quite a list."

"I didn't kill nobody."

"From where I'm standing it looks like you boys killed Harlan over at the Pendleton farm. Now why would you kill an innocent fisherman?"

"I didn't kill no Harlan. Don't even know a Harlan."

"If I were you I'd be tying that strip of cloth around my leg."

He grimaced in pain, blood flowing more freely as he struggled to get a tourniquet tied. Nick considered helping him, but the guy looked like he wasn't about to die—yet. A little angst might help him get some much needed information.

"Well, I'm sure a judge will sort this all out. You don't look like the type who survives well in one of those high security prisons. Am I wrong?"

"Look, I was just following Barry's orders. Damn, Junior."

"What about Junior?"

"He kidnapped those people and killed the guy at his pond. You shoulda' heard Barry. Never seen him so pissed off. Thought he was goin' to kill Junior with his bare hands until that Lou Lou woman showed up."

"Lou Lou?"

With a tourniquet in place, his bleeding stopped for the time being, he seemed to relax a bit, even though Nick could see pain etched across his face.

"Yeah, a woman. Seemed to know Barry and Junior. Some history or something."

"Where is this woman now?"

"She tied us up, then took off with Junior."

"You're telling me a lone woman came into your operation here, tied all of you big, strong neo-Nazis up and took off with Junior?"

"Well, yeah. She had a gun and she was pretty good with it too."

"So where do you think Barry's gone."

"You won't be able to stop him. Once Barry has made up his mind, there's just no stoppin' him."

"And what would I need to stop him from doing?"

"Killin' that Marine and his girlfriend, Junior, and the woman, Lou Lou, of course."

Nick could hear ambulance sirens from a distance.

"And one more thing. Why are you telling me all of this?"

He looked up with weak smile at Nick, his face pale from pain and blood loss. "Cause Jayson Moore is with him. After he helps Barry take care of them, he's comin' after you. Wouldn't want to be you at all, mister."

31 MEETING THE PENDLETONS

MaryLou drove the state highway from Hearne back to Pflugerville, wondering how on earth she had gotten herself entangled in the Pendleton clan once again. She recalled the first time she met Earl Sr., how terrified she was of meeting her biological father. Her expectations for him matched the knowledge her tearful mother had divulged about a trucker she had met at a truck stop. Funny how assumptions can be so off-base.

Fifteen years ago, MaryLou, had gone out to the Pendleton farm, driving up a long dirt track to a white farm house. She had stepped up on the porch, hesitating for a moment, then knocked on the door. She hadn't seen Earl Sr. standing at his barn door watching her, probably assuming she had something to sell or some religion to hawk.

"Can I help you?"

She startled, not expecting anyone behind her.

"Oh, god, you scared me."

"Sorry. Saw you come up to my house from the barn. If you're selling something, I'm not interested."

He stood tall with the muscles of a man who labored for a living.

"No sir. I'm not selling anything."

"Then what are you pushing? You one of them Baptists or a UT student wanting money for whales or baby seals or some other crap?"

"Pushing? No, I'm not here to..."

"Yes?"

She turned to leave. "Maybe this was a mistake."

"Slow down, young lady. Obviously you have your reasons for being here. Why don't you just tell me what it is you want."

She turned back to face him. He looked older than she had imagined, his kind eyes looking out to her from a face weathered with age and experience. "I, I don't want anything. I just wanted to say, I just wanted to tell you..."

"Take a deep breath and just spit it out."

"You're my father."

He paused a beat, his eyes studying her. "What?"

"Nineteen years ago in Gonzalez, the truck stop off Highway 183?"

"Yeah, I know the truck stop."

"My Mom met you there. Apparently that's when I came into the picture."

"You're saying me and your Mom...in Gonzalez...nineteen years ago?"

"Yes sir."

He looked down at his feet, then over her shoulder to a distant point, then directly into her eyes. "I don't know what you're playing at, but I don't appreciate you coming onto my property accusing me of, of..."

"I'm not accusing you. I'm just saying, you're my father."

"Get outta here. Now. Don't come back."

"I just wanted to—"

"Go!"

MaryLou had left the Pendleton farm in tears. She had expected some awkwardness, but not total denial. Was having her as a daughter so terrible? She drove down the road, anger and rejection clouding her vision, when a blaring horn and flashing lights from behind startled her. Mary-Lou's first thought involved a police speed trap, her heart pounding in her throat. Then she realized the vehicle behind her looked more like a pickup truck than a police car. The truck pulled up beside her. She could see Earl Sr. motioning for her to pull off the road. MaryLou slowed down, easing onto the shoulder, Earl Sr.'s truck coming up behind her. They both got out of their vehicles, MaryLou wiping tears away, Earl Sr., his face pinched, as if attempting to hold back a multitude of emotions.

"I'm sorry, Mr. Pendleton. I didn't—"

"I remember."

"What?"

"I remember your Mom. I remember the truck stop and the night we had together."

"So," she said measuredly. "You're my dad."

"Well, I surely wouldn't mind having a beautiful daughter like you in my family, but maybe we better not get ahead of ourselves."

"What do you mean?"

"Seems like I recall people do blood tests for this sort of thing."

"But my Mom says you're the one. She said you were the only one that summer."

"Did she now." MaryLou thought she caught the barest hint of a smile in his eyes. "Well, in any case, let's be sure."

"You said you remembered. If you remember after nineteen years it must have been a pretty memorable meeting."

Earl Sr.'s eyes stared off into a distant past.

"Yeah, meeting your Mom definitely was a memorable experience."

"So why didn't you two stay together? I mean, she was a waitress and you were a truck driver. Its not like you had any commitments holding you apart."

"Just one of those things. We had our moment, then just moved on."

After blood tests confirmed MaryLou's genetic link to Earl Sr., he opened his home and his heart to her. She had decided to stay the summer with the Pendletons, Earl Sr. and her new half brothers, Junior and Caleb, being part of a family she had never had growing up in Gonzalez. She would hang out on the porch while the boys did chores, then the three of them would go down to the pond to smoke some weed and cool off in the water. Caleb, lean and strong, spent much of his time away from the farm focused on a girl who would eventually be his wife and Carl's mother. Junior stayed around, lingering with her as they talked about life, the shape of clouds, and what cows must be thinking.

Then Barry Swenson walked into her life. A slightly pudgy red headed teen, he lived down the road near Thrall, helping Earl Sr. with the extra load of work during the summer. The first time she met him, he had driven up to the barn in a green Ford Pinto his parents had given him for making the National Honor Society. The very same Ford Pinto that had been moved inside their school gym the previous summer, wheels removed, with the words "Barry Is A Pussy" painted across its sides. After the incident with his car, Junior had told her Barry had noticeably shifted from a smart, awkward, fat kid to an overly confident, angry teen. The Panther's star linebacker, rumored to be the mastermind behind moving Barry's car to a gym, would die in a mysterious fiery crash just before Home Coming. Of course, no one thought Barry had anything to do with the incident. He definitely had the motive, but no one imagined he had the means.

His repainted car slid to a halt, dust kicking up, then his door popping open. A still physically awkward, plump Barry in cowboy boots, faded Levis, and an already dirty white tee shirt stepped out of his car.

MaryLou watched him from the porch, instinctively repulsed by his presence, even at a distance, sensing danger. She didn't know what it was, but something wasn't quite right with him. He reached into his Pinto for a cowboy hat, then turned, noticing her for the first time. He walked like a penguin, shifting his weight on short legs. His eyes stayed fixed on her, never blinking. His face twitched nervously, his right hand tapping on his leg like he was just barely under control, ready to explode in violence or laugh hysterically in any given moment. She couldn't hold his gaze, didn't want to, but realized he was determined. His determination scared her. He paused at the steps, putting one foot on the second step, leaning against the railing.

"I'm Barry. What's your name?"

She could see lust in his eyes, searching her, scanning her face, her neck, shoulders, resting on her breasts until she instinctively lifted a hand to her shoulder to protect herself.

"MaryLou."

He slowly scanned between her legs, licked his lips returning to her breasts. She felt exposed. Violated.

MaryLou said, "Do you mind?"

Barry's incessant tapping stopped momentarily. "What?"

"The way you're looking at me. It's creeping me out."

"Now that's no way to talk to me. I'm just trying to be friendly."

"No, you're not."

He tapped his hand on the railing again. "Why are you being mean to me? I just want to be friends."

"We don't even know each other, Barry."

He stepped up onto the porch, speaking as if the last exchange had never happened, as if a switch had flipped drawing on a more confident, cocky version of Barry.

"MaryLou. Now that's a pretty name for a pretty girl. Are you Junior's girlfriend? I'd think he'd tell me if he had a new girlfriend. Especially a hot little thing like you. You his girlfriend?"

She wanted to run, to escape, but found herself feeling trapped on the porch swing, compelled to answer his questions.

"No."

"No? Now that's some of the best news I've heard in a while. But if you're not his girlfriend, who are you?"

"I'm his sister."

"Sister? You're shittin' me."

"Half-sister. Junior's dad is my dad too."

"Well I'll be fucked! A sister. And a goddamn pretty sister at that. Well, well, well."

"Don't you have work to do or something?"

"There you go trying to get rid of me again." He moved closer, hands at his sides, a young man full of virile confidence. "I ask 'cause I have a feeling me and you? Yeah, we're going to hit it off." He plopped onto the swing, his weight flexing wood, chains groaning from the effort. He put his arm across her back until MaryLou could smell his sour sweat. "Yeah, we're going to hit it off big time."

She stood up, walking to the door. "I've got to go inside, do some chores for Earl Sr."

"Do you now? Well, I'll be here all summer darling, ready to take you to places you've never been before."

She opened the screen door, trying to muster some power within her. "You really use that line with girls?"

His piercing blue eyes bore into her, an angry edge in his voice. "That's no line, MaryLou. You and me, it's destiny. By the time this summer's done," he cocked his head, his eyes scanning up her body as if he could see right through her clothes, "I'll know more about you than you know about yourself. Believe it."

During the week, each time Barry worked the farm, she would be sure to stand near Junior or Earl Sr., but even at a distance she could feel his stalking eyes burning her. On a Friday, Caleb had left for the summer to go fishing with some friends down near Galveston, Earl Sr. went into town for some supplies, and Junior had disappeared into the fields to mend fences. MaryLou stayed at the house, dusting, washing dishes, then finally sweeping off the porch. Barry's green Pinto pulled up. She thought about running into the house, but had determined she would not be bullied around by a creep like Barry. She kept sweeping, ignoring his presence, until his footfalls pounded on wood steps.

"MaryLou. How are you doing, darling? Haven't seen much of you since our last visit."

Her back still turned to him, she said, "I've been busy." She focused on keeping her voice even, not wanting to give him the pleasure of knowing he scared her.

"Busy, eh. I know how that is." She felt a large arm wrap around her waist. "How 'bout if me and you get busy. Hmmm? Whatduya think?" He buried his face in her neck, his hot wet tongue licking up to her ear lobe. She tried to pull away, but his sunburned arm held her locked in place. She swung her broom back in an effort to hit him, but he grabbed the broom handle with his free hand, pulling it out of her hands as if she was a toddler, then tossed it over the railing to the ground below.

"Barry. Stop." She tried to free herself, but his grip only tightened as his free hand now painfully squeezed her breast. Before she knew what had happened, he slipped his hand under her belt, down her waist, his thick fingers forcing their way between her legs, her feet now up off the ground.

"Goddammit Barry. Stop! No!"

She kicked, throwing her elbows back in a vain attempt to hurt him, to stop him. In return, he tightened his vise grip around her waist, forcing air from her lungs, while holding her suspended on his hip, his fingers probing her with such force, if she had been able to breathe, she would have screamed. Reaching back she dug fingernails into his face.

"You goddamn bitch!" He slammed her against the wall, his stunning blow narrowing her world to a long, dark tunnel, her body crumpling to the floor. Partially conscious, she remembered feeling his weight crushing her, each thrust ramming her head painfully against the wall. Then darkness.

Coming back to consciousness, he stood above her, pulling his pants up, looking as if he wanted to spit on her. MaryLou curled up, shock and pain overwhelming her.

"Don't go crying you little cunt. You know you fucking wanted it. Yeah. You wanted it, you bitch."

She heard Junior's voice. "What the hell? Barry, what the hell are you doing?"

"We're just having a little fun, Junior. That's a real slut you have for a sister."

Junior yelled, "You sonvabitch!"

She heard their fight, bodies crashing against the house, strained grunts, fists on flesh, bodies banging down the steps. She couldn't watch, she couldn't care. She had fallen into a deep, dark well, her body ripped inside out. Then there was silence.

Sometime later she heard Junior's voice again. "MaryLou? Jesus. MaryLou, I'm sorry. I'm so sorry." He helped her pull her clothes back on, carried her inside, then laid her down carefully on her bed.

She looked up at Junior, his left eye swollen shut, blood streaming down the right side of his face, his upper lip split. "Its not like he said Junior."

"I know. I know."

"Its not like he said. He, he..."

"I know. I know, MaryLou. You're still my MaryLou. My LouLou."

~*~

When Earl Sr. returned from town to find out MaryLou had been savagely raped and one of his sons severely beaten, he flew into a rage like nothing Junior had never seen. Shotgun in hand, Earl Sr. went to his pickup truck, driving away with such speed, he almost lost control, his back wheels swinging back and forth behind him. Junior heard him come back two hours later, the front door slamming behind him, a familiar sound of a beer bottle being pulled from the fridge and then slapped down on the counter.

Junior asked, "Did you find him?"

Earl Sr. looked at him, taking a long pull from his bottle. "The son of a bitch has run off. Fuckin' coward."

"Shouldn't we call the cops, Dad?

Earl Sr. glared at Junior. "He'll just say she wanted it."

"He beat her up. She sure as hell didn't want to be beaten up."

"He'll say she likes it rough. She asked for it. I'm not putting her through all that. The cops won't help her. They'll just make it worse."

Junior reached for the phone.

"Unless you want me to close up that other eye of yours, put the damned phone down, Junior. We'll take care of this. She's one of ours. We'll take care of it."

But Earl Sr. didn't take care of it. Not because he didn't want to, but Barry had disappeared. A few years later they found out he had joined the Army shipping out to the deserts of Iraq, then gone to school, culminating in a dental degree, in Michigan.

~*~

They all tried to put Barry's attack behind them. Earl Sr. buried himself in work, while Junior and MaryLou sought relief in bags of weed Junior bought from two middle aged Vietnam vets who sat by a small BBQ joint at a deserted crossing of two country roads.

"I miss the old MaryLou."

She stared straight ahead, taking a deep toke of weed, holding soothing smoke deep in her lungs before exhaling.

"You know, the one who liked to laugh and talk about movies?"

"Did I do something to make him think—"

"That's bullshit. You did nothin'. Even if you did, you sure as hell weren't asking to be beaten up and raped."

"So you're saying I did do something."

"No, I'm not saying that at all. You did nothin' LouLou. Nothin'. Barry's a lowlife sonvabitch. If anybody's to blame here its me not getting there in time to keep that bastard away."

MaryLou took another long toke, then passed the joint to Junior. She had been feeling victimized since Barry's attack, but for some reason, maybe it was the weed or maybe she had just tired of being a victim, she felt a growing anger and determination to bring the fight right to Barry Swenson. "One of these days, I'm going to find that bastard, Junior. When I do, I'm going to kill him."

Junior looked at the smoldering ember of his joint, pondering her words, then took a drag. "I'll hold him down while you cut his balls off. How does that sound?"

"Sounds good Junior. Sounds real good."

~*~

The first morning MaryLou felt sick to her stomach, she put it off to too much weed and beer, vowing to slow down a bit. But after a string of days feeling nauseous followed by her period being late, she panicked. She borrowed Junior's truck, driving twenty miles to find a drug store in Austin away from nosey Pflugerville eyes. A pregnancy test confirmed her fears. She was indeed pregnant and Barry had to be the father.

She sat by the pond with Junior on a warm late summer day, watching water spiders dance across its surface. A dragon fly hovered like some prehistoric craft looking for a place to land.

"I'm really sorry, MaryLou. Really. Barry is a total psycho shit."

"What am I going to do Junior? I can't tell my Mom about any of this, she'll kill me."

"Kill you? He raped you, MaryLou."

"I know he...I know what he did. But my Mom, I can't tell her what happened. I can't, I can't do this. Not with him. Not this way."

A turtle moved slowly off a fallen tree trunk, sliding into the water with a plopping sound.

Junior asked, "What do you want to do?"

She spoke softly, revealing her dark secret. "I want to get an abortion."

"Are you sure, MaryLou?"

Her eyes flashed anger. "Yes, I'm sure, Junior. I can't have this baby. I can't."

"Okay. I get it. I'm sorry. I get it. Well, I'm not going to let you do this by yourself, Lou Lou. I'm your brother, half-brother at least. You don't have to be alone for this."

Junior leaned toward MaryLou, enfolding her in his arms. MaryLou let Junior hold her. With her world spinning out of control, his arms offered an anchor in waters she wished she didn't have to navigate. The following week, without telling anyone what they were doing, Junior took her to a clinic for the procedure, paying the fee.

Afterwards she felt empty and alone. Walking into their kitchen the next morning she found Earl Sr. sitting at the kitchen table nursing a cup of steaming coffee.

"Mornin', MaryLou."

"Morning, Dad." Over the last few weeks, after the blood test had confirmed Earl Sr.'s part in MaryLou's life, she had begun to experiment with calling him 'Dad'. Something he seemed to like.

"How you doin', darling?"

She felt so empty, his concern couldn't reach into the place deep inside she now kept protected.

"I'm okay."

"I know where you were yesterday."

Panic gripped her. She wasn't sure where this was going and she didn't have any reserves to muster much in the way of protection. She wordlessly stepped over to the counter, busying herself with making some toast.

Earl Sr. continued, staring into his coffee. "I just want you to know I understand." She turned to meet his eyes, his face etched in pain. "As far as I'm concerned, you're still my MaryLou. I just want you to know that."

He stood up, walked over kissing the top of her head, then stepped out through the back door. MaryLou stood at the counter, weeping, her toast burning to black.

~*~

With each passing year, her memory of Barry's attack, what she soon referred to as "The Situation", festered like a pustule in her gut. "The Situation" had influenced her in so many ways: a law enforcement degree, her time with the CIA, and now as a special operative inside Homeland Security. In fact, without her Agency resources she wouldn't have known Barry Swenson had multiple interests from drug distribution to manufacturing of amphetamines, a rumored toxic waste scam, and potential terrorist activity based on his unique, crazy political theory. When she heard Barry might be back in Central Texas, she decided to use his politics as a justification for her assignment in Pflugerville. Her cover as a Houston Chronicle reporter seemed a good one, but she hadn't counted on Nick walking into her life. Until that night with him she had always considered a relationship baggage she couldn't afford to carry around, but now she had stumbled upon someone completely unexpected. Saying they clicked just seemed trite. They had exploded into a convulsive heap of absolute bliss.

The other wildcard, which was proving to be a thorn in her side, was Junior. Over the years she had helped Junior when she could, he being adept at getting himself into trouble, she being adept at fixing trouble. She still couldn't believe Junior had managed to get himself entangled with Barry Swenson. How could he do anything with that fat fucking bastard? The original plan, which thanks to Junior was now in the tank, had been to come to Central Texas, find Barry Swenson, kill him, and leave. She didn't have a clear plan "B" yet, but somehow she was going to have to protect Junior and come up with a solution, a lasting solution, for Barry Swenson.

Pulling into her motel, she reached down to check her Glock taped underneath the seat and then, stepping out of the car, quickly slipped a back up gun in her back waist band. She looked around to be sure no one had followed, then stepped silently into her room.

32 BOTTOMS UP

After giving statements and arranging for a tow truck for Quentin's patrol car, Nick and Quentin hitched a ride with another Pflugerville officer, dropping Carl back at the farmhouse. At the Justice Center Nick got out, shaking Quentin's hand.

"Thanks for your help back there buddy."

Quentin held Nick's firm handshake. "There's an APB out on them both. We'll get them."

"I know you will."

Parting ways, Nick drove over to MaryLou's motel to make sure she was doing okay. Opening her door at his knock, he could see MaryLou had clearly made a full recovery, her face flush, eyes alert. She wore a white terrycloth robe, her hair wet from a shower. She left the chain locked.

"Nick, didn't expect to see you today."

Her voice sounded odd, hollow to Nick. Maybe she hadn't quite recovered yet.

"Looks like you're doing better. That's good. Mind if I come in?"

"Sure. Of course."

She paused turning to scan the room over her shoulder, as if she had something to hide, then unchained her door, pulling it open. Nick couldn't put his finger on it, but something about MaryLou felt off. He coached himself to stop being a private investigator for once and just try to be Nick Sibelius with this woman he knew he was falling for. They stood awkwardly in her room, Nick unsure what to say.

"You left the hospital looking pretty green. Just wanted to drop by to be sure you had everything you needed."

"You're really sweet, Nick. No, I'm okay."

"I passed by earlier today. Noticed your car was gone."

MaryLou gave him an odd look, which he interpreted as her wondering if he had decided to stalk her.

"I'm not stalking you, by the way. Just passed by. I figured you must have gone out to find a drug store."

"Well, yes. That's right. Just something to settle my stomach. Thank goodness it worked."

"So you're feeling better."

"Not all the way yet, but I'm doing better, Nick."

They looked again at each other. Nick couldn't understand the change in MaryLou. Last night she seemed to be a soul he had known all his life. And the lovemaking. But today she seemed distant, almost like another woman, an identical twin sister who had never met him. Maybe he had come on too strong, too fast. Or a six month drought of being with a woman, of feeling connected to another human being for that matter, made him come across as desperate, needy, or worse.

"MaryLou, about last night."

"Last night was wonderful, Nick." She looked into his eyes, her smile edged with sadness.

Nick hesitated. He didn't understand what was happening, but it felt like they stood on a very thin plate of glass. A wrong word would shatter what they had both shared the night before. "Yes, MaryLou. Wonderful. Look, I just came by to check on you. I better get on down the road."

She walked back to the sink, pulling out two glasses. "A drink?"

"I don't know." Nick couldn't shake the feeling if he stayed much longer he'd begin to lose her. "I probably should be going."

"Just one drink, Nick." She poured some Jack Daniels into two plastic cups, turning to hand Nick one, kissing him lightly on his cheek. "Then I'll send you on your way. Bottoms up."

They both took a sip of amber liquid. MaryLou asked, "What's happening?" Nick took another sip of whiskey. "I'm a reporter, Nick. You know how we are. Always need to know what's going on."

"It looks like Junior has been creating quite a bit of havoc along with his buddy, Barry."

"Our guy with the farm has a buddy. How nice."

"Look, I know you want to cover this story. I respect your professionalism, but Barry Swenson is a dangerous guy. And he's got a killer named Jayson working for him. He killed a Houston police officer."

"I remember hearing about it. Awful."

"You've got to stay away from this mess, MaryLou."

"I do appreciate your concern, Nick, but I'm as good or better at what I do than you are. I've been doing fine without police protection all of these years."

"I didn't mean to insult you. I just don't want you to get hurt."

"I don't want you to get hurt either, but I'm not going to keep you from doing your job."

"Touché." He raised his glass to MaryLou. "Just be careful."

"Always. So what's your next step? Hunt this Barry character down?"

"I've got lots of loose ends. Besides Barry, I've got Junior and apparently some woman named Mary who's somehow connected to all of this."

MaryLou set her glass down on a nightstand, turning her back to Nick. "Mary?"

"She's Junior's sister. She sounds a bit scary too. She apparently kept all of Barry's boys under control. They were convinced she'd kill them all if she wanted."

MaryLou turned around smiling. "Really. I'd like to meet this Mary. Maybe I can do an interview once you track her down."

"That would be quite the interview. Mary Pendleton, violent sociopath or Central Texas debutant."

MaryLou looked almost hurt. Nick realized he needed to shut up and get out of there before he erased all of their progress from last night.

"What, you don't like my title for your interview?"

"Why don't you leave writing to the professionals, Sibelius."

"Yeah, you're probably right." *Leave Nick. Leave now.*

MaryLou slipped one hand into her robe, smoothing a fold. In spite of wanting to leave, Nick couldn't help but ponder how easily he could slip the knot from her waist.

"So where is my favorite private investigator off to now?"

Snapping back to reality he said, "I'm going over to Rev. Anderson's house, just to check in with him."

MaryLou reached up to stroke Nick's face. She looked like she had something to say, almost as if she needed to unburden herself. Nick reminded himself to leave his interrogation instincts out of his relationships.

She said, "Be careful, Nick. None of this is worth you getting hurt."

Nick brought her hand to his lips, feeling her pulse through the warmth of her wrist. "I've been doing this a long time too, MaryLou. Don't worry. Barry, Junior and this Mary have more to worry about from me, than I do from them."

With those words he gently kissed her lips, then opened the door, stepping out into a hot Texas summer evening's fading light.

33 ESCAPE FROM THE SANDS

Junior had been sitting in room 104 of the Sands Motel for several hours. He tried out the thousand fingers massage, hoping to distract himself with some sort of sexual experience. But instead of being caressed by long, soft fingers of a hundred buxom, naked women, he felt like one of those play pieces in an electric football set, vibrating without direction across a playing field. He remembered why he had smashed his electronic football game to pieces after Harlan had repeatedly beaten him when they were kids. Of course, thinking about Harlan plunged him back into despair, then anger about his friend's drowning.

"Jesus, Harlan. You can beat me at fucking electric football, but you don't have enough common sense not to drown yourself? I thought you were some kind of goddamn fisherman. Don't you people know how to swim?"

He dug up a Gideon Bible in his bed stand. Normally Junior wouldn't bother to read a Bible, or much of anything else for that matter. He did read the lingerie section of the Sears & Roebuck catalog and those nudie pictures of tribal women in *National Geographic* when he was a kid. As an adult he preferred the *Victoria's Secret* catalog and cable television. However, he found himself sitting on the edge of a convex shaped bed, staring at an old color TV with only six channels, the reception so bad on four of them he really only had two. If two lousy channels weren't enough, some asshole had turned on the parental control to block porno on channel 6. So he found himself alone in a cheap motel room without porn or a Longhorn football game. Other than jacking off, and he was just too rattled about recent developments to conjure up enough of a female fantasy to do the deed without visual assistance, he only had a Gideon Bible as his last refuge of entertainment. He opened the book, thumbing through pages, when he came upon a chapter having something to do with working. How weird. So he started reading this chapter called "job", when he discovered the story was about some guy named "job." *Who would name their kid job? That's like calling someone Chore or Shitwork.* He laughed for a moment thinking about how funny it would be calling Carl, Shitwork, instead of Carl. Reading through the first couple of chapters, skipping a few bits just because they were so godawful boring, he learned this "job" guy got totally screwed over by God. Killed his family, destroyed his property. A real heavenly shit fest.

"Damn. That's what's happenin' to me. God's crapping all over my business. Shit!"

He kept on reading, hoping he'd find a solution to his problems by the end of the second chapter, but as best as he could tell, God really didn't give a flip about this "job" guy. He was just screwing with him to win a bet with a bunch of assholes. Probably angels. Angel assholes.

Realizing God not only wouldn't help him out, but didn't actually give a shit, left Junior with only one clear choice in his mind. He needed to get the hell out of this motel, find Carl, then get Barry to help him get Sibelius off his ass. And then, for MaryLou, he'd put an end to Barry Swenson. Yessir, time to take care of business. Besides, if he stayed at this motel, he'd just get MaryLou more involved in whatever God had intended for him. No, she had saved him one too many times. All he had ever done the last few years was hurt her.

He stepped outside of his room, looking across the parking lot for a car he might be able to steal. Junior had never stolen a car. Wasn't really sure how to steal one. But he had watched a lot of TV and knew you had to break in, then jam a screw driver in the ignition, or something like that. His eye caught sight of a yellow Corvette. *Now that's a nice ride.* He casually approached the car, looking inside, then glancing around to be sure no one had the drop on him. Pulling a handle he confirmed its owner had locked the doors. An idea came to him to shatter the driver's side glass with a powerful thrust of his elbow. With a mighty blow his elbow met the equivalent of a titanium wall, pain flashing up his arm, the car alarm coming to life. Panic gripping him, he hobbled away from the 'vette, hiding behind a big SUV. The yellow sports car screamed, honking and blaring, lights flashing, but no one came out to check on the vehicle. Come to think of it, Junior couldn't remember a time when someone actually checked on a car alarm going off, everyone assuming some vibration or other had just set the thing going. Finally the blaring stopped and Junior caught his breath. He found a large rock nearby and he knew what to do. Limping back to the 'vette he looked quickly around, then smashed his rock into the window, glass spidering out in all directions. He kept hitting it, breaking away small pieces of glass, the car alarm once again screaming, until he could reach in, releasing a lock to open the door. He now sat on a glass strewn leather upholstered seat. No screw driver. *Shit. Wait. Those guys on TV are always wiring shit together under the dash.* He leaned under the steering wheel looking for wires, almost believing there might be two marked wires which plugged into each other to start the car. No such luck.

Sitting up, he noticed the door to room 210 opening. Panic gripped him once again. He struggled out of his bucket seat. Favoring his hurt leg, he hopped away from the scene of his crime hoping he could put sufficient distance between himself and the car to make him look like a witness rather than a thief. The couple in 210, a balding guy in his fifties and he wasn't sure at this distance, but a woman who looked an awful lot like that tease of a waitress Jennifer at the Bluebonnet Cafe, stepped onto the balcony, not giving any heed to a Corvette having a complete freak out.

He waited for them to leave and the 'vette to calm down. Then a young couple in a orange and black Smart car pulled up to the office, jumping out, laughing and holding hands. Their car looked liked someone had driven a VW bug into a trash compactor and flipped the switch. Junior knew for sure the thing had to be smaller than his four wheeler back at his farm. While he had rather stolen a hot sports car or at least a nice roomy SUV instead of a clown car, they had left their keys in the ignition with the engine running. Maybe God had decided to help him out a bit after all. Junior wedged himself into the driver's seat, putting his successfully stolen tiny car into Drive, then took off down the highway to Carl, to Barry and hopefully, to get his recent business enterprise, as well as his life, out of the crapper.

34 PREPARATIONS

Barry felt pretty pissed off. Junior seemed intent on completely destroying his operations. Some of his best men had been killed by Nick Sibelius and a Pflugerville cop. At least he had Jayson, who had a proven track record in the cop killing department. He hadn't bothered to look in his back seat until now, so seeing a girl, bound and gagged, gave him a start.

"What's this, Jayson? You were supposed to kill them both."

The big, blond hulk kept his eyes on the road.

"Ran into a snag. Didn't have time to off both of them, but I can pull off, slit her throat, then leave her in a ditch, if you like." Jayson made this offer as if he were suggesting where to go eat for dinner.

"I appreciate your enthusiasm, Jayson. I do. However, I think I have a way to rid ourselves of several problems at once." He turned to Ayisha, her face swollen from the bashing she had taken in Jayson's hands. Barry reached back, ripping duct tape from her mouth. She took in large gulps of air. "Dear, I need to know where you live." Ayisha, her eyes filled with fear, stared, her voice caught in the back of her throat. "Let me rephrase my question. Either you tell me where you live or I'll let Jayson do you right here, then we'll beat the address out of you. Now, which will it be?"

"Magnolia. 1007 Magnolia."

"You're sure now? Because if you're lying to me, there are far worse things I can have Jayson do to you. So, are you sure?"

"Yes. 1007 Magnolia."

"Excellent." Barry taped her mouth again. "You can punch her address into my GPS after we make our preparations."

Given the success of his criminal endeavors to date, he was not about to let some small town cop, a barely employed private investigator, and a teenage girl get in his way. Once he dealt with them, Junior and Carl would be easy pickings. Which just left MaryLou. Now she'd be tricky given the skills she had shown earlier in the day and an intensity fueled by their past history. He'd have to think through a strategy trapping her in a way, which for old times sake, he'd be able to tie her up, strip her down, do her, then take her out. *Yeah, I'm gonna plan something very special for you, my dear. A reunion of sorts. A farewell reunion.* Barry felt himself get hard just thinking about it.

Fortunately his Hummer had already been packed with weapons and ammunition, so he had the tools he needed. Their first stop was his West Austin home where they swapped out his black Hummer for a white Dodge Ram pickup with a club cab. Jayson moved Ayisha to the back seat and the weapons and ammo under a hard top cover of the truck bed. While Jayson did the heavy lifting, Barry worked at a table in his garage building a small, but effective explosive device.

Having completed their preparations, Jayson left with Ayisha tied up in his back seat, while Barry stayed at his house. Parking across from the Bluebonnet Cafe, Jayson waited for Officer Quentin Matthews to show for his regular afternoon cup of coffee. He waited over two hours, wondering if Barry might have his information about the cop's habits wrong, when Quentin pulled up in a patrol car.

Jayson muttered to himself. "Look who's stopping in for his last meal."

A bag hanging from his shoulder, Jason walked casually toward his target, pausing once to gaze into a storefront window, pretending to be a shopper, not a killer. Stepping beside a front wheel of Quentin's replacement cruiser, he dropped some change he had in his hand. Bending down to gather his coins, he slipped his hand into his messenger bag, pulling out a small cigar box which he placed on a tire, hidden by the car's front fender. Having gathered his coins, he resumed walking, then made the block back to his truck. He thought about waiting around for the big bang, but Barry's instructions were clear.

"Plant the bomb, then use the girl as bait to kill Sibelius."

35 HOLY, WHOLLY, HOLE-Y

Junior drove up to the farmhouse wanting to find Carl quickly, then get to Barry's before he had another encounter with law enforcement or Sibelius or the Marine. He pulled his Smart car up beside Carl's pickup truck, his dogs barking, then jumping with excitement when they recognized him.

"Carl! Carl, get out here!"

No answer. He went into his house, calling out Carl's name, searching room by room for his nephew.

"Dammit Carl. I told you to stay in the house."

Junior walked across to the barn. Not finding his nephew there, he walked down to the pond, then through burnt and still smoldering woods to Carl's no longer existing hiding place. He walked back to the barn, rechecking every corner, then again back to the farmhouse. Not finding his nephew left Junior with two options in his mind. Either Carl got picked off by Jayson and his body would never be found, or his idiot nephew did the very thing he told him not to do, namely leave. In which case, Jayson would eventually find him and his body would never be found. He had to get to Barry's—now.

Driving away Junior stopped at a nearby convenience store for a cherry slushy. Then he pulled back onto the road for his drive into Austin. Half a mile away from the convenience store, he could see a police car ahead of him on the next rise. At first he panicked, but taking a big draw on his slushy straw he got a brain freeze realization that about the last place law enforcement would look for him would be in some euro clown car. However, Junior had about ten miles before he would be turning towards Austin. The idea of trailing behind a police car for miles didn't strike him as a very smart thing to do. He laughed.

"Maybe that's why they call this thing a Smart car."

He slowed to the shoulder, waiting until the police car disappeared behind a crest, then pulled a u-turn back down the same road. Junior decided to just wait for a few minutes back at his farm out of sight. Driving up to the farmhouse once again he couldn't believe his eyes. The nephew he assumed had been killed and buried in an unmarked grave, sat calmly on the porch swing. Junior accelerated up the drive, slamming on his brakes just in front of the house, leaving Carl with the impression of a dust devil roaring to life.

Carl stopped swinging, probably wondering what had just arrived in a billowing cloud of dirt. Junior kicked open his car door, struggling to get out in a way which would convey his anger while not hurting his knee too much. Instead, he looked like some kind of circus clown in a dust storm.

Carl asked, "Junior, is that you?"

Junior finally extricated himself from his car, pulled up his pants, then straightened his shirt.

"Of course it's me Carl. Where the hell have you been? I thought Barry had gotten ahold of you."

"The police came and got me."

Junior's heart skipped a beat realizing how close he must have been to a face to face encounter with the law. "What did they want?"

"To show them Barry's farm."

Junior climbed the porch stairs. "You told them to fuck off I trust."

"They kind of had the upper hand, if you know what I mean."

He stopped at the top step. "So you told them about Barry?"

"They seemed to already know. I just showed them his place."

"How did that go?"

"Pretty bad. Bullets flying and shit. Dead guys everywhere, Junior. Never seen nothin' like it."

Junior joined Carl on the porch swing. "So the police killed Barry. Well, that's a relief."

"No, Barry got away. That Jayson fellow too." Carl stopped the swing. "Wait, I thought Barry was your friend."

"He got away? Barry's out there somewhere?" Junior shook his head in disbelief. "Holy shit."

"So he's not your friend?"

"Friends don't try to stab you to death, Carl. So no, he ain't my friend no more."

The swing creaked rhythmically as they pondered Barry roaming the countryside free.

"Sorry, Junior."

"Sorry about what, Carl? Making me have to kidnap people? Taking a police officer to Barry's compound so Barry has one more reason to hate my guts? What? What are so sorry about, Carl?"

"Well, I meant I was sorry you lost your friend, Harlan."

Junior rose from the swing. "Come on. Let's go."

"Where to?"

"I don't think you're in much of a position to be asking questions, Carl. Just get in the car."

"In that thing?" Carl laughed. "Where did you steal it from, some roadside freak circus?"

"No, I stole it from a motel parking lot. Thank you very much. Now get in the car."

"Let's take my truck. If someone sees us in a clown car we'll be hearing about it for years."

"Carl, if we take your truck, the police and Barry will spot us on sight. If they do, no one will hear from us for years."

"Why's that?"

"We'll be kill't dead...or worse. Now get in the goddamn car."

~*~

While speeding toward West Austin, Carl, scrunched in beside Junior, nervously banged out a rhythm on the dash.

In exasperation Junior said, "Carl, will you please stop banging on the car."

"What? Oh, this? Sorry, guess I'm just a bit nervous."

"What do you have to be nervous about? I'm the one whose way of life is about to be crushed like a cheap can of beer by a drunk good ol' boy."

"Well, where are we goin'?"

"To see my business associate. He's going to be pissed off, but I figure he's our best chance of sorting this whole thing out."

"I thought you said he tried to kill you with a knife?"

"Yes, but he acted in the heat of the moment. Barry and I go way back. I helped him avoid a very bad situation once. He owes me."

Pulling up to Barry's expansive house, they both wrestled themselves out of the car, then straightened up, walking tall, trying to regain some of their dignity after spending so much time in a vehicle as far from a pickup truck as a ukulele is from one of Willie Nelson's guitars.

Junior rang Barry's doorbell, saying to Carl, "Just be yourself, Carl. Well, on second thought, just be quiet. I'll handle this."

Barry looked surprised to see Junior and Carl at the doorstep of his ranch style home. Junior had hoped to be ushered through to a back patio where they would talk over business with a cold beer. Instead, Barry ushered them through his door, tasered Carl, who crashed on an imported Italian marble floor in spasms, then put a gun to Junior's head. While Junior begged for mercy, Barry strapped him down to a dentist chair in a back room of his house. The room looked exactly like a dental exam room, complete with chair, x-ray machine, even a flat screen TV in a corner where he could see CNN covering a story about a bombing somewhere, while Neil Diamond sang softly in the background.

Barry came into Junior's line of sight, dressed in pale blue scrubs. "Last time we spoke I thought we had come to an agreement. You were supposed to take care of business, Junior."

"Well, yes, but our situation has gotten a bit more complicated." He tugged at his bindings. "Is this really necessary, Barry?"

"What's gotten complicated, Junior?"

"The police are after me and I've got some private investigator chasing me too."

"How do your concerns impact me, Junior?"

"What? Well, if I'm in jail you don't have a place for your environmental resources or storage for the meth. And if you don't have a place to dump that shit, then Jayson will be after your ass too, that's what."

Barry worked cubby fingers into a blue surgical glove. "Good point." His glove snapped into place as if to emphasize agreement. "So what are you going to do about it?"

"Me? I need your help, Barry. If we're going to stay in business I need some help with the police and Sibelius. Why don't you untie me? We can go have a beer and figure out how to handle all of this."

"So I'm supposed to provide you with the business opportunity of a lifetime and clean up your mistakes too. Is that it?"

"Look, I figure you need me." He watched Barry move around to the other side of his chair next to a set of tools attached to long cables. "Hey, what are you doin'?"

Junior had tried to resist, but Barry's gun at his temple convinced him to open wide while Barry inserted some contraption keeping Junior's mouth wide open.

"I'm going to help you, Junior, because it appears you are too incompetent to handle this yourself. I'm going to make sure you get on with things."

Junior tried to say something like, "What are you doing you crazy fuck?" However, all he could get out was, "Ah, ah ah ah ah ah-ah-ah."

For what seemed like hours but was only minutes, Junior lived a nightmare. The red-headed dentist methodically drilled holes through several teeth. Pain like bolts of lightening shot through his mouth exploding behind his eyeballs, then racing down his spine, leaving him screaming. Writhing in agony, his fingernails tore into his armrests, while Barry sat first beside him, then enthusiastically astride him, his drill screaming, a burning odor of hot tooth enamel filling the room. Junior cried and whimpered, even after Barry's contraption keeping his mouth open was removed and his bindings were cut. Unable to focus, he stared blankly at overhead fluorescents, each breath passing air through gaping holes in his teeth, sending new pangs of a pain he had never felt in his entire life coursing through his body. Junior knew for a fact God had definitely decided to dive deep into his shit and totally fuck him over.

A voice called out to him through his pain, "Junior. Junior!"

Junior pulled himself out of his agony long enough to focus on Barry's plump face.

"Whah?" Junior said, unable to move his lips without setting off a chain reaction of pain.

"First thing you're going to do, Junior, is kill the Ayisha girl. Do you understand? Kill her."

"Bah..."

"No buts, Junior. Until those holes get filled in, you my friend, will be in absolute agony. If you try to go to a regular dentist, the cops will find you. I'm the only one who can fix you up again. So, if I were you, I'd get my ass over there and kill her as soon as possible."

"Whah bow Cah?"

"Carl? Your snitch of a nephew who led police to my door? I'm going to make him beg me to kill him."

"No."

Barry grabbed a stainless steel pick, placing its point next to Junior's eye. "What did you say to me?"

Junior froze, his eye following Barry's movement. "Pleah, no."

Barry hovered his sharp instrument by Junior's face, then stepped back, tossing his tool across the room.

"Fine. Take your twitchy friend there with you. But if you disappoint me, he'll be the first to die."

Junior forced himself out of the dentist chair, shuffling with his bad leg over to Carl who was just coming to from his encounter with Barry's taser. Together they held each other up, leaving Barry's house at gunpoint, then finally falling back into their Smart car.

Carl massaged his neck, sore from convulsions. "That didn't quite go as planned, did it Junior?"

Junior glanced at his own swollen pasty white face in the rear view mirror. "Fah you..."

"What?"

"Fah! You! Fah You!" His shouting increasing his pain, Junior pounded on his steering wheel crying. "Ah, fah, fah."

36 VIEW TO A KILL

Jayson remembered Nick Sibelius, especially the priceless look on his face when he put a bullet in his partner's brain. Sibelius was the only person who could testify against him about killing a cop. With a little luck, he'd lure Sibelius into his trap with the girl, kill them both, then destroy any evidence by burning down the house.

A delay in planting his bomb meant he was now driving into Ayisha's neighborhood at dusk, shadows lengthening with a setting sun. He rumbled by manicured lawns, perfect gardens and driveways filled with SUVs and four door sedans. Jayson parked about a block away from the Anderson home, which stood in a cul de sac backing onto a golf course. While most houses in this development had six foot high cedar privacy fences, houses next to the golf course, by housing association regulation, did not. Jayson waited for darkness, then checked for any evening joggers. Seeing none, he lifted Ayisha on his shoulder like a sack, then tossed her easily over a three foot high decorative wrought iron fence. She grunted on impact. *Good. Bait always works better if it's alive.*

Jayson picked her up again, making his way behind her house, where he dumped her by a brick wall. Peering through a sliding glass door, careful not to reveal himself, Jayson couldn't believe his luck. At a kitchen table sat an older black man, who had to be the girl's father, and Nick Sibelius. Surprise would be on his side, but he'd need to be sure to deal with Sibelius first. He searched the back yard for something heavy enough to shatter a sliding glass door. He decided on a large, concrete bird bath. He lifted the bath from its base, making a point of staying out of sight, then waited, listening to the two men talk.

"So you believe Jayson Moore has my girl? Dear Lord."

"I'm doing everything in my power to locate her. I will find her."

"Find her, Nick. You've got to find her. How's the boy, by the way?"

"He's hanging on, barely. You should know, he fought for her. That's why he's lying in a hospital bed."

"He fought for her. That's good. I guess I'll give him a second chance if..." His voice trailed off.

"I'll find her, Rev. Anderson. I promise."

Jayson took a few deep breaths. Ever since he knocked one of his dealers unconscious with a pit bull, his back had been killing him. Who knew those dogs were so damn heavy? Counting to three, he heaved the concrete bath through the door, glass shattering into large shards. In one swift motion, he drew his gun. Nick, initially startled, had instinctively moved to protect Anderson. Jayson fired. A mist of red blood exploded from Nick's arm, as he fell to the glass covered floor. Jayson turned to shoot Anderson when, what felt like a giant baseball bat slamming against his thigh, flung him back onto the patio. He looked up to see Sibelius prone, pointing his gun, yelling. Jayson grabbed a terrified Ayisha, lifting her to her feet, wrapping his powerful left arm around her neck, then jammed his gun into her temple.

Nick had moved, leaning against a door way, his left arm bleeding, but his weapon pointed directly at Jayson. "Put your gun down, Jayson. It's over."

"It's not over, Sibelius. Not by a long shot. Now throw down your gun or I'm going to splatter this girl's brains all over her daddy's patio, just like I offed your partner. Do you hear me?"

The black guy, the minister, stood behind and to Nick's left, tension in his voice. "Calm down, Jayson. That's your name, right? This doesn't have to end this way. She's innocent."

"Don't fucking tell me how this is going to end, Reverend. Sibelius, throw down your gun!"

Nick spoke, keeping his eyes on Jason. "Let me handle this, Reverend. Look, Jayson..."

"What kind of name is Sibelius anyway. What is that? French?"

"Jayson..."

"You goddamn cheese eating surrender monkey, don't even think about telling me what to do! Now throw down your gun."

Jayson started counting.

"One. Two..."

Nick tossed his gun away.

"What do you know? Surrendered just like all you people do. Now on your knees. You too, your holiness."

Nick stood motionless. Blood flowing out of Jayson's leg also drained his strength. Jayson knew he needed to get his business done quickly.

"On your fucking knees!"

Nick motioned to Anderson and they both dropped to their knees.

"Jayson, this isn't going to end well for you."

"Really? Seems to me I've got this pretty little girl all to myself and I've got you on your knees ready to die. Looks to me like things are going really well."

"How about the big hole in your leg? If you don't let me get you some help soon, you'll bleed out like a stuck pig."

"Good point, officer. Oh wait. That's ex-officer, right? I mean, who wants to work with a guy who let's his partner die?" Jayson momentarily lifted his gun off the target, his mind becoming cloudy, then once again aimed his weapon directly at Nick's head. "The sooner I shoot your ass, the sooner I can use your belt for a tourniquet."

Jayson watched his quarry's fixed stare, anticipating his pleasure at blowing Sibelius' head up like a ripe watermelon. He slowly squeezed his trigger.

Nick gazed down the barrel of Jayson's gun, the murderer's finger closing on the trigger. He sighed. Clearly his ticket was about to be punched. Without warning Jayson's face exploded in a spray of red mist and bloody chunks, his dead body crumpling to the floor, a distant crack of a rifle sounding almost simultaneously, Ayisha screaming, and Nick diving to avoid what should have been a certain kill shot from Jayson's gun.

~*~

Junior couldn't believe how much his face hurt. He tried to keep his mouth shut, breathing only through his nose to avoid what felt like frozen ice picks being jammed into his jaw. Along with Carl, he had gotten back into the Smart car, driving with murderous intent to Ayisha's house. Junior, at heart not a killer—people just seemed to die within his vicinity pretty much completely out of his control—decided he had enough. He was determined to march into the girl's house, put a bullet in her head, her daddy, and the dog, if they had one. He'd take out every living thing: hamsters, cats, fish, everything. He'd show that crazy fuck Barry he meant business. Old Barry would show up to assess the damage and it would look like Junior poured blood all over the walls. Yeah, old Barry would learn not to fucking mess with Junior Pendleton.

His plan, which he thought was pretty damned good for a guy with multiple holes in his teeth, consisted of approaching her house from behind by crossing through a golf course fairway. He parked on the street, walking to a crossing intersection with a dead end facing a golf course and surrounded with trees. Stepping over a barrier, Carl followed him, then walked into a small grove of trees. A loud clap, like a gun being fired at close range, startled them. Given what had transpired lately, they both instinctively hit the ground. Then, to Junior's astonishment, Mary-Lou came crashing out of the woods, a high powered rifle with a telescopic sight slung across her chest.

"Lou Lou? Is that you?"

MaryLou immediately pointed her rifle in his direction, then seeing Junior, albeit a swollen, battered Junior, lying on the ground next to a concrete barrier, lowered her weapon.

"Junior? What are you doing here? And what happened to you?"

"Barry."

"Barry? Toxic waste Barry did this to you?"

Carl spoke up much to Junior's relief. Junior wasn't sure he could speak much more without passing out in pain.

"He zapped me with a taser, then drilled a bunch of holes in Uncle Junior's teeth. Barry's crazy."

MaryLou glared at them. "Junior, didn't I tell you to stay in the motel? I put you there so something like this wouldn't happen."

"Sorry." He winced from the air moving through his holes.

"Don't tell me you're sorry, Junior. Just do what I tell you to do."

Junior asked, "Was that you shooting, Lou Lou?"

MaryLou sighed, pulling Junior up by his shirt. "Yeah, about that. You don't have to worry about Jayson anymore."

"Are you saying you killed Jayson? Hot damn!" Junior grimaced. "Really?"

MaryLou started walking. "Let's go."

"I am ever so grateful, Lou Lou. Probably not as satisfying as taking out Barry, but then..."

She turned on Junior. "It wasn't satisfying, Junior. So let's just drop it. What's important right now is you two need to get far away from here. Do you understand? And this time, stay put or I'll take care of you, too."

Junior looked at Lou Lou's eyes for a slight tease, but all he got was a stone cold stare. She definitely meant business. He nodded his agreement. Leaving his stolen Smart car, they piled into MaryLou's Prius, driving back roads away from Austin west toward Fredericksburg.

~*~

Barry had parked a block from Ayisha's house to watch his plan unfold. Hopefully Junior would interrupt Jayson killing Sibelius, then, Jayson would kill everyone in sight. At first things looked promising. Junior had parked on a street by the golf course with a clear path to the girl's house. They had walked into a small grove of woods. He presumed they would stalk their way behind her house, enter through a back door, then get caught up in Jayson's one man Armageddon. Training his binoculars on the house he could see someone. *Wait, it looks like a big white guy. Yes, it's Jayson.* Barry saw Jayson, a strangle hold on the girl with a gun pointed down at somebody. If Junior will just get a move on, hell, this will be all wrapped up in a few seconds. A gun fired, then Jayson's head exploded, his body falling, the girl wresting herself away. Barry had no idea Junior was such a great shot. Hell, his shot came from over a hundred yards. He waited for more gunfire, but only silence reigned. *If*

Junior's smart enough to not let himself get killed by Jayson, how could he miss a teenaged girl? What is he thinking?

He ran back to his car, driving quickly down the street to where he assumed Junior had parked. *Clearly I'm going to need to drill a few more holes!* Cresting a hill he saw a woman putting a rifle in the trunk of a Prius. Carl opened a back door to get in and Junior sat in the passenger seat. The woman looked around, not recognizing Barry's car, then got in the Prius and drove away. MaryLou.

Barry let his frustration get the better of him, banging on his dash so hard his custom ordered wood grain panel cracked. Taking in several deep breaths, he regained control, then shifted into his business mode by mapping out pros and cons in his mind about his current situation.

Pros:

1. Jayson appears to be very dead which means I now own my toxic waste and metamphetamine businesses completely. *

He added the asterisk to celebrate his success.

After one "pro" he just couldn't think of anything else positive about the current turn of events. So he switched to listing his Cons:

1. The girl is still alive—kill her.

2. Her boyfriend may still be alive—kill him.

3. Nick Sibelius is still alive—kill him.

4. Junior's nephew Carl can't be trusted—kill him.

5. Junior has become too much trouble—kill him.

6. MaryLou is not only a pain in the ass, but she can shoot—kill her so she doesn't kill me.

He considered his pros and cons, checking to be sure he hadn't left out any important items. Having satisfied himself with his chart's completeness, he felt an inner peace the knowledge of knowing next steps always gave him. He knew he should probably be delegating more work. However, his delegations to Jayson and Junior simply didn't measure up to his standards. Great entrepreneurs sometimes had to take things into their own hands. After all, having made a high risk move into environmental resource management, he was honor bound to protect his investment.

Following MaryLou's Prius, a plan formed about how to proceed with Cons four, five and six in a way which enabled him to also tic off Cons one, two and three from his list. He adjusted his air conditioning to a comfortable seventy degrees, telling his voice controlled stereo to play his favorite Bee Gees Greatest Hits. A trademark Bee Gees falsetto sound revved up like pack of singing beavers in heat. "Yes, this is going to be a very good day."

37 MARCUS' LAST RIDE

Marcus Caruthers sat in the driver's seat of his 1959 Persian pink Chrysler Imperial. The car had belonged to his mother, God rest her soul. She had died just in time, since Austin Police impounded his Porsche after a cop clocked him at 140 mph in a 55mph zone. He would have gotten away if he hadn't tried a short cut across a median to a service road. How was he supposed to know a road crew had left piles of re-bar and concrete barriers there overnight? The impact pretty much crushed his 911's front end right up to its windscreen. Thank God for air bags and his racing grade five-point seat belt.

So, he lost his wheels and his license. Mom's old Imperial, looking something like a battleship in a sea of pleasure craft on the road to a Pride Parade, had antique car tags. Marcus figured antique tags meant her car didn't have to meet the same regulations, like emissions and safety equipment, as a modern car. If those regulations were bypassed, then surely having a driver's license had to be optional. This was Texas after all.

He sat at a light near Pflugerville High School, raising his Shiner beer in salute to educators who toiled in the trenches everyday. Then he downed its contents, tossing his bottle behind him, which clanked against other bottles he had tossed in his back seat over the last two hours. On a whim he turned onto Main, where street lights caught his attention. Being a fast driver, he had never really taken time to look at a streetlight. Really look at one. Its light hurt his staring eyes, but for the sake of art or philosophy or something, he continued to gaze, to take in its luminosity. His big ship of a car began swaying. For a moment he thought he might have actually gone to sea. A red flashing light passed overhead. He liked the contrast of red against a yellow streetlight box. Just before everything exploded into a fiery gold, Marcus let out a long, delicious belch of a lifetime. The next moment he pondered the momentous roar of yellow, red, and gold when combined. And if any chunks of Marcus could have had a thought after the explosion, they would have considered how quiet things are when everything goes to black.

~*~

Quentin had stepped into the Bluebonnet Cafe for a quick bite before he continued his search for Jayson Moore and Barry Swenson. A black Hummer, not the most inconspicuous of vehicles, should be easy to locate. But up to this point, he hadn't heard any hints on his radio about two fugitives or a Hummer. Finishing up a plate of chicken fried steak, green beans, and mashed potatoes, he took one last sip of coffee, then pushed away from the cafe counter.

"See you tomorrow, Stacey."

She looked up from the kitchen delivery bay, loading plates of food up her left arm with a method honed by years of experience. "Sure Quentin. Be safe out there now."

Quentin reached for the front door handle. "Safety first."

He smiled turning to push the door open when, in a blinding flash reminding him way too much of Iraq, his cruiser exploded, along with a car behind it. A blast, knocking him off his feet, sent shattered glass across the cafe, razor sharp pieces impaling diners sitting near windows. Quentin lay on the floor, stunned, his ears ringing. He reached for his radio to call in for help, but if his call was answered, he couldn't hear their response. He tried to rise, when an excruciating pain pulled him back to the floor. Reaching down, he felt a large shard which had found its way into his abdomen just under his protective vest. He lifted a hand dripping with blood to his eyes, then saw Stacey's face above him slowly fade out of focus.

38 COST OF DOING BUSINESS

From a discreet distance Barry followed MaryLou's blue Prius from a main highway onto a two lane shoulderless county road. He knew exactly what he wanted to do, but felt a bit perturbed his brand new pearl white Lexus would have to be damaged to get the job done. However, they were on a fairly deserted narrow road miles from help, affording him a perfect opportunity to check off several of his to-do items. He consoled himself with a certain knowledge his beautiful car would be "stolen" then destroyed in a terrible fire later in the week. His totaled car would provide insurance funds to get a BMW or maybe one of those new Mercedes.

He gazed out his front window, darkness punctuated by two red taillights. He checked his back mirror for headlights, but only distant city lights illuminated a night sky. Accelerating, Barry quickly overtook MaryLou who, unaware of Barry's presence, moved partially onto the shoulder to allow him to pass. Barry laughed at this act of Texas courtesy, then angled his Lexus into her car with such force and speed she slid right off the road, down an embankment. Rolling over and over, flattening small cedars and yucca, her car finally came to a rest upside down at the bottom of a ravine. Barry slammed on his brakes. Getting out of his car he looked around, ready to drive off quickly, if necessary. Not seeing anyone approaching in either direction, he went around to the passenger side of his car to assess the damage. His front fender had been dented, scrapping away beautiful pearl white paint. His bumper sagged at one end.

"Damn. Well, that's the price of business."

He finally got around to looking down the ravine at MaryLou's overturned car, a mechanical version of a road kill armadillo. He had hoped it would burst into flame leaving cadavers burnt to a crisp, their teeth oddly destroyed from such a traumatic accident. Barry could not contain a brief smile at his creativity for always finding new ways to use his dentistry skills. Unfortunately, her car just sat there upside down. He cursed, realizing he not only busted up his Lexus, but he wasn't wearing the right shoes for walking down steep embankments into ravines. He struggled in his penny loafers to not slip on tall, dry grass. However, momentum, a lack of traction, and his genetically disposed lack of coordination won out. He fell on his backside, sliding down the embankment. Arriving at her car in a scruffy heap, he could see a conscious Junior hanging upside down from his seat belt and MaryLou beside Junior moving slightly at his approach. He had hoped rolling their car into a ravine would be sufficient to kill them all. Barry, adept at making split second decisions on his feet with his hands down someone's throat, immediately shifted his plan to account for his two survivors. Not wanting to have any hassles, he pulled out a hypodermic needle he always kept with him in case he needed to incapacitate someone. Barry lived by the Boy Scout motto "Be Prepared" he had enthusiastically followed as a young Eagle Scout and now as an adult. He thrust his needle into MaryLou's arm.

"Barry? Is that you?"

Junior, even though he was upside down, must have recognized Barry's loafers through the car window. "Yes, Junior."

"What are you doing here?"

"I was following you when someone, might have been that Ayisha girl's Daddy, knocked you down this ravine."

"Ayisha's Daddy? Why would he do that?'

"You tried to kill his daughter, Junior. Let's get you out of there."

He squirmed to glance over at the woman hanging upside down in the driver's seat. "Lou Lou. We've got to help Lou Lou."

"Let's get you out, then we can both get her out."

Junior looked over at his nephew. "And Carl!"

Barry went around back to check on Carl. He lay crumpled on the roof, his face covered in blood, apparently not breathing. At least one of them cooperated with Barry's cunning plan.

"Looks like this one didn't make it. Is this Carl? Can't tell with all the blood."

"Aw, not Carl. He's my nephew. Dumb as an empty box of Fruit Loops, but I still love him. No, not Carl." Junior began banging his fists against the roof in despair, while Barry placed a small timed explosive on the overturned vehicle's fuel tank. With Barry's help, Junior released his seatbelt, crashing to the roof below him, then he crawled through broken glass out the car window.

"Come on, Junior. Help me get Lou Lou before this thing explodes."

"You think it's gonna explode?"

"Absolutely. These things always explode. So the sooner we get her out and get some distance between ourselves and this car, the better. Once we get to my car I'll call 911 for some help."

Junior, who felt dazed and more than a little confused, followed Barry's direction. Lou Lou seemed to be unconscious, but she was breathing. Carl just looked like a bloody mess.

Together they dragged an unconscious Lou Lou up the embankment placing her in Barry's backseat. Junior noticed a large dent on Barry's usually meticulous Lexus as he got in.

"Man, looks like you were in a wreck, too."

"Yeah. About a week ago some old lady ran right into me."

Junior looked back down into the ravine. "We gotta call 911. We need to help Carl."

"I don't think Carl's going to make it, if he's even alive right now." An explosion rocked them. A plume of flame lit up the night, expanding out as tall, dry grass ignited. "No, Carl is definitely not going to make it, Junior."

~*~

Junior had always felt annoyed by his brother's son. As far as he was concerned, the boy was as dumb as a golden retriever and not as good a swimmer. After his sister-in-law ran off with a rodeo star and Caleb had died, Junior took on the role of father, trying to help him into adulthood, even though Carl felt like a millstone around his neck. One positive thing coming out of Junior's duties was having Carl around to do shit work, which had definitely increased Junior's quality of life. Even though Junior didn't really like Carl, he loved him like family. He definitely didn't like the idea of Carl dying in a car wreck, or worse, burning to death. He considered bolting from Barry's car when he felt the muzzle of a gun firmly pressed against his rib cage.

Barry said, "We've got more important business to take care of my dentally challenged colleague."

Junior, tears streaming down his face from dental pain and grief about his nephew, didn't say a word on the long drive to Barry's house. All he could think about was Carl lying dead in the overturned car, Harlan floating dead on the pond, and a throbbing pain in his mouth. Once home, Barry pulled into his garage, its door closing behind them to hide his damaged car and the unconscious woman they were about to remove. Junior helped Barry carry Mary Lou into his dental room, Barry all the while assuring Junior his intentions were honorable, insisting his chair was simply a medical necessity for a woman in her unconscious condition. Barry then gave Junior something for his pain, which, before he fell in a narcotic haze to the floor, did indeed relieve him from his misery.

~*~

"I see you're waking up."

Junior opened his eyes to a ceiling with inset fluorescent spotlights, a pasty dry mouth, aching teeth and a massive headache.

"What did you do?"

"I'm taking care of business, Junior. Something you should have done days ago."

"Carl..."

"He's dead, Junior."

"Carl? Carl's dead. Oh God..."

"He was a loose end, Junior. You would've had to kill him sometime anyway. This way you don't have to feel guilty, since his death was purely an accident."

"Carl. Carl, I'm sorry..."

"Will you please get over this whole Carl fixation, Junior. We've got things to do."

Junior heard Barry busy at something which sounded like someone stripping tape from a dispenser. He kept his eyes closed, holding his head in his hands to keep the throbbing at bay. After a time, Junior said, "It's because of my job. I read all about it in a Gideon Bible. God is gunning for me."

"Your job? I don't know what you're babbling about, but your job Junior, is to keep prying eyes away from our business enterprise. That's your job. To date, you've been nothing but worthless. Tell you the truth, Junior. I've lost quite a bit of faith in you. At first I thought you had really taken the bull by the horns, offing Jayson with a high powered rifle. Then I discover you were just hiding, as usual, in some bushes and she was doing all the shooting."

Barry nodded in the direction of his dental chair. Junior looked up to see MaryLou, completely naked, her arms, legs and head firmly affixed to a beige dental chair, wrapped in clear plastic shipping wrap from head to toe, her mouth held open with a vise-like contraption.

"What the hell are you doing?" Junior rose up to defend her, but Barry, anticipating Junior's mood, had a gun pointed directly at his head.

"So here is how this is going to go, Junior."

"Cut her loose!"

"If you want her to stay alive, you'll shut up and listen."

Junior fell back, almost whimpering, "Lou Lou."

"You see Junior, I think your heart has been in the right place, but you just haven't been motivated correctly. I thought drilling holes in your head would work. Most people's self-survival instinct would have been enough to propel them into action. But not Junior Pendleton. No, you need a different kind of incentive and I believe I have found just the right thing. I'm going to start feeding your Lou Lou here toxic waste." Barry took what looked like a sports bottle with an extra long straw, shoving the tube down MaryLou's throat and squeezing the bottle until she gagged, choking, brownish green liquid dribbling down her cheek.

"What was that? What are you doing?"

"Medical waste, Junior. Toxic, radioactive. Won't kill her with one dosage, but if she keeps drinking, and she definitely looks to me like a girl who loves to stay hydrated, then she'll be dead in twenty four hours."

"Please stop, Barry. What do you want? Please, just tell me what you want."

"I want you to kill the girl, her boyfriend and Sibelius. Here's a digital camera. Kill them and take their picture so I know they're dead. Bring back pictures of three dead people, she lives. Less than three, she's dead. Got it?"

"Please, Barry. Please don't kill her. Kill me, but not her."

Barry laughed. "I'm not killing her, Junior. You are, unless you bring me those pictures. Now get out of here. You have twenty four hours."

39 A BREAK

Nick watched Ayisha's father, sitting on the patio, cradling his daughter in his lap, oblivious to blood pooling around him from their dead attacker. How Jayson had stood there holding a gun at Nick with his leg leaking blood like an open faucet was pretty amazing. But the shot taking Jayson's face clean off was even more amazing. Someone, someone with skills, had been out in the woods. Junior came to mind, but while he seemed to want to shoot everything in sight, Nick couldn't imagine his marksmanship to be anywhere nearing the precision required for this kill shot. Of course, a nasty piece of work like Jayson Moore probably had a number of enemies waiting in the wings for an opportunity to gun him down. Nick would have seriously considered that theory, if not for the unusual timing. Someone didn't want Jayson to pull the trigger. Were they protecting Ayisha? There was someone else in the mix. This Mary woman? Although why would she want to kill Jayson and why would she want to protect Ayisha? Then a thought occurred to him. What if this person was trying to protect him?

After getting treated by an EMT for what turned out to be a crease needing a few stitches, Nick walked across the field to look for any evidence of a gun being fired. He knew it was a bit of a long shot and sure enough, he found nothing unusual to help establish a gun had been fired. No casings. Nothing. Another sign this shooter must be a professional. Some neighbors gathered outside, drawn from their homes by the commotion in their usually quiet community. Chatting with them, Nick learned someone had parked a distinctive little orange and black Smart car, which he discovered still parked nearby. Other cars had come and gone, but no one could remember much about them. He had Alice check for stolen cars in the last two days. She found an orange and black Smart car with matching plates stolen about a hundred miles east near Hearne at a Dunes Motel. Nick couldn't think of any criminals he had ever run across who would willingly steal a miniature car, then drive almost a hundred miles to assassinate a neo-Nazi drug dealer from one hundred yards.

Then Alice called back with a break.

"Looks like our boy Carl escaped a fiery wreck out in the hill country. He's at a local hospital and he's asking for you by name. And Nick, Quentin Matthews is there as well."

"He's checking on Carl?"

"No, Nick. There was another explosion tonight. Someone put a bomb in Quentin's car. Killed a man and injured about five or six others, including Quentin. He's in surgery right now."

Nick rushed downtown to Austin's trauma center at Brackenridge Hospital. Quentin was still in surgery. Since Nick wasn't a police officer or family, they weren't going to release any information. However, he found out from several of his colleagues Quentin had taken a shard of glass in his abdomen. He gave them his cell phone number, requesting a call with any news about his friend. Then he found Carl lying in bed, his face bruised, one eye swollen shut, but the rest of him appearing to still be in one piece. He stared at a TV suspended across his room, a glazed look in his one good eye, which brightened up when Nick walked in.

"How you doing, Carl? I heard you had a pretty bad accident."

"No accident. We were knocked off the road. We rolled and rolled down that hill. I was sure we were goners. I got knocked out somehow. I wake up, Junior and Lou Lou are gone and then everything blows up."

"Slow down, Carl. You said Lou Lou. Who is Lou Lou?"

"Not sure, but she and Junior seem to know each other. Anyway, I came to and they were gone. If I hadn't gotten out of the car, I'd be dead. My doc said she didn't know how I got out, but it was an awfully good thing I did. Otherwise I would have been fried to a crisp."

"So how did you find yourself driving down a road in the hill country with Junior and this Lou Lou?"

Carl looked straight ahead, focusing his attention on Emeril Lagasse making étouffée on TV.

"Carl, if someone's trying to kill you, giving me the silent treatment will not help you at all."

"I don't know. Junior's already pretty pissed at me."

"Are you worried about your uncle, Carl?"

"Yeah."

"Well, if you want to help your uncle, you're going to have to trust me. Why don't you tell me what's going on."

Carl eyed his remote, then muted Emeril mid-roux. "I don't know exactly what Uncle Junior's doing, but he's got some sort of business arrangement with Barry. And this Barry guy is crazy."

"Why do you say he's crazy?"

"Would you call drilling holes in a man's teeth normal? He electrocuted the shit out of me. After we left his place, Uncle Junior seemed pretty upset. Next thing I know we're sneaking around in some bushes by a golf course, then I hear a big old gun fire. We run to our car and out walks this Lou Lou holding a rifle. We end up in her car and let me tell you, she's pretty pissed at Junior."

"So, Lou Lou fired the gun?"

"She said something about having taken care of Jayson, then went off on Junior about leaving some motel."

"Where were you going before your wreck?"

"Someplace west near Fredericksburg I think. She wanted Junior to lay low for awhile to give her time to deal with Barry. Only he dealt with us first."

Nick looked at Carl's heart monitor beeping a steady rhythm.

"Carl, tell me why you and Junior were in those bushes by the golf course to start with."

"Barry. He wanted Junior to kill the girl he found at his farm. You know, the one you thought I had done something bad to?"

"Your plan was to kill her, but Jayson, then this Lou Lou, beat you to the punch. Right?"

Carl nervously scanned the room his one good eye as if looking for an escape route. His heart monitor pulsed faster. "Yessir. But it was them or us."

"I'd like to get your confession in writing, Carl."

"I don't want to do no confessing. I asked for you 'cause Uncle Junior's in trouble."

"Yes, he is."

"No, not trouble with you. Something worse. Trouble with Barry. I think Barry's goin' to kill 'em both."

"How do you know he wants to kill them?"

"Well, he sure didn't mind running us off the road and leaving me for dead."

40 GIVE ME THE FINGER

After leaving Carl, Nick learned Quentin had come out of surgery, been moved to recovery for an hour, then on to ICU. He decided to return to his office just to check in with Alice and gather some information on Carl's accident. Since the car they rolled appeared to belong to this Lou Lou, he'd be able to get more information about her. Alice looked up with her typical sparkling personality.

"How's Quentin doing?"

"He's a fighter. He'll make it."

"Well that's good to know. And how's Carl?"

"A bit banged up, but he's going to survive to pee on picnic tables in the future."

Her lips twisted into a frown, her brow furrowing. "I just don't know why anyone would want to kill Carl. He's harmless."

Nick walked toward his office door.

"I'm going to be in my office for a bit, doing some research. But you can interrupt me if you need something."

Nick had just booted up his computer when Alice called from the front office, a hint of tension in her voice. "Nick, I need you to come out here. Now, please."

He stepped through the door, imagining Alice was going to try cheering him up. Instead he found her sitting at a desk. A bruised and bloodied Junior stood behind her, pointing a gun at her head.

Nick traded a look with Alice. She was calm. Focused.

"Junior. What are you doing?"

Junior eyed Nick nervously, his swollen face pale and dripping with sweat, the gun shaking in his hand.

"Look Sibelius. I don't want to kill this girl." He glanced at Alice. "You are a girl, aren't you? But I will. I will, I tell you. So you just do what I say. You hear me?"

Nick kept his right side slightly behind the door, his holstered gun hidden from Junior's view.

Junior said, "Let me see those hands!"

Nick hesitated, then tossed his gun on an upholstered chair in his office out of Junior's line of sight. He stepped away from the door, raising his hands.

"What's going on, Junior?"

"Nothin's goin' on."

"Something's got to be going on. You're standing in my office with a gun pointed at Alice's head. And to be honest, Junior, you look like shit."

"Well, I haven't had a very good day."

Nick took a step toward Junior.

"You know, Junior, my Mom used to say just because you've had a bad day is no reason to take it out on other folk."

Junior nervously swung his gun around to Nick. "Don't take another step, goddammit! You don't think I'll use this?"

Nick stopped, slowly lowering his hands.

"You don't want to hurt anyone, Junior."

Junior swung his gun back around to Alice, its muzzle an inch from her ear. "Its not me. I don't kill people."

"What about Harlan?"

"Not my fault. The idiot drowned hisself. I was just standin' around in the vicinity."

"So this is how you want to be remembered, Junior?"

"Remembered? Nobody's goin' to remember me. I'm just trying to keep Lou Lou alive, and me too, for that matter."

"Lou Lou. So, Lou Lou is with you?"

"She's with Barry. But that's enough of your questions. I got to get down to business."

Nick kept his eyes on Junior. "I don't think it's true, Junior."

"What ain't true?"

"It's not true you won't be remembered. I know Carl will remember you."

Junior's shoulders slumped, then he cried, "Carl's dead! And you're going to be too."

"Carl's not dead, Junior. I saw him just a few minutes ago in a hospital room."

Junior relaxed, the gun drifting away from his intended target. "What? You're lying to me."

"God's truth, Junior. He almost got killed in a car wreck. I believe you were in the car with him?"

Junior lowered his gun.

"But there was a fire. He's alive?"

"I can take you to see him, but first you've got to give me the gun."

"I can't. I can't. Barry's going to kill her if I don't kill you and the girl."

"Junior, I keep hearing you're not the killer type, in spite of all the bodies and gunshots associated with you recently. Here's your chance to prove it. Give me your gun. I'll take care of Barry and do my best to save Lou Lou."

Nick held out his hand, gesturing for Junior to hand him his gun.

"I don't know."

With reflexes Nick hadn't known she possessed, Alice, in one motion, rose out of her chair grabbing Junior's gun, twisting it back forcefully. Junior screamed in pain, his gun falling to the floor. Nick kicked it away, as Alice pinned Junior's arms behind his back. Junior's trigger finger, broken and dislocated, hung at an odd angle from his hand.

Alice leaned into his ear. "And yes, Junior. I am a girl." Alice, letting him fall to his knees, left Junior crying and cursing.

"Just kill me now. Come on. Do it! I'm done. I can't do this no more. God's doing everything He can think of to beat my ass right into the ground. Jesus, Jesus this hurts. Goddammit!"

Nick tossed Alice a pair of handcuffs, then he pulled Junior up off the floor, depositing him onto a nearby chair. Alice had picked up Junior's gun, removing its clip, emptying the chamber, then laying the gun's components on her desk.

Nick said, "I'm impressed, Alice. I didn't know you had that skill set."

"There's a lot about me you don't know, Nick. Two tours in Iraq leave you with a few skills. Of course, I was Al back then. Besides," she shot Junior an angry look. "I don't like people pointing guns at me."

Nick nodded, focusing on Junior. "I'll keep it in mind for the future."

Alice reached across her desk to pick up a ringing phone.

"Hi, Frank. No, nothing much. Nick and I were just shooting the breeze. What's that? Sure. Hold on." She raised the handset towards Nick saying, "Frank at the Pflugerville Police Department. Wants to know if you have anyone who can identify Jayson Moore."

Nick grabbed ahold of the receiver. "Frank. Yes. As a matter of fact, I've got someone here who worked with Jayson. We'll be right over."

Nick handed the receiver back to Alice. "Junior, looks like we're going to a morgue and while we go, you're going to tell me what you know. Alice, would you find out everything you can about this wreck Carl and our friend Junior here were in earlier today? I especially want to know about the car's owner."

~*~

Nick walked over to his rent-a-wreck Cadillac, motioning for Junior to get in.

"Mighty fancy ride for a private investigator, Nick. I thought you guys drove around in black SUV's and such."

Nick glared at him, his eyes forcing Junior into the passenger seat. Driving downtown gave Nick some time to question Junior and hopefully fill in some of the gaps. Junior told his story from meeting Barry, to kidnapping Ayisha and Delton to Harlan's drowning. He explained how LouLou had rescued him from Barry's intensifying craziness. And how Barry forced him with his dental drill to go after Nick, Ayisha and her boyfriend.

Nick, listening to Junior's chronicle of mayhem, finally said, "Who is this Lou Lou to you Junior? Sounds like you two know each other."

"She's my half-sister. My Daddy had her with some woman in Gonzalez."

"Does she come around often?"

"Hadn't seen her in a couple of years. Not her fault. I'm a bit of an asshole."

"Sounds like an insightful woman, Junior."

They walked into the morgue, three stainless steel tables sat in the middle of a room, a bank of what looked like giant filing cabinets against one wall. Dr. Gus Garcia, a slender Hispanic man with jet black hair and goatee, sat behind a desk, reading a newspaper and eating potato chips from a bag.

"You must be Nick. Frank told me to be on the lookout for you." He set his chips down, coming around his desk, wiping grease and salt onto his lab coat, then shaking Nick's hand. He turned to Junior, catching himself when he realized Junior's hands were cuffed behind his back.

"Good to meet you." Junior muttered.

"Which one of you will be identifying our body?"

Nick said, "Junior will."

Dr. Garcia scanned Junior, finally resting on his face. "I understand you know the deceased."

"If you mean Jason Moore, yeah, I know him."

"Do you think you can identify him without seeing his face?"

"Why would I want to do that? Wouldn't it be easier if I could see his face?"

Gus looked at Nick with consternation.

"You didn't tell him, did you?"

"I guess it just didn't come up, Gus. You see, Junior, you can't see his face because Jayson doesn't have a face anymore. So we've got to go with other things like tattoos, birthmarks, that sort of thing."

"No face? Shit. Okay. Let me think. Sure. He's got Old Glory with swastikas for stars on one arm and a lone star flag on the other. Oh, and he has a knife wound on his stomach and bullet hole in his left shoulder." He glanced to Gus and Nick. "I saw him with his shirt off. Okay?"

Gus said, "Why don't you come over here and take a look."

At the same time Nick's cell phone rang. Alice was calling in.

"Nick, the car was a rental."

"Okay. Who was the renter?"

"You're not going to believe this one. I'm sure there's a good explanation."

"Come on, Alice. Who rented the car?"

"You know the reporter you've been hanging around with lately?"

"Did she already find out who rented it?"

"Well, no Nick. The reporter, MaryLou Perkins, she rented it."

Alice's words were a sledge hammer to his chest. "Excuse me?"

Alice repeated, "MaryLou Perkins. I'm sorry."

"There's nothing to be sorry about, Alice. You're doing your job." Nick pulled his phone away, forcing himself to stay focused. He put it back to his ear. "Alice, call the Houston Chronicle and find out if they have a reporter by the name of MaryLou Perkins."

Nick hung up the phone, his head clouded, his heart up in his throat. He couldn't get a full breath.

Gus asked, "Everything okay, Nick?"

Nick turned, a ferocity boiling up inside of him. "Junior, is Lou Lou also known as MaryLou Perkins?"

Junior, reacting to Nick's sudden anger cowered like a small animal discovering it had accidentally entered a lion cage.

Nick repeated his question. "Junior, is she MaryLou Perkins?"

"Yeah. Who else would Lou Lou be?"

Nick took a moment to process this information. The woman he knew as a reporter from Houston, his lover, was actually Junior Pendelton's half sister. She had murdered Jayson Moore with a high powered rifle right in front of him. He eyed Junior, saying what they both knew to be true.

"And Barry has MaryLou."

"It's worse than that. Barry has MaryLou naked and tied down to a dental chair with her mouth propped open. The goddamn sonvabitch said he was going to force her to drink toxic waste until she dies, unless I got back there within twenty four hours with photos of three dead people: you, Ayisha and her boyfriend."

"You're telling me this now?" Nick had Junior by his shirt, every molecule in his body wanting to slam him headfirst into one of the steel tables. "You stupid—Goddammit, Junior!"

"Nick." Gus intervened. "Nick! I wouldn't blame you for a second, but maybe you might want to spend less time beating the crap out of this fool, and instead, figure out how to help this MaryLou woman."

Nick paused, reason beginning to rise up above his rage. Glaring at Junior, he said to Gus, "Give me one of his fingers."

"Excuse me?"

"His fingers, Gus. Give me a finger."

"Now Nick, the guys in Pflugerville asked me to take good care of you, but I can't go around removing parts off dead bodies."

Nick pushed Junior out of his way, reaching over to a tray by an examination table, picking up an electric autopsy saw. With a whir from its stainless steel blade, he cut off one of Jayson's fingers. Gus stood watching, his mouth agape. "You can't just come in here and cut off chunks of my cadavers!"

Nick put the finger in a towel, slipped it into his pocket, then walked over to Junior.

"Come on, Junior. We're leaving. Now."

As the door slammed shut, Nick heard Gus yell, "I expect that finger back on my desk by tomorrow morning. You hear me, Sibelius?"

41 DENTAL APPOINTMENT

Back on the road with Nick, Junior recalled how the man had threatened to shove a shotgun up his ass. At the time he felt pretty intimidated, but with some time and distance from the incident, Junior had decided the private investigator was just being overly dramatic. Now, as Nick swerved through traffic, his face a picture of murderous intensity, a dead man's severed finger in his pocket, Junior realized Nick was the kind of man who followed through on his threats. Given the sad path his life had taken lately, Junior was determined not to tempt fate, because surely, if he gave the Lord an opportunity, God would provide another shotgun for Nick. So he spoke only when spoken to, which consisted primarily of giving directions. Arriving at Barry's house, Nick parked about a block away.

"Okay Junior. This is what you're going to do. I want you to take this finger..."

Nick handed Junior a bloodied cloth. He could feel the fleshy cylinder of Jayson's finger between his own.

"Take this finger and use it as proof you killed me. Got it?"

"But he wants the couple dead too. Bringing him one finger is not going to make him happy."

"I'm not trying to make him happy, Junior. Just buying some time. So go in there, tell him you're still working the job, but as a gesture of good faith, you're bringing him a finger, just to let him know you mean business."

"I don't know, Nick—"

"Junior, you've got a choice to make here. Do you give a crap about MaryLou?"

"Sure I do. She's helped me out more than once. I don't want to leave her to some twisted fuck like Barry."

"If you want to help MaryLou, then I need you to take the finger to Barry. Let me handle the rest."

"Alright, but I don't have a good feeling about this."

Junior got out of Nick's rent-a-wreck, Jayson's finger wrapped in a cloth in his pocket. With each step toward Barry's house he felt like a convicted murderer walking to his execution. Nick was certainly one angry cuss, but Barry was crazy like a coyote on crack. This was not going to be pretty.

~*~

While Junior walked to Barry's front door, Nick made his way to the back, looking for an open window or door. He figured he'd have to climb decking to gain access, but the first door he tried opened. Apparently Barry felt quite safe. He entered a spa-like room with a stationary bike, an ergometer, an elliptical, and free weights. At the far end he opened another door which led to an indoor sauna and shower, then another room equipped to be a home theater complete with leather lounge chairs. He crossed back over the training room stepping with care down stairs to a floor below. He hoped Junior had, by now, knocked on Barry's door, getting his full attention.

~*~

Junior stood at Barry's front door knowing this had to end badly, but also knowing he owed Lou Lou. He couldn't let Barry kill her, but he knew he wouldn't be able to kill everyone Barry wanted him to kill in the remaining fifteen or so hours he had left. He knocked on Barry's door several times, figuring if Barry was busy in his dental room, it would take awhile just to get to his front door. The door suddenly opened and a cheerful Barry greeted him.

"Well, Junior. I take it you've done the deed. Fantastic!"

"Hi, Barry."

"Do come in. Come in." He ushered Junior into the foyer, striding the hall with the clear expectation of being followed. "I'm a man of my word, so show me those pictures and we'll see to MaryLou."

"I, uh, I haven't quite finished yet."

Barry stopped in his tracks, his shoulders visibly tightening, his fists clenched.

"What did you say?"

"I said I haven't quite finished."

"Then why are you here, Junior?"

"Well, I know how important killin' these people is to you, so I thought I'd bring you a piece of one of 'em, just to let you know I'm takin' care of business. Maybe loosen MaryLou's binding just a tad."

Barry turned, his interest peaked. "You brought me a piece of one of them?"

"Yeah." Junior held out a bloodied cloth.

"And this is?"

"Nick Sibelius."

~*~

Nick stepped onto the lower floor, walking down a hallway, checking each room as he passed. Junior had said the room where Barry had MaryLou was down a flight of stairs. This had to be the floor, but he couldn't find the room. He went back to the two bedrooms, checking closets for false walls. Nothing. He stepped once again into the study. Barry had a glass case filled with antique dental tools. On a large walnut desk sat a human skull alongside a model of a soda can sized oil barrel with a message printed on its side.

Swenson Environmental Resourcing, Inc.

Safe, Economical, Discreet.

The barrel had a slot for coins. Who would design a piggy bank for an illegal toxic waste disposal business? He had just about given up on finding the room when a full length mirror caught his eye. He ran a hand around the edge, then pressed against the mirror. It popped open with a click. Peering down a dark staircase he felt for a light switch, but couldn't find one. He used the dim light from the study to inch his way down the stairs to a landing, his hand finding a door and its knob. He opened the door, stepping into darkness marked by blinking green and red lights. Crouching on the floor, he waited for his eyes to adjust, listening for sounds.

~*~

Barry took Junior's package, opening the cloth to see what part of Nick Sibelius Junior had brought him. He felt a little pissed at Junior for not having completed his job yet, especially when he knew full well Lou Lou, not Junior, had actually killed Jayson. However, he did have another fifteen hours and the thought of holding Sibelius' ear, or nose, or better yet, his prick, gave him a bit of a thrill. He wished he had told Junior to bring him body parts instead of pictures. He'd have to remember that for the next time. Opening Junior's cloth, his initial excitement faded. Junior had just brought a finger. How mundane. But wait! Barry noticed something had been marked on this digit or maybe it was a tattoo. Sort of a human fortune cookie. He always liked fortune cookies. While Junior hadn't brought back a very interesting part of Sibelius, at least there might be a fortune or a saying or something. He picked it up, examining the thick, cold, stubby, black haired metatarsal. Barry could immediately see Sibelius apparently hadn't had a manicure in quite some time. People who don't stick their fingers in other people's mouths for a living just don't understand the value of a good manicure. Lots of black hair. He didn't remember Sibelius being quite so hairy. Then he noticed writing. Not a tattoo, but writing, by hand, printed with a ball point pen. He read his fortune out loud.

"HELLO, YOU SICK S.O.B."

Blood drained from Junior's face, shock overtaking him. "Hello? Are you sure it doesn't say something like 'surrender'? Maybe, 'reach for the sky or I'll shoot'?"

"Is this some kind of joke, Junior?"

"No, Barry. I don't know how it got on there. I mean who writes shit on cut off fingers?"

"Who's with you, Junior?"

Barry pulled a gun from his waistband, pointing his weapon directly between Junior's eyes.

"Now hold on, Barry."

"Who is with you?"

"Aw hell, Barry. He made me do it."

"Who?"

"Nick Sibelius."

"He's here? Now?"

Junior nodded yes.

"Let's go."

"Where we going?"

"We're going to see your sister. Let's go."

~*~

As Nick's eyes adjusted, he remembered his cell phone. He tapped his flashlight app to illuminate the space. He found himself in an exact replica of every dental exam room he had ever seen, except the chair seemed to have some kind of a thick pad tied to it. Touching the plastic pad, he felt warmth. Scanning the chair with his phone he realized the pad was MaryLou firmly affixed to the chair with clear shipping film, her mouth forced open with surgical steel mouth forceps. Holstering his gun he tried to hold his phone for light, removing plastic film with his other hand, but Barry had applied multiple layers preventing him from simply tearing the binding away. He felt in his pocket for a small knife, then carefully cut through layers until he finally had access to a locking mechanism on the forceps holding her mouth open.

"It's me, MaryLou. Nick. You're going to be okay. Just hang in there."

He couldn't tell how she was doing or if she was even conscious. So he moved quickly to cut through, and pull away film, working first to release her chest so she could breath more easily, then cut at bands of film holding her head down on the chair. Her head and shoulders free, he saw her eyes blink, then she twisted her neck in his cell phone's dim light.

"I'll have your hands free in a moment MaryLou." He removed the mouth forceps. She opened and closed her mouth several times, stretching muscles, then licked chapped, cracked lips. She spoke in a breathy voice.

"Nick, thank God. How did you find me?"

"Junior."

For a time neither spoke, only Nick's knife tearing at film filled the silence.

"So then, you know."

"Know what, Lou Lou? You're really Junior's sister? You've been lying to me all this time? Or how about you making a complete ass of me?"

"Nick, I'm sorry. I didn't know what to do."

"Looks to me like you knew exactly what to do."

"Nick—"

"Let's just get you out of here. Okay? We can talk about the rest of this later."

Nick had cut through enough film to release MaryLou's arms. He then took off his shirt.

"Here, take this. Don't know where your clothes are."

MaryLou wrapped his shirt around her. "Thanks."

He moved to cut through film around her legs, when light flooded the room. Footsteps clanged on metal. Squinting against bright fluorescents, he pulled out his gun, looking up to see Barry guiding Junior down a metal spiral staircase. Barry had his gun trained on the back of Junior's head.

Barry said, "I see you found the other entrance to my little play pen."

Nick said, "Drop your gun, Barry. Its over."

"What, you don't care if I splatter Junior's brains all over the place?"

"Go ahead, Barry. I could care less."

"Oh, Nick. You're just too funny." Barry nodded appreciatively at MaryLou. "Nice shirt, MaryLou. I'd give you your panties, but…"

He pulled some white panties from his pocket, bringing them up to his nose, inhaling deeply.

"My, my." He dabbed his brow with her panties, then returned them to his pocket. "By the way, you did some fine shooting today. You took down that big old aryan like you were shooting a twelve point buck."

He looked over to Nick again. "So, Nick. You're okay with me killing your girlfriend's brother? Really?"

Nick stood motionless, his eyes fixed on Barry.

"Put your gun down or I'll blow Junior's brains all over everything. I don't think your girlfriend there will want to do you after her brother's head explodes all over her."

Nick looked to MaryLou, hoping the shooting skills she demonstrated earlier with a rifle would translate into the only play they had for survival. "You win, Barry."

He chuckled. "I always do."

Barry moved his gun away from Junior toward Nick. At the same time Nick tossed his gun to MaryLou while diving to the right, yelling at Junior to duck. Barry tracked Nick with his gun. Junior, having been hit in the head numerous times by various pieces of farm equipment and who had only survived to adulthood because he finally ducked without thought when anyone said the word, immediately dropped on Nick's command. As Junior fell away from Barry, MaryLou caught Nick's gun in both hands, leaned backwards arching her back, and fired once, twice, a third time into a stunned, and now dead, Dr. Barry Swenson, DDS.

For a moment everyone held their position. Nick looked at Junior who sat on the floor rubbing his head. He had apparently smashed into an x-ray machine when he ducked away from Barry. Nick turned to MaryLou.

She lay back, gun in hand, still bound to the chair from her hips down. Her voice, given the circumstances, was calm. "Can I have a little help with these bindings?"

Nick paused, considering what he wanted to say. *Thank God you're alive! I love you. We'll run away from here to a new life, together. I'll keep you safe. I promise.*

"Why don't you get your brother to help you. I need to figure out what to tell the police when they get here. By the way, nice shooting, Lou Lou." He spit her name out like he was expelling a foul liquid from his mouth.

"Nick."

"I really don't want to hear it, Lou Lou. You've lied to me and now I find you're somehow tangled up in Junior's mess. It won't be difficult to prove you murdered Jayson Moore." He wanted to wrap his hands around her throat. Just strangle the living shit out her. He wanted to kiss her, hold her, feel her hair brush against his face. He wanted to put a bullet in her head.

She said, "I saved your life."

"I don't recall asking you to save me, Mary…Lou Lou. You blew his goddamn face off with a high powered rifle!" *How many Chronicle reporters can hit a Nazi's face at three hundred yards? Who the hell are you?*

"If I had known what an ass you can be, maybe I would have let Jayson put a bullet in you, you selfish, self-centered…"

Nick's eyes burned with anger. His insides hurt like hell. He wanted to slap her, to beat her, to force her to love him. "MaryLou, you can't shoot a man down with a rifle, then expect me to turn the other way." *But you do. Goddammit, you do.*

MaryLou ripped away strands of plastic film from her legs.

"So that's the thanks I get? You're giving me up to the police for murder?"

"And aiding and abetting a felon."

"You're really going to do this?"

"What the hell do you expect me to do? Let you walk? If you had trusted me. If you had come to me earlier, maybe... But I can't just let this slide." *Why didn't you trust me?*

"What's going to happen to Junior?"

"Well let's see here, Lou Lou." Nick purposefully exaggerated her name. "Since wounding a transient, shooting at a hot air balloon, and killing a trespasser, all of which his fancy lawyer got him off the hook, he has racked up kidnapping, manslaughter, if not murder for Harlan, attempted murder, aggravated assault on a law enforcement officer, illegal toxic waste disposal, arson, car theft, and conspiracy to commit murder with our favorite, now dead, dentist Barry. You've been a reporter for a few years, so you tell me. What do you think is going to happen to Junior?"

MaryLou turned to her brother, "Dammit, Junior."

Nick extended his hand to MaryLou, "So my gun?"

She looked up at Nick, resignation in her voice, the gun's muzzle pointed in Nick's direction. "I don't think so, Nick."

Nick felt sucker punched, actually having to inhale deeply to physically catch his breath. "MaryLou." His eyes moved from his gun to MaryLou's determined gaze. "MaryLou, what are you doing?"

A part of him expected her to lower the gun, to love him, to surrender body and soul to him. But MaryLou kept the gun trained on him, each passing second bringing with it the reality and pain of her betrayal. "You want to dig this hole deeper? Is that what you want, MaryLou?"

Junior pleaded, "Please Lou Lou, you don't need to do this."

"Junior, come over here and cut me out of this damned plastic wrap."

Junior pulled a small knife out of his pocket, cutting film away from her legs.

Nick said, "Help me understand, MaryLou. Why would you want to help this idiot who we both know is a danger to the general population and probably himself?"

Junior interrupted, "He's right, Lou Lou. I am a danger 'cause God's after my ass."

MaryLou said, "I feel responsible for him, Nick. There's history."

"What history could possibly lead you to want to go to prison to protect him?"

"It's complicated."

"Un-complicate it."

"You don't have to tell him shit, MaryLou," Junior said.

"Tell me what? You were spanked as a child, so now you're a lying bitch who kills people?"

She winced at his words. "When I was a teenager living here something terrible happened. I got pregnant."

Nick looked over to Junior, "Junior?"

"God no. Like you say, I'm a twisted little bitch Nick, but not that twisted. Somebody else."

"So you're a cold blooded killer because you got banged up as a teenager. Is that what you're trying to tell me?"

"If you'll shut up for a second, I'll tell you. I was pregnant because Barry raped me."

They stood in silence letting her words reverberate in the room. Nick took a deep breath.

"Okay." He wanted to hold her, to take the pain away, but he didn't know how. "So you came here to kill him?"

"I don't know. I came here to settle the score somehow. Put him away for good, possibly kill him if he resisted arrest."

"So you're a cop now."

"Homeland Security."

Nick couldn't believe where she was going with this fantasy. "Right, MaryLou. You're a rogue agent who has come back to kill the man who raped you as a teenager."

He looked into her determined expression, her eyes confirming the truth of his words.

"He was a domestic terrorist, Nick."

"My god. You are with Homeland Security. You came here to kill Barry. MaryLou." He stepped toward her.

"Stay back, Nick. I love you, but I'm in this pretty deep. You don't need this, you don't need me, in your life."

But I do want you in my life. "I get Barry, but why are you helping Junior?"

"After the Situation, the rape, I discovered I was pregnant. Junior stood by me. I owe him a lot. I was alone Nick. Junior was the only person there for me when I really needed help."

Her words hung in the air for what felt like minutes, echoing off the walls of Barry's personal dental exam room, then fading to silence. They stayed motionless, each unsure of what to do or say next.

MaryLou spoke first. "Nick. Say something."

He paused, considering what he wanted to say. *If I had been there I would have protected you. I would have killed the son of a bitch Barry myself. I love you.*

"I'm sorry. I'm sorry for what you went through. I understand you feel a debt to Junior, but you can't run away from this, MaryLou. You've aided and abetted a felon and you shot Jayson Moore."

"Well, so did you! I get penalized for being a better shot? And don't I get some credit for saving your life? If I hadn't shot Jayson, he would have killed all of you."

"You didn't show up with a high powered rifle to save anybody. You and I both know you planned to shoot Jayson to keep him from killing Junior."

"Look, I didn't have a choice. Okay? What do you expect me to do, let the bastard kill him?"

"You could have told me what was going on. You should have told me, MaryLou." *Why didn't you trust me?*

"I was afraid if I told you the truth I'd lose you."

Nick shook his head. "Are you telling me the truth now?"

She wiped a tear away from her face, wagging the gun nervously in Nick's direction. "Now Junior and I are going to get out of here, and you're going to let us go."

"And why would I do that, MaryLou?"

"Because my dear, if you try to stop us, I'll have to shoot you. Don't doubt it, Nick. I would deeply regret it, but I cannot let myself be arrested and I'm not letting Junior go to prison."

She looked toward Junior, keeping the gun trained on Nick. "Take a roll of duct tape and bind Nick's hands behind his back. Turn around, Nick."

Nick studied MaryLou's face. The woman he knew, the woman he loved, seemed to be invaded by the soul of Lou Lou. He turned his back as instructed. "MaryLou, don't do this."

Junior picked up the tape. "Are you sure you want me to do this Lou Lou?"

"Just do what I say, Junior, and maybe we'll both get out of this in one piece. Okay?"

Junior pulled Nick's arms behind his back, taping his wrists together, then binding his feet. Nick willed Junior to bind him painfully tight, to distract him from the blade MaryLou's words had shoved into his heart. She found her clothes, dressing quickly, leaving Nick's shirt on the dental chair. When Junior had completed his work, she motioned him to follow her out the door. She turned back to Nick. "I'm sorry, Nick. I really am."

Nick watched her leave, frustrated he let them get away, embarrassed to have been overpowered by a woman and her idiot half-brother, and angry he let his need get in the way of his common sense. But Junior had failed to deliver the distracting pain Nick wanted in his bindings, so what shook him more was a panic deep inside he might never see MaryLou alive again.

42 CHASING REALITY

Two Austin Police officers responding to a call about shots being fired, stormed into a suburban home, weapons at the ready. They eventually found a typical dental examination room, only this one included mounds of plastic wrap, a somewhat corpulent red headed dead man with blood pooled around him, and a shirtless man bound with silver duct tape claiming to be a private investigator.

The two officers scanned the room, quickly determining any danger had past. Officer J. Smith walked up to Nick, returning his gun to its holster, face flushed with adrenaline. "Got some ID?"

The man frowned. "Happy to oblige, but you'll have to get this tape off of me."

Smith pulled out a pocket knife, cutting through layers of tape while his partner looked on, hand resting on his weapon. Just in case. Once released from his bonds, the private investigator showed them his credentials.

"So you mind telling me," Smith looked carefully at the man's identification. "Nick Sibelius, Private Dick, what the hell went down here?"

Nick put on his shirt. "I've been building a case against the doctor there. Kidnapping. I tracked him down to this house, only to discover someone else wanted him just as badly. It looked like the doctor, dentist actually, had tied someone down to his personal dental chair. I guess whoever it was escaped."

Officer Smith handed Nick's credentials back. "No shit." He looked to his partner, a black cop in his late twenties. "Hey Sid, you hear that? Tied to a damned dental chair."

Nick slipped his wallet into a back pocket. "When I came in, I found him dead on the floor. The shooter got the drop on me. Taped me up and ran."

186

Smith glanced at Sid who had the same doubt sketched across his face, the cop knew in his own gut. This guy was hiding something. "So you're saying you found this guy already dead and then were tied up at gunpoint by an unknown assailant?" He scanned Nick's over six foot tall frame. "He must have been one big sonofabitch."

Nick shrugged. "No, not all that big. Just got the drop on me."

Sid gave out a slow sigh. "And you let him take your weapon. I think you might be having a really shitty day, private investigator."

"Yeah, you can say that again. I just started this business and now I've been disarmed and some bastard has my gun."

Smith and Sid nodded in recognition of the serious implications of losing a gun.

"Jesus, I just hope he doesn't use my gun to..." Nick looked to Smith, his voice trailing off. "I've got to get it back."

Sid said, "You'll need to come downtown to make a statement."

"Absolutely. I'll come down now tomorrow morning."

"That's really thoughtful of you, but we'd rather you ride downtown with us. Now."

~*~

MaryLou had left Nick tied up with Barry to delay any attempt to come after them. Her plan was working. Having gone through the entire scenario several times with two different detectives, he sat alone in an interrogation room. When the door opened again a balding man in a tailored suit, french cuffs with gold cufflinks, a handkerchief in his breast pocket, stepped inside, placing a brown leather briefcase on the floor.

"You must Nick Sibelius."

Nick looked at him, uncertain where this conversation was going.

"Alice called me. She's a remarkable woman, isn't she?"

"Yes, she is. Are you an attorney?"

"John Mathers of Mathers, Smiley and Pritcher, Attorneys at Law." He reached across the table, a gold ring on his manicured finger. "I've gotten you released. Come with me."

Nick followed Mathers down a hallway and out of Police Headquarters. Alice sat in the driver's side of her pink convertible Ford Thunderbird.

Mathers left Nick at the passenger door, walking around to Alice's side of the car. He took her hand, offering a gentle kiss. "As promised my dear."

"Thank you, Walter. You are a angel."

"No, you are my dear."

Nick watched the two lovebirds continue chirping to each other, when Alice finally said goodbye, pulling away from the curb.

"Thanks, Alice."

"Your very welcome, Nick."

"Does he, uh, know about…"

She turned to him, looking like a cat with a mouse tail hanging out of her mouth. "Does he know I'm evolving? Of course he does. You don't approve?"

"I just don't want to see you get hurt."

"I'm a big girl, Nick. But you're very sweet to be concerned. I'll let him know if he gets out of line, my Nicholas will be there to protect me."

"Alice?"

"Yes, Nicholas."

"Don't ever call me Nicholas."

"Yes, Nick."

Alice dropped him off at his car in West Austin. He drove to his trailer to pick up a spare pistol and a shotgun, then he headed east on Highway 290 toward Tyler. MaryLou would be running somewhere she felt safe, somewhere familiar. Nick's head knew MaryLou probably had gotten on Interstate 35 heading south to Mexico, but his heart told him she would head for East Texas to her grandparents old farmhouse. Unfortunately, East Texas consists of the eastern side of a huge state and he had no idea about the location of this farmhouse.

His phone lit up with Pflugerville Police Chief Frank Waterstone's photo on the screen, interrupted his thoughts. Nick considered not answering his call, but maybe this was news about Quentin.

"Hello, Frank. Thanks for hooking me up with Gus down at the morgue. How's Quentin?"

"Quentin is stable and it's looking good. But that's not why I called. Nick, what in God's name are you doing? I've heard a bizarre story from Gus about you cutting a finger off a corpse, and the Austin Police Department, not my police department, the Austin Police Department, is telling me you were at a murder scene."

"Frank—"

"It's enough some mystery shooter blew Jayson Moore's brains out all over Anderson's granite countertops and I've got a dead guy floating in Pendleton's pond—"

"I did get Anderson's daughter back to him, Frank—"

"Did you know her boyfriend is a goddamned decorated Marine?"

"No, I didn't know."

"I know you're a good friend of Quentin, but what the hell's going on?"

"Frank, it's a bit hard to explain."

"Try."

"I had a lead about a drug dealer, the dead dentist. I heard he was planning on attacking the girl. So I went to the Anderson's house. Unfortunately, one of Barry Swenson's thugs surprised us, threatening to kill Ayisha." Nick paused, realizing he was about to go down a path of no return. "I think the dentist, Swenson, shot Jayson. Swenson had some illegal toxic waste dumping scheme going and apparently Jayson had double-crossed him."

"Toxic dumping inside Pflugerville?"

"Yeah, on Junior Pendleton's property."

"You're kidding? Earl Pendleton's son?"

"I have a feeling we're going to find a lot of toxic waste on his farm."

"Great. That's all I need. I've got people dying left and right, an American hero almost beaten to death, and a toxic waste dump inside city limits. The new mayor is going to have my ass on a silver platter. You better come by my office so we can talk all of this through."

"I might not be able to make a meeting today."

"Like hell. I need to get this straightened out ASAP."

"I'm kind of on the road right now."

"Nick—"

"I've got a lead on Junior. I can tie this whole thing up."

"Nick, you're not a cop anymore. You're job is not to chase criminals all over Texas. Let the state guys handle this. Besides, you're making them nervous in Austin. They think there might be more to this than you being overpowered by an unknown assailant, Junior, I assume." The Chief paused as if waiting for Nick's confession. "So what more is happening Nick? You and I both know Junior may be good against an inebriated transient or a hot air balloon, but overpowering you? I don't think so."

"I appreciate your confidence, but he caught me off guard. It happens."

"Nick I don't know why you're not telling me everything, but you need to understand the consequences here. I don't care how tight you are with Quentin, I cannot intervene if you go after these people. Do you understand what I'm saying?"

"Yeah, I understand."

"So what's it going to be?"

"I'll be in touch, Frank." With those words he pressed the End button.

Five minutes later his phone rang again, only this time Alice's picture came up.

"Nick, what's going on? I just got an earful from Chief Waterston a few minutes ago. He wanted me to tell him where you were. Demanded, really. Of course, I don't know where you are."

"I'm on the road. I'll probably be out a day or two."

"I checked with the Houston Chronicle. There's no one working there with the name MaryLou Perkins. When I went to do a little digging on her myself, I ran into a brick wall."

"What do you mean, a brick wall?

"I mean its like she's some secret agent or something. There's nothing about her anywhere. Like she doesn't exist."

Nick let Alice's information sink in. "Maybe she's in the Witness Protection Program."

"Nope. Checked it out. She doesn't exist Nick."

Nick realized if she was a Homeland Security agent, then she wouldn't want anyone to know anything about her. He could get Alice to check with Homeland Security regarding an agent named MaryLou Perkins, but if she really was an agent, the inquiry would only raise flags and make it more difficult for MaryLou to slip out of this mess she had gotten herself in. Nick looked down an undulating black asphalt road, feeling like he was trying to complete a puzzle with missing pieces.

"Can I trust you, Alice?"

"I'm a bit hurt you have to ask, but yes, you can trust me. What's going on?"

"I need your help. I'm driving east towards Tyler hoping to find Junior. I think he might hide away in a farmhouse out here."

"Now, why would you think that?"

"It's not important. Is there anyway you can do a search of farmhouses built in the early 1900's? The original owner would have been named Perkins."

"Well, yes, I should be able to do a search of land records. It's going to take some time."

"I need this information yesterday, Alice."

"Exactly who are you looking for?"

"I'm looking for Junior. He ran into some difficulties earlier today. Now he's running away. I want to stop him before he gets himself into even deeper trouble. Can you do this for me Alice?"

"You got it, Nick."

"And if Frank calls back..."

Alice acted out her response. "I tried to call him Frank, but the cell phone reception in East Texas is a bit spotty."

"I owe you, Alice."

"Yes, you do. We'll discuss it on my next performance review."

Nick ended their conversation wondering if he'd have the opportunity to give Alice another performance review. No matter what outcome the next few hours might bring, he felt pretty certain his private investigation license would be worthless when he got back, if he got back. Driving on, an inner voice of reason questioned why he'd risk everything for a woman who had lied to him about her identity. His heart quickly responded she had now saved his life twice, and even if she hadn't, he had to believe in her. She had to be real.

43 HIDEOUT

Leaving Barry's dental nightmare house, MaryLou had wanted to make a quick getaway, but Junior insisted they go to the hospital to pick up Carl. Even though Barry was dead, he didn't want to take a chance with any repercussions against Carl from the police or one of Barry's other associates. Junior found him in a hospital gown sitting in a wheelchair, looking at a collection of vintage surgical tools enclosed in a glass cabinet in the front lobby.

"Let's go, Carl."

Carl banged his wheelchair hard against the display case trying to turn around in response to Junior's voice. "Junior! You're okay!"

"Of course I'm okay. Let's go."

Junior rolled Carl out of the lobby into an awaiting Lexus, which sped away from the hospital. After a quick stop at a drug store for several tubes of Orajel for Junior's teeth, they turned toward East Texas. Once on the highway, MaryLou briefly let the reality of losing Nick enter her consciousness, but feeling her eyes begin to swell with tears, she chastised herself for being weak and not staying focused. She looked at her battered half brother, then in the mirror at Carl who busily texted on his phone.

"Carl, do not tell anyone where we are. Understood?"

"Yes ma'am. Just playing games, nothing important."

Junior said, "Lou Lou."

"Junior, I really don't want to hear it."

"Let's go south on I35 to Mexico."

"Don't you think Mexico's a little obvious, Junior?"

"What do you mean?"

"Everybody goes to Mexico when they're running from the law, Junior."

"Well then, if everybody does it, it must be a good idea."

"Junior, Nick is going to drive down I35 looking for Barry's car. You can count on it."

Junior had to think about this for a minute. Going to Mexico seemed like the right thing to do. The bad guys always went to Mexico in the movies. But Lou Lou had a point. Nick would certainly be onto them if they headed south. But if not Mexico, where?

"So where should we go if we're not going to Mexico?"

MaryLou hesitated to answer, as if she was thinking through a difficult strategy. "Well, Junior. One possibility is a farmhouse I know about in East Texas. It belonged to my grandparents, but no one lives there anymore. If we go there no one will ever find us."

"So we'd be like, off the grid. There'd be no way to find us."

MaryLou's plan and a supply of benzocaine settled Junior down enough for him to sit quietly in the passenger seat, watching flat farmland gradually shift to undulating forested hills. Carl played games in the back seat on his smartphone. The road became a black two lane ribbon through green pines and cottonwoods. They took a right turn down a dirt road, a cloud of red dust kicking up behind them, the sun crowded out by a forest canopy. After several miles, MaryLou turned onto a narrow track, their car occasionally bottoming out against the ground, until they came to a small, single story white framed house surrounded by a chain link fence.

Carl spoke up. "Where are we, Lou Lou?"

"Somewhere we won't be found, Carl. We'll be safe here for awhile."

MaryLou opened a creaking, rusted fence gate, walking on stones to the front porch, the very same white limestone rocks on which she had played her own version of hopscotch as a little girl. Stepping onto the porch she could feel boards strain in protest underfoot. The screen door had a fine coating of red dust from dry soil, creaking loudly as she pulled it open.

Junior said, "Does somebody live here, Lou Lou?"

"Not anymore."

"Who's house did you say this was?"

She turned the front door knob, smiling at how the door to this house, even when abandoned, stood unlocked, as always. She could still hear her Granddad saying if a man had so little trust in God that he had to resort to locked doors, then his soul was in much more peril than his possessions. Even in death, Granddad's soul seemed to be doing just fine.

"My grandparents used to live here."

The door opened into a hallway. Before a remodel in the 1950's, this "dogtrot" breezeway had been an open space between two halves of the house. Turning to her right, the living room sat empty. Old faded red and green flower pattern wall paper clung loosely to wall lathe work. Brown water stains marked a corner by the ceiling. Pine slats ten inches wide and ten feet long covered in several years of dust, made up the floor. An odor of pine and musty decay hovered around them.

"I used to come visit my grandparents here as a little girl."

Junior asked, "Have they passed on?"

She turned to her left, walking into the kitchen, an ancient Hotpoint Automatic stove in white enamel sat with one of its four doors, an oven door, opened wide like some beast waiting to be fed. A fridge, the same 1950's Hotpoint appliance MaryLou remembered with fondness, sat with its door slightly ajar. For a moment she could once again see her Grandmom, who may have first coined the saying, "Life is short, eat dessert first", reach into the freezer box for a container of Neapolitan ice cream on a warm summer day.

"Yes. My Granddad died when I was in high school, just before I met you. And my Grandmom died a few years later. They willed this house to my Mom, but she just couldn't bring herself to spend much time out here. I guess being here felt too much like losing them."

"I can understand. When my brother Calab died, I felt like someone had taken an axe and lobbed off a big part of me."

MaryLou said, "I wish I had known Calab better."

"Well, he left on a fishing trip just a couple of days after you showed up your first summer with us. I suppose if he had been around these last few months probably none of this would have happened."

"What does your brother have to do with Barry's toxic waste dumping scheme?"

"Daddy always used to say when God was giving out brains, Calab must have cut in line and gotten an extra helping."

"Pretty smart, huh."

"Yeah. Daddy also used to say I must've been peeing against a tree which explains how I missed the whole handing out brains thing altogether. But don't get me wrong. I loved my brother. We did everything together, even after we grew up. I think we were meant to always be together.

"Why do you say that?"

"Well, whenever Calab wasn't around, especially after he died, everything, and I mean everything, turned to shit. Calab went on a band trip and I accidentally set the front lawn on fire with some firecrackers. If Daddy hadn't helped with a garden hose, I might have burned our whole house down. Then he goes fishing and I let Barry, well, you know. And now that Caleb's gone, well..." Junior fell silent, MaryLou imagining him reeling off in his mind all of the disasters befalling him, and those around him, since Calab flipped his truck over, breaking his neck.

"You know, Lou Lou, I didn't call you when I realized how bad things were getting 'cause I didn't want to drag you into this mess.

MaryLou looked at Junior, then began opening cabinet doors looking for any canned food or other items than might be useful. "Of course, Junior. I know. Look, we're going to turn our luck around. Starting today. Okay? I know we've both had a bad run here, but beginning today, we're both going to have a better life."

"Lou Lou, why are you doing this? You already have a life, you've got a job and I think you're into that Sibelius guy. Why are you doing this?"

"We're family, Junior."

Junior crossed his arms, resting his backside against the counter. "That's bullshit."

"Bullshit? What do you mean, bullshit?"

"I mean I'm your half brother. You and I both know the only reason I'm you're half brother is cause my daddy drank too much and your momma lacked good sense. Think about it. She has a baby with a drunk trucker who drives off in his rig, then never looks back. How stupid is that?"

MaryLou felt a painful sting when her open palm smacked Junior across his face before she consciously recognized a rage welling up inside of her.

She said, "As stupid as continually trying to help my moron of a half brother?"

Junior had bent slightly over, holding his left cheek in his hands, too shocked to say anything, when with a surprisingly similar amount of force, MaryLou smacked the open palm of her left hand across the other side of his face. Her slap revived Junior's tooth pain he had been suppressing with benzocaine.

"Jesus, Lou Lou!"

Junior had opened a wound in her heart and she didn't feel like staunching its bleeding. "And for some goddamned stupid reason I'm still being loyal, saving your ass from a sociopathic dentist and the police."

Junior protected his face with his hands. "I'm not a moron."

She shoved him forcefully against the fridge, slamming the big appliance into a wall. "I've lost Nick because of you, Junior."

MaryLou looked at her half brother cringing against the refrigerator. If she had a cast iron skillet handy in this moment, she would gladly beat the life out of this pathetic excuse for a half brother. Instead, she let out a cry of anguish and frustration sounding like a cross between a coyote and a mean ass cat. Turning on her heels, she walked out of the house, the screen door slamming shut behind her.

Junior said quietly to himself, "I'm sorry about Nick, MaryLou. I really am." Knowing she had left, he let his hands drop. Then, more as an act of maintaining his male dignity than anger, he kicked a cabinet door below the counter, which immediately popped open, slamming painfully into his shin. "Ow, goddammit! And I'm not a moron!"

44 TWITTER MAN

Carl never quite made it to the house, having been distracted by a path across a back pasture leading down a hill into some woods. The same strange attraction which led him to make a home in a small patch of woods at his Uncle Junior's now took hold of him once again. Only this time, Carl's world had expanded with a smartphone he had purchased with money he made doing Junior's shit work. He smiled to himself each time he looked at his brand new phone thinking about getting something smart out of something shitty.

~*~

After getting him out of jail, Junior had told him to stay at the house and not do anything until he returned. Carl had figured Junior just didn't want him to get into anymore trouble. How would going into town to buy a phone cause any trouble? So he had jumped in his truck, driving to a little storefront by a Chinese restaurant on Pecan Street he had seen a few weeks ago.

The windows were covered with Great Deals!!!! Special Sale!!! Lowest Prices!!! Best Satellite with Your Favorite Channels!!! Cell Phones!!! Copies!!! Faxes!!! Checks Cashed!!! Money Orders!!! all displayed in bold red, blue or white, along with a somewhat faded yellow "Support Our Troops" ribbon decal affixed to a glass door, as well as American Express and Mastercard emblems. Walking in, a man in his twenties with black hair and dark skin, paced back and forth, waving his arms as he spoke on a phone in a language Carl had never heard. He knew the man wasn't Mexican or Chinese or Vietnamese, his skin being a little too dark and his language all wrong. Didn't those people at the all-you-can-eat Indian restaurant he had gone to with Junior's now dead brother Calab a couple of years ago look a bit like this guy? Then he remembered where he had recently seen someone who looked exactly like this guy. On Fox cable news. He was one of those Islamic terrorists who liked to strap bombs and crap to themselves yelling *alalalala* just before they had sex with some virgins. Or something like that. In any case, this guy looked like one of those terrorists, which is why Carl jumped, letting out a little cry when the young man hung up his phone, directing his attention to Carl.

"May I help, sir?"

"Ahh. What? Uh, yeah. Uh, thanks. Okay."

"Looking for anything in particular?"

Like a bomb? "Uh, yeah, I was looking for a cell phone. You carry cell phones?"

"Of course we do. Let me show you what we have." The salesman came around from behind the counter, Carl ready to dive for cover at the first sign of an AK-47 locked and loaded in his direction. The salesman stood by a wall of cell phones looking at his potential customer who had gone into a partial crouch, one hand on the counter, as if he was about to leap into the air.

"Everything okay, sir?"

The young terrorist must have left his gun behind the counter after he realized who he was up against. Carl relaxed a bit. He did, after all, want to get a cell phone and he wanted to get back home before Uncle Junior returned.

"Sure. Yeah, I'm fine. So, these are your phones?"

After demonstrating a few models, Carl decided on a phone fitting his rather meager budget which didn't seem too complicated. About thirty minutes later he left with a phone having more features than he understood and a monthly bill which would get out of reach very quickly. However, the terrorist salesman had told him his phone was very popular and unlike some of those flip phones, his was a "man's phone." Carl hadn't realized cell phones were so gender specific. Even though his salesman would probably be on Fox news after his plot was uncovered, Carl certainly didn't want to walk around with some girlie phone by accident.

On his way out to MaryLou's place in East Texas cell phone coverage had been a bit spotty, so he spent most of his time playing games, instead of posting to Twitter. He hadn't heard of Twitter until he got his phone. Now he tweeted with all sorts of people. Famous people. Yessir, he got tweets from no less than Jeff Gordon and Taylor Swift. Fucking NASCAR driver, Jeff Gordon! Like right now Carl checked and discovered Jeff was eating french fries at a diner in Charlotte, North Carolina. Jeff said until he got a carbon fiber hood on his car, the only carbon fiber he had was a fork on his bicycle. Carl tried to imagine what a carbon fiber fork would look like and why it was better than stainless steel forks his Mom always used at her dinner table. Then he realized he could Tweet Jeff back.

"Hey Jeff. LOL@carbon fork. My Mom uses stainless:-)"

~*~

Once they got to MaryLou's house in East Texas, he had tried to see what Taylor Swift was up to, but it seemed ever since he Tweeted her "U Have Gr8t Tits^^:-))" he hadn't been able to access her page, although he figured she still followed him. Walking into some woods behind the house, he considered writing to the Twitter people about this technical problem. Then he came upon a lush, grassy space better than anything he had made back at Uncle Junior's. Carl remembered his smartphone had a camera. If anything would get Taylor Swift to pay attention to him, it would be when she saw he owned some prime Texas land, or at least thought he owned some land. So he held his phone at arm's length to take in both his face and the splendor of his woods, snapping a selfie. He thought he'd have to wait for a print of his picture once he figured out how to do that sort of thing. For now he'd just tweet Taylor about the photo. But then his phone asked him if he wanted to send his picture or post it to Twitter or Facebook. He couldn't believe how cool his phone was and how much he really liked his salesman, even if he was a terrorist.With the press of a button, a photo of Carl posted as a Tweet to all of his followers: Jeff Gordon, Taylor Swift, and Alice Coleman.

45 HELLFIRE AND DAMNATION

Driving down an undulating two lane road with an occasional truck loaded down with pine logs rumbling past in the opposite direction, Nick questioned his sanity. How did he go from acting like someone with training and experience in law enforcement to lying about a crime and protecting a woman who had killed two people? Of course, the two people she killed were both about to kill him. If only MaryLou hadn't run off with Junior. Clearly shooting Barry Swenson had been an act of self defense. And yes, she did have a hunting rifle with a long range scope when she took out Jayson. But in her defense, if she hadn't been there, he and several others would be dead. He owed her. No, him owing her was only part of the truth. He loved her. He wanted this woman in his life.

Jesus, Nick, you sure know how to pick 'em. Couldn't you find a nice girl who wasn't a sniper and related to an idiot?

Then he thought about the revelation at Barry's house. He understood MaryLou might feel an obligation to help out Junior because her brother had been there for her when she needed him. But those events transpired fifteen years ago. Surely there's a statute of limitations on feeling obligated. Nick had always worked with evidence, objective facts. But these objective facts would not add up to an outcome he wanted. He wanted MaryLou.

So I'm driving to nowhere in particular to find her. Man, you've completely lost it.

Alice called.

"You won't believe this, Nick."

"You found tax records on the house?"

"Better. Carl Tweeted a photo to me geotagged by his phone. I've got an exact latitude and longitude of his location. Got a GPS in your car?"

Nick didn't know what a geotagged photo was, but he gladly input the lat/long into his GPS, hit 'go to', which brought up a map with a magenta line taking him directly to Carl, to Junior, but most importantly, to MaryLou.

After about an hour of driving Nick approached a narrow track which, according to his GPS, didn't exist and which he figured must be the drive to her family's farmhouse. Nick pulled off the dirt road, slowly making his way up the track by foot, moving into some trees as he approached a white frame house. MaryLou sat on a porch swing looking beautiful and burdened. Then the front door opened and Junior emerged holding a glass of iced tea and a bottle of beer. Nick thought about coming up behind them, using the element of surprise, but instead, he found himself walking across the front lawn, gun holstered, as they sat on the porch watching his approach.

MaryLou spoke first. "Nick?"

Junior set his beer down, standing. "How the hell did you find us? You some kind of damned hound dog or something?" Junior reached for a shotgun leaning up against the porch railing, but MaryLou held him back with a hand.

She said, "How did you find us?"

"Carl. It appears he likes to Twitter and sent a photo of this place to Alice."

Junior shook his head in utter disbelief, "Stupid sonvabitch."

Nick said, "I wouldn't be too hard on him, Junior. I imagine like me, he doesn't know much about geotagging. Besides, you've had your share of screw ups lately."

"Geotagging?" Junior pushed past MaryLou, picking up his shotgun. "You're right. Never heard of it. So why are you here? There's nothin' good can come of this."

Nick ignored Junior's shotgun, focusing on MaryLou. "As far as anyone knows, this entire mess is Junior's. You don't need to get entangled in any of this. You shot Jayson and Barry, both to save me. No one's going to convict you for self-defense."

"You don't understand. It's too late, Nick."

"MaryLou, listen to me. There's nowhere to run. Do you plan on hiding out the rest of your life? Let me take you both in. You know you can trust me."

MaryLou seemed to ponder Nicks words. "I do trust you, Nick. But I can't. No, I won't let you lie about a murder to protect me." She smiled, looking over at Junior who pumped his shotgun. "And you know Junior here wouldn't last long in prison."

Junior added, "Yeah, I'm not about to be the girlfriend for some big ass tattooed sonvabitch."

MaryLou shrugged as if the consequences would unfold no matter what they did.

Junior said, "This is how this is going to play out. Lou Lou and I are going to get into our car and you're goin' to let us go."

Nick said, "And why would I let you go again?"

With his shotgun trained on Nick, Junior moved to the car. Nick could see anguish in MaryLou's eyes. She had a gun, but he knew she wouldn't use it. However Junior had a bad habit of accidentally killing people. MaryLou got in on the driver's side of the Lexus while Junior kept Nick at a safe distance. Then he jumped into the passenger side slamming his door. Nick watched them pull away leaving a cloud of dust behind.

"Nick?"

He pulled his weapon turning to see Carl standing by the side of the house.

"Carl?"

"Yessir. What are you doing here?"

"Well, I was looking for your Uncle."

"He's around here somewhere. Want me to get him for you?"

"Actually, he just drove away with MaryLou."

"What? They drove off without me?"

"I think they want you to come with me. My car's down the road."

~*~

MaryLou pushed the Lexus hard. Knowing Nick, he wouldn't wait long to pick up the chase.

Junior yelled, "Damn."

"What?"

"I shoulda disabled his car. Damn." He banged a hand down hard on the dash. "They always do it in the movies."

MaryLou drove to a county road, then sped away, the engine straining. Coming to another lumber road, she slammed on her brakes, turning with tires screaming across asphalt onto a dirt track.

~*~

Nick had guessed MaryLou would continue to head east away from Austin. A cloud of red dust marked her escape route. He turned off the highway onto a dirt road, accelerating. MaryLou had some distance on Nick, but he figured she hadn't counted on his years of off road driving experience. Of course, he usually didn't drive off road in a Cadillac. His engine roared, rocks banging against his Caddy's underbody, it's soft suspension slamming his undercarriage repeatedly into the rough road.

Carl screamed "Jesus! Crap! Watch out! Slow down, man. You're goin' to kill us. For the love of Jesus, slow down!"

But Nick only drove faster with a recklessness fueled by fear and desire. He flew down the dirt road, his big car heaving and banging, a huge, thick cloud of dust rising after them. Seeing red taillights flash through a plume of billowing dust behind his quarry, he stomped down on his accelerator, slamming into the rear of MaryLou's Lexus. They swerved, bending metal screeched, blinding dust enveloping them. Cresting a hill, the cars went airborne, then slammed down hard on the road. Nick momentarily lost control, his tail end swinging wildly around, slipping off the road's edge, then slamming into a tree. The Lexus sped away.

"You okay Carl?"

"Jesus, Nick. You're goin' to kill us dead."

Nick gunned his engine, but his car wouldn't move forward. Getting out, he could see the rear tires suspended over a ditch.

"Get out, Carl. We've got some work to do."

~*~

MaryLou slammed on her brakes, her car skidding across the dirt.

Junior said, "What are you doing, MaryLou?"

"We're not going to get away this time, Junior."

MaryLou had stepped out of her car, looking down the road where Nick had crashed.

"What do you mean we're not going to get away? He drove right off the road. We've got to go, Lou Lou."

"I can't do this, Junior. He doesn't deserve this from me."

"He doesn't deserve it? So what do you propose?"

"I'm going to surrender. That's all I can do."

Junior put his arm around MaryLou saying, "I never meant for you to be hurt by all of this, Lou Lou. I guess after Daddy, God had it in for me."

"What do you mean, after Daddy?"

Junior looked to MaryLou, then back to the ground. "Well, I sort pushed him into our tractor's power take-off."

"You what? "

"Power take-off. You hook up a Bush Hog to a—"

"I know what a PTO is, Junior. But Daddy…you murdered him?"

"No, I didn't murder him. It was an accident. A really bad accident. Lou Lou?"

MaryLou kicked Junior's feet out from under him, slamming him down on the ground. Straddling him, she hit him across his face, blood and a tooth spraying into red sandy dirt. She hit him again, and again. He didn't resist, he didn't make a sound. Junior lay under her, surrendering to her rage. Tears streamed down her face as she held two fistfuls of Junior's tee shirt, ready to slam his head with finality into hard, packed Texas soil. Gulping air, she leaned her head back, her anguished cry silencing all life around them. She let go of him.

Junior, his face bruised, cut and bleeding, said, "I am truly sorry, Lou Lou."

She looked at her half brother, a good man who could only do bad. "I know you are, Junior. I know."

MaryLou got up, brushing off dust and wiping her bloodied hands on her jeans. Once Junior lifted himself from the ground, they both stood by her car, watching the dirt road, when MaryLou spoke again. "You need to make a run for it, Junior. Go into the woods, then keep heading east. Don't stop until you're in Louisiana. Then its up to you to stay out of sight. I can keep Nick away from you for now, but you've got to do the rest. Do you understand?"

"What do you mean, you can keep Nick away for now? What happens to you?"

"Don't worry about me, Junior. Look, you're my only family, now that my Mom's passed. I don't know why I keep on trying to save you, but it's got to stop today. I'm going to do this one last thing, then you're on your own. Okay?"

"I'm not exactly sure why you keep trying to save me anyway, Lou Lou. But let me just say, I sure don't like where you're going with this."

"Junior, you stupid sonofabitch! Just do what I tell you to do or so help me..."

Junior held out his arms in surrender. "Okay. Okay. I'll do what you say. Let me go take a pee, then we can carry out your plan. Jeeze."

Junior walked into the woods finding a nice peeing tree when he noticed a small cabin tucked away hidden by foliage. He made his way over to the cabin, a plan beginning to form in his mind. He had seen a YouTube video where this good ol' boy blew up a propane tank by setting it on fire. This cabin just happened to have a barbecue pit with a propane tank. Sweet. He piled paper and wood up around the tank. After making sure the grill was off and the tank valve was on, he put a flame to his pile of kindling with his lighter, cut the hose and ran like hell. He reappeared out of the woods, breathing hard but with a big smile of drilled and broken teeth on his swollen face.

"Okay Junior, its time for you...what are you smiling about?"

"I've fixed everything, Lou Lou. No need for us to split up or you to get arrested."

"What did you do, Junior?"

"Well..." An explosion boomed in the woods, then a ball of flame rose up about fifty yards away from them.

"What did you do, Junior?"

Junior yelled out above a now roaring fire, "I've created what they call a diversion."

"Jesus Christ, Junior!"

Dry East Texas timber proved to be kindling just waiting for a spark. Within minutes the woods were ablaze, flames jumping across the road setting trees and brush along their escape route on fire.

"How are you supposed to get away if your road for escape is on fire, Junior? Did you think about that?"

"Aw, hell. Damnation, I'm sorry, Lou Lou. I just thought, you know —"

"Please stop thinking, Junior. Just stop."

MaryLou paced back and forth across the road trying to think what to do. In other circumstances, with Nick out of the mix, she'd just disable her pursuer and drive away. However, her original plan might still work. Junior could run into the woods away from this fire. She could still find a way to disarm Nick, take his car and get away. She'd lose Nick for good, but at least he'd still be alive. However, now she had no guarantee the fire would stay behind them. If Junior died in a fire, she'd never forgive herself. Her half brother was dumb as a stump, but he was a related stump. One thing was for certain. She didn't want to be trapped with a fire at her back.

"Get in the car Junior."

"But Lou Lou—"

"Get in the car. I know what I'm talking about."

MaryLou revved her engine, sliding the Lexus' tail back around to retrace their escape route. However, Nick's car pulled to an abrupt halt, blocking their path.

Jumping out of his car Nick yelled, "MaryLou, stop right where you are!"

Nick had his weapon drawn, but pointed to the ground. MaryLou leaned out her window.

"Nick, just let us pass."

"It ends here MaryLou. Now."

"I'm sorry, Nick, but this can't be the end." MaryLou smiled one last time, nodding to say goodbye, then gunning her engine, tires throwing dirt and rocks, she did a one-eighty.

Junior cried out, "MaryLou, what are you doing!"

"I'm making lemonade, Junior." Her car raced towards flames climbing up pine trees, black smoke turning day to night.

MaryLou looked over at the man, her brother, who had been so kind and caring to her when she was scared and completely alone. She knew he didn't mean to cause all of the mayhem which seemed to follow him like a plague. But to kill Earl, Sr. To kill their father. No, this time her path would diverge from Junior's. She reached over, released his seatbelt, then in one swift motion, opened his door.

"What are you doing, Lou Lou?"

"I'm helping you do the right thing, Junior." With those words she shoved Junior out the open door.

~*~

At first Nick froze in place unable to believe the scene before him. MaryLou could have surrendered. She could have stepped out of her car and he would have found some way to make everything okay. Instead, she drove right into a raging forest fire like some kamikaze pilot. Only the target she destroyed was his heart. He felt like someone had planted a pitch axe in his chest. He fell to his knees, his insides screaming her name. All of his darkness, all of his pain from the death of his partner, losing his job, his wife leaving him, a loneliness which had defined him, MaryLou driving through fire to get away from him, everything overtook him in one dark, ugly thick sludge of pain. He sat in the dirt, hell encircling him, his life cut and bleeding out. The fire breathed, whirling red dust and black smoke, enveloping him. Hell had come for Nick Sibelius and he resigned himself to his fate.

Then he heard a voice nearby, "Nick!" The voice rose over an intensifying roar of flames. Carl, on hands and knees, his face blackened with soot, labored to breathe. Nick figured he must have been trying to save Junior. He grabbed Carl, pulling him to his feet. Carl could barely walk, his lungs wheezing with smoke, so Nick dragged him away from the flames like he was moving a heavy bale of hay.

Another voice called out a short distance away. "Help me. Help…"

Carl coughed out his words. "You hear something, Nick?"

Nick left Carl propped up against his car. Pulling out a handkerchief to cover his face, he plunged back into the inferno. He found Junior lying in a ditch, coughing and choking on smoke, his arm broken. Carrying him away from the flames, Junior repeated over and over again, "I'm sorry, Lou Lou! I'm so sorry."

46 WISH YOU WERE HERE

For several days after seeing Mary Lou drive to her fiery death, Nick stayed at his trailer having rediscovered his old friend Jack Daniels and an endless stream of trash on cable. Carl, feeling a special bond with Nick since being pulled out of the flames, came by. Nick scared him away, screaming obscenities, swinging a Louisville Slugger. Then Quentin showed up, released from the hospital, walking with a cane. Nick, wearing jeans and a faded blue tee shirt he hadn't bothered to change out in three days, sat on a lawn chair watching his friend drive up, then get out of his red Ford Mustang.

"Hey Nick. Thought I'd drop by, check in on you."

"Did you now. Well, here I am, Quen."

Quentin grabbed a beer from an ice chest, taking a seat in a lawn chair next to Nick. "Nick, we've been friends a long time. I was there when Denny died, your marriage fell apart, and when you lost your job in Houston. I've been there through all the shit."

"Yes you have, Quen. Hell, I even managed to just about get you blown up. I'm pretty good at getting friends killed, you know."

"You had no control over a psychopath like Barry Swenson. Don't flatter yourself."

Nick locked eyes with his best friend. "So what do you want Quentin? You want a medal or something?"

"Yeah, a medal would be nice." Quentin took a long drink from his beer. "You know Nick, you can be one of the biggest assholes on this planet. But no matter what, we're still friends. I may not like it, hell, you may not like it. But even in the pathetic state you're in right now, I know you've got my back."

"Why are you here Quen? To tell me everything's going to be alright?"

He shook his head. "No, I imagine things are going to get a bit worse before they get better. I guess I just want you to know I'm still here for you. You don't have to walk this alone."

They both sat in silence, a red tail hawk circled above, screeching a few hundred feet away. A white tail deer stood by a live oak, her black eyes alert for danger.

"Why do you think she did it, Quen? Why did she leave me? Why did she kill herself driving into that fire?"

"Don't know, buddy. Maybe the only way she knew how to keep what she had with you was to destroy who she was."

"Yeah. Maybe."

~*~

Four weeks after losing Mary Lou, Nick stepped into his office. Alice looked more feminine, softer than the last time he had seen her. He guessed Walter Mathers had been giving her some wardrobe pointers. She stood near the coffee pot in a cream business suit, her skirt just at her knees, wearing sensible pumps. She turned, frowning.

"Nick?"

"Alice, how have you been?"

She set her cup down, stepping up to give him a hug. Then she slapped him across his shoulder.

"How am I doing? Well let's see. I haven't been paid in a month, so today I'm packing my stuff."

"You're quitting?"

"No I'm not quitting. My boss," Alice thrusted a sharp finger into Nick's chest, "abandoned his business. A girl has to do what a girl has to do."

She threw a large tape dispenser into a box sitting on top of her desk. Then walked past Nick to her desk chair.

"Alice, I'm sorry."

"Oh, so you're paying me, I don't know, sometime this year?"

She forcefully yanked the middle drawer of her desk out, pens and paper clips flying into the air. Then she dumped its contents into her box. She looked up from her labors.

"Don't even think about giving me any grief. I at least get to keep my damned stapler."

Nick grabbed the box from her. "Alice, I know I've disappointed you. You're right. I don't have enough business to keep you on. But I'll make sure you're paid for last month and an additional two weeks. I promise."

She plopped down in her chair. "It's not the money Nick. Walter takes very good care of me. It's you. I'm mad at you for letting a woman do this to you."

Nick poured some coffee into a cup, then thinking better of drinking her brew, set it to one side. "Blinded by love, Alice. That's my only defense."

"Well I played football in college, Nicholas. My coach always said your best defense is a strong offense. So get off your butt and live your life, or so help me God I'll conjure up my inner man and beat the holy crap out of you."

Nick set her box back down on her desk. "Yeah, well, thanks for the advice." He turned to walk out the door, then paused. "You can keep your stapler, Alice."

~*~

During the next six months Nick traveled three times to East Texas, sifting through a charred landscape and the rusting husk of Barry's burned out Lexus, where Mary Lou had disappeared from his life. Finally after his third visit, he acknowledged to himself such intense heat from a forest fire had simply reduced her to ashes. Dust to dust. Ashes to ashes.

For a time he thought he might end up in prison. Travis County Forensics had determined DNA on Barry Swenson's plastic shipping film did not match Junior's. However, Nick had the foresight to hire Junior's attorney and Alice's boyfriend, John Mathers' of Mathers, Smiley and Pritcher, Attorneys at Law. He successfully demonstrated to Judge Harlow the prosecution did not have sufficient evidence to take Nick to trial. How could a jury convict a man of homicide when he was found wrapped up tight with duct tape and no murder weapon had ever been located?

He did begin to pick up a few clients. A woman hired him to follow her husband, who turned out not to be having an affair, but taking dance lessons to surprise her on their twentieth anniversary. A couple had him locate their son, who had gone missing since returning from his fourth tour in Iraq and Afghanistan. He had checked himself into a rehab clinic, hoping to clean up a drug problem he had developed before seeing his parents. One day on an impulse Nick gave Alice a call.

"Alice, how you doing?"

"Nick, good to hear from you. Oh, I'm doing okay I guess. You know about Quentin I suppose?"

"Yeah I heard. Quentin Matthews, Police Chief. That's a big promotion for him. I guess Frank is now enjoying a nice retirement."

"Yeah. After all of the mayhem in Pflugerville, he didn't have much of a chance with the new mayor. So its been six months, Nick. Why am I hearing from you now?"

"Sorry I haven't called earlier, I just had, well, I've had a lot to process. But I think I've got a path forward."

"That's great Nick. I'm happy for you. Well, I better run along. My shift starts in about an hour."

"What happened to Walter?"

"He wanted me barefoot in his kitchen and I wanted to work."

"So you split up?"

"Heavens no. I got a job at a local coffee shop."

"If you have a couple more minutes, I'd like to make a job offer."

"Really? Doing what?" He could hear skepticism in her voice.

"I didn't realize what you brought to the table, your skill set, until we had the incident with Junior. You're not only good with people, you can handle yourself and you know your way around a computer. I could really use a colleague, a woman like you."

"Can you afford me?"

"No. You won't be able to quit your barista job at first, but as my business picks up I'll be able to pay you more. What do you say?"

Alice didn't hesitate. "I'm in Nick. I'm starting to think working under fluorescent lighting all the time is beginning to wash out both my skin tone and my brain."

"That's great Alice. Not the skin and brain thing. The working with me thing."

~*~

When Nick got back to his trailer he found a note taped to his door and a small package. He tossed the package on his kitchen counter, then read the note.

Nick,

I guess you know I got the farm, Daddy being dead, Uncle Junior being in jail, and Aunt Mary Lou out in a blaze of glory. Anyway, Uncle Junior asked me to hold a service for his sister. Him being in jail and all, I figured it's the least I could do. We have a spot for her in our family plot. (One of the few places Uncle Junior didn't bury toxic waste.) Even though we don't have a body, Junior thought it would be nice to have a memorial stone in her honor. I know you liked Mary Lou and figured you'd want to be there. Saturday at 2pm.

Carl

The service felt interminably long to Nick, his sadness weighing each step, cold winter air heavy and thick. Driving back home he unconsciously played a reel of clips of his time with Mary Lou. Her voice, her laugh, her eyes, the softness of her skin all seemed to be fading from memory. He had lost her, but he couldn't help feeling he had gained from their brief time together. She had opened his heart again, after his wife's betrayal, after feeling so alone. While he hadn't been able to save her, he could still honor her by staying open to life, instead of crawling back into the dark hole he knew so well.

He got home, drank a couple of beers, then noticed a small box he had tossed on the counter a few days ago. He didn't recall ordering anything on line, but he couldn't rule out a drunk session on eBay. He hoped to God he hadn't bought anything really expensive. Rifling through a drawer, he found a paring knife, slitting the box open. Moving its flaps back he found a small cloth pouch. At least it wasn't a gold Rolex or something else his meager credit card balance couldn't handle.

Nick grabbed another beer out of his fridge, then plopped down on the sofa, dropping the pouch on his coffee table. He flipped open his laptop, hoping to distract himself with email or some mindless web browsing. He hadn't checked his email in a few days and about fifty messages awaited him: a Nigerian prince who wanted money, various spams ranging from sex to guns to financial schemes, a message from Quentin just checking in, one from an old friend on the Houston police force which he flagged for response, and then junk mail from an unfamiliar address, 08924ssml@gmail.com.

He hesitated for a moment, then against his better judgement he clicked on the message, just in case an old acquaintance was trying to reach him with a new address. A window opened to a picture of a woman sitting on a low stone wall, the Golden Gate Bridge behind her. He clicked to enlarge the image, his chest tightening. Could it be? The caption read, *"Wish You Were Here. Love, MaryLou"*

MaryLou? Someone was playing a joke. A really bad joke. He forced himself to read the message.

I'm sorry for all the pain I've caused you, Nick. Maybe one day I can make things right. Take care of yourself.

Mary Lou

P.S. Hope you got my package.

Nick looked at the photo again, his heart racing. He found the pouch, expecting Denny's St. Sebastian necklace to drop into the palm of his hand. She might be alive, but Mary Lou would never be coming back into his life. Instead, he found a silver chain and a small oval pendant with a Roman soldier standing with a spear. The inscription read, Saint Florian Protect Us." Nick smiled. A few of his firefighting buddies in Houston had this pendant. The patron saint of fire fighters.

"Mary Lou. My god, you're...alive." He cried laughter. "She survived."

Mary Lou was alive. He immediately crafted an email telling her how much he loved her, how he couldn't believe she had survived, how happy he was they'd be able to have a life together now. He clicked send, watching his email program upload his message. His computer dinged with an error message telling him his email had bounced. He tried several more times, each attempt failing, then realized she must not want to be found. At least not yet. Just knowing she was alive had to be enough for now.

He opened his trailer door, letting cold February air scented with mesquite and cedar fill his senses. Large, billowing cumulous clouds floated across a deep blue sky. Nick got into his pickup, smiled to himself, then rolled down his windows. He drove to the highway, letting the cold winter air remind him how good it was to be alive.

END

ABOUT THE AUTHOR

Richard Hacker, after living many years in Texas, moved to Seattle, Washington. He may be wanted by authorities for transporting Texas BBQ across state lines. His writing has been recognized by the Writer's League of Texas and the Pacific Northwest Writers Association.

www.richardhacker.com

Follow the author on:
Facebook: www.facebook.com/RWHacker
Twitter: @Richard_Hacker

PREVIEW THE NEXT NICK SIBELIUS NOVEL

Coming Soon!

All Hat and No Cattle

Murder, Drugs, & H2O: Nowhere Else But Texas

Nick Sibelius Series, Book 2

by R.W.Hacker

TARGET #5

Charity's universe demanded blood for the pain she endured.

She sat in her black Nissan Leaf, silent but for the sound of the impatient tapping of her fingers on the steering wheel. Her eyes fixed on a red roof tiled Spanish revival number in the cul-de-sac of Island Palms Cove, a street lined with multi-million dollar mansions along a custom built peninsula on Lake Austin. Ignoring the opulence, she watched a fire red Ferrari 430, license plate number HNJ 793.

Her hopped up, speed addicted, hacker of a cousin Larry had provided, as usual, the required critical information. She'd handed him her standard envelop with his "medication" and a license plate number. Several hours later, he emailed an encrypted file with all of the particulars, including a code for the security gate. Charity would make Daniel Hoyt pay for his disrespect of cyclists.

She pondered the idea of sticking a gun in Hoyt's, mouth. She'd pull the trigger, watching his brain matter splatter across the mirrored surface of his fucking Italian super car. The thought of how sun-baked blood and brain would absolutely eat right through the clear coat, destroying his mirror finish, gave her a visceral pleasure. Balance. She reminded herself

Sitting in her carbon zero car, she downed a non-fat latte, one power bar and an electrolyte packed coconut water. Her hip ached and the need to take a piss rose with some urgency. For a moment she considered packing it in for the day, knowing she could come back tomorrow. Tapping an iPod strapped to her arm, a high energy male voice filled her ear buds.

"Are you haunted by demons? Do you find your plans faltering? Do you let your fear of failure stop you from achieving your goals?"

Charity spoke out loud to her demons – the lazy, fat, loser demons who always haunted her whenever she "hit the wall" during a race or a workout.

"Come on, Charity! Push it! Push through it, goddamn it! Let's go. Let's go!"

The podcast continued. *"How do you approach life? 'Fire, ready, aim'? To live with intention, to live consciously in the world, you must rearrange your world from 'fire, ready, aim' to 'ready, aim, fire!'"*

Charity stepped out of the car into a warm, humid summer morning. She scanned the area, then pulled down her black tech fabric riding shorts. Squatting, she kept her legs far enough apart to avoid the splashing stream of urine. While peeing felt good, the indignity of the moment set off her ongoing anger at God. Men had pricks they could just hang out at will to pee.

If God was a woman, then women, whenever the mood or necessity warranted, would be able to yank a man's prick right off, like the tail of a chameleon, who scurries away nub-butted while you hold the still twitching member in your hand.

The energetic male voice pulled her back to the task at hand, *"What is 'Ready'? You are ready when mind, body and spirit, when your whole being is a coiled spring for action. Can you feel your creative, life spirit tension about to explode?"*

Charity repeated her mantra. "Yes, I am Ready. I am a coiled spring. I am a creative explosion."

Finishing, she pulled her shorts up over her long and freckled muscular legs, watching her quads flex as she smoothed the leg band. As had been the pattern for the last three days, Hoyt had not left his house before 6:30 am. She checked her pink GPS enabled training watch. 5:05 am. Plenty of time.

"Readiness is not sufficient. To be powerful you must AIM. A for Attitude, the attitude of a winner. I for Intention, intending with heart, mind and soul the reality you will create. And M for Manifestation, making your power real in the world."

Charity summarized the teaching reverberating around her. "I am ready. I am a winner. I will manifest my power to create life exactly how I want it. Let's go, Charity."

Pulling the trunk release, she reached for her Iron Divas black and pink workout bag with a white skeleton riding a pink road bike, the skeletal rider's long flaming hair trailing behind, teeth gritted ferociously. She took in a breath and slightly bent her knees, feeling the strain of her triceps flexing under the load of the bag. Her focus on Hoyt had taken her off the daily workout regimen. Just one more reason she hated this sonofabitch. Opening the bag, she pulled out a one liter opaque plastic bottle filled with a batch of highly concentrated fox urine she had purchased at Hill Country Outfitters the day before.

"I am a winner. I will prevail."

Moving quickly, she jogged the two blocks to an expansive home with terra cotta roof tiles and her target red sports car in the driveway. She crept to the driver's side of the Ferrari, checking the door. No alarm.

Even though she had a "smash and go" plan if needed, it pissed her off the egotistical jerk assumed no one would dare mess with his ride. She worked fast. Placing a gel pack on the driver's side door to dampen the sound, she punched a quarter inch hole through the carbon fiber door with a titanium drill bit. She slipped a plastic hose fitted with a tiny spray nozzle on the end through the hole, then connected the free end of the hose to a small, battery powered pump, which in turn connected by a hose to the urine filled bottle. She flipped the switch. The sulphur smell of urine filled the morning air as liquid flowed through clear plastic tubing, disappearing into Hoyt's sports car's door. A fine mist sprayed out the nozzle onto the interior and custom red and black racing seats. Her pump strained, having emptied the container. She pulled the hose out, causing some liquid to dribble down the door, splashing onto the drive. Charity took a breath in through her nose, the stench like diarrhea and burnt hair causing her to gag, acidic vomit coming up in her mouth.

Be strong. Be confident. Be courageous.

Closing her eyes she regained her focus, put the equipment back into her bag and twisted a bullet shaped tampon into the hole, its pale blue string dangling in the air.

She ran back, tossing her gear in the trunk, then drove to the Laguna Gloria Museum parking lot to put on her cycling shoes, helmet, gloves and riding glasses. 5:55 am. She lifted her pink Guru Evolo carbon road bike off the roof rack, checked tire pressure and brakes, then clipped in, heading back to Hoyt's house. Her legs burned as she conquered the gradual slope of Mount Bonnell Road. She was strong, powerful, in control. Hoyt had begun his crucible of becoming her fifth target. But as she shifted through the gears, Charity reminded herself while Target #5 would be fun, she had come to Austin with a singular purpose: to kill her brother's murderer.

Yes, the Universe demands a balance of blood for pain.

~*~

Dan Hoyt awoke on his back, drool running down the side of his cheek and a woman's leg draped uncomfortably across his crotch. He turned his head to see a red 5:33 floating in the darkness. He tried to squirm out from under the leg. "Got to get up."

He couldn't remember what the woman's leg had been attached to. Julie? Janice? Didn't matter. He pushed the leg aside, turning to get out of bed. The leg spoke up.

"You getting up? Come on back to bed, baby."

Jenny? Janet? The name associated with the talking leg just would not come to him. Not that knowing her name was a big deal, he had found over the years, however, women seemed to get a bit bitchy in the morning if you couldn't remember their names.

"No, I've got to get up. Lots to do today. But you stay right there. After last night, you definitely deserve some extra rest."

He had absolutely no idea what had happened last night.

The leg's drowsy voice spoke in the darkness. "You weren't so bad yourself."

Whatshername must have been lousy, given he couldn't remember having sex with her. Telling her the truth wouldn't get him out the door any faster, but lying to her would at least keep her quiet. He leaned over in the darkness, finding a breast to kiss, which he assumed belonged to the leg.

"Mmmm. You leaving so soon?" The breast spoke, but with the voice of a different woman. The night was coming back to him. Two very hot women, tequila shots, short black dresses pulled up to panty level as the smaller one sat on the lap of the taller one, miraculously stuffed into the passenger seat of his Ferrari. They were undressed and all over each other almost before he could get them to the bedroom. He hadn't been able to find the damned Viagra. Hoyt figured with two he'd get it up, but once again his cock had let the team down. He kept the lights off, feeling a bit exposed for not being able to perform, especially under such optimal conditions.

"Yeah, lots to do girls. Make yourselves at home. I'll leave some money for a taxi."

He closed the bathroom door, flipping the light switch. Hoyt stared at a squinting naked thirty four year old man without an erection in the full length wall mirror. He showered, shaved, pulled on a pair of creased jeans, a white starched shirt with silver and turquoise cuff links, a pair of hand made quill ostrich skin boots and a Stetson hat with diamond encrusted headband. He opened the door to the two women, one spooning behind the other, in the middle of his bed.

The stress lately had really taken a toll on his sex life. When, at first, he couldn't get it up, he panicked a bit thinking it might be prostate cancer or some other horrible malady his money couldn't fix. The doctor ruled out all of the usual suspects, which left him with stress.

Stress. Yes, he felt stressed because of the deal he had in the works, but Jesus. Be a man Hoyt. Stress.

Fortunately, the Viagra worked, when he could find the goddamn bottle. But this seemed to be the way his luck fell lately. He manages to hook up with two cute darlings, get them home and then nothing. His balls chimed in. *They must be lesbians, otherwise...* Hoyt liked the way his boys thought.

Going downstairs he stepped into an expansive kitchen, all granite, stainless steel, hardwoods and glass. Flipping on the flat screen suspended under a cabinet, weather woman Samantha Fox in bright primary colors, red this morning, stood by a map devoid of clouds with temperatures in the 100's. A message ran below pronouncing water rationing in effect. He pushed a couple of buttons on the espresso machine, cursing when he realized he had forgotten to place his cup under the complicated machine's nozzle. Coffee splashed into the drip pan until he shoved his cup in place. Leaving the kitchen he made his way to the front door with a partial mug of steaming coffee. While the morning so far had been a bust, he couldn't help but smile thinking about his drive out to the project south of Austin in his Ferrari. He loved his Ferrari like a man loves his woman. He loved the smell of her, the sounds she made as he ran through her gears, the thrust of clutching her, the scream of her tires as he stretched her around a corner. He loved the looks of all of those people who could never be him, who could never sit in her black and red racing seats, know the feel of her shifter, the rush of air flowing over her sleek, graceful body.

He pressed the button on the fob to open the door and with a flash of lights the alarm set. While wrangling two semi-inebriated randy women out of the car, he managed to lock the doors, but had failed to set the alarm. Fortunately he lived in a cul-de-sac of million dollar homes with an aura of security, so accidentally leaving the alarm off was not a big deal. He pressed the button again, hearing the locks release. With a coffee mug in his right hand, he opened the door with his left, looking up the street as a woman in black and pink lycra on a pink road bike rolled by silently. He wondered how he had missed seeing her in the neighborhood before. Watching the curves of her athletic body, he vowed to get several bottles of Viagra placed strategically in his homes, offices and vehicles before the end of the day.

As the door opened a thick putrescent stench solidified his brain into something resembling a lump of head cheese. His nostrils burned, eyes watering uncontrollably. His right hand, no longer responding to his brain, dropped his coffee, shattering the ceramic cup into pieces. His bowels released while his stomach spasmed, simultaneously soiling his jeans and sending his morning coffee and all of last night's dinner spewing across the interior of his beloved Ferrari. The overwhelming odor of what he could only imagine was the diarrhea of dead, rotting rats in a soup of burnt chicken intestines consumed him, voiding his lungs of air. He fell to his knees gasping, continuing to vomit uncontrollably until he had nothing left to give.

The woman on the pink bike had circled back around, he assumed to help him out. The thought of the two lesbians upstairs laughing at his limp dick and now another woman helping him because he shit his pants and projectile vomited all over his car really pissed him off.

She hadn't stopped, but Hoyt, raising a hand as if to repel her attention, preemptively called out. "I'm fine. No problem."

Willing himself to a standing position, he stepped away from the car, pulling out a cell phone, angrily pounding a phone number.

"Charlie!"

"Mornin' boss. What's up?"

"I'll tell you what's up. Some goddamn sonofabitch just destroyed my fucking Ferrari, that's what's up, Charlie! Get over here now. And didn't you tell me you had some kind of private eye friend?"

"Yeah, I keep his truck..."

"Well, call him. Now."

"It's awful early, Mr. Hoyt."

"I'd don't give a flying fuck what time it is Charlie. Call him and have him meet me here in an hour. I don't know who did this, but they have no idea who they're fucking with."

"Want me to get a latte for you on the way over?"

"No I don't want a goddamn latte. Just get your ass over here. Now!"

BUSINESS OPPORTUNITY

In hindsight, Nick would wish he had stayed in bed, dreaming about a naked woman sitting on a camel in a snowstorm. Instead, he sat on a lawn chair in front of his silver bullet shaped Airstream trailer east of Pflugerville, a cup of coffee in one hand, a breakfast taco in the other, watching the sky gradually turn from a deep violet to orange and then a deep blue. Water restrictions left the grass surrounding his trailer, once a lush green blanket of St. Augustine, a crispy brown shag carpet. The turf crackled underfoot and bone dry soil split open crevasses like hundreds of little mouths agape begging for water.

This excuse for a lawn mimicked the sorry state of his life. After finding his anesthesiologist wife astride a trauma doc on her lunch break, Nick's life had taken a decidedly downward spiral, culminating in being fired from the Houston Police, punctuated with the rim shot of a nasty divorce. Then he fell in love, or maybe lust, with the sister of a murderer, which did not put him in a positive relationship with the local police department. To his horror she drove like a banshee into a raging forest fire, the locals pronouncing her dead. He thought he'd lost her too, until an anonymous email hinted at her survival. Alive or dead, he hadn't heard from her since the fire over a year ago. A year is a long time to hold onto a faint hope. Now he sat in front of his trailer just outside of the same little town staring at the sorry state of his lawn and contemplating the equally sad state of his life.

His lawn needed, Nick needed, a long, cool drink of life giving water. He looked to a cloudless morning sky predicting the continued demise of his grass. Nick wondered if he'd be able to find the water which would bring him back to life before he completely dried up and blew away.

When his cell phone rang from the trailer, he poured dregs of his coffee onto the parched earth and stepped inside to take the call.

"Nick Sibelius."

"Nick, man I'm glad you picked up this early." Charlie Samuels. The mechanic who kept his pick-up moving in a forward direction. *Why is*

Charlie calling me at 6:30 in the morning? Does Ford have a major re-call for spontaneously combustive trucks?

"Charlie?"

"Uh, morning Nick. So sorry to bother you this early."

"Everything okay? Do I have a critical piece missing from my truck or something?"

"No, no. I'm not calling about your truck. I just remembered the last conversation we had."

"Yeah, my clutch would probably be good for another twenty thousand miles."

"No, I mean the part about your business. Private investigations. You are in the private investigation business, right?"

"Yeah, that's what I do."

Nick's business plan demanded a swank address among the hills and million dollar homes of west Austin. His bank account, however, forced him to settle for a decomposing northeast Austin industrial park built in the early 70's on a plot of land contaminated by two decades of toxic waste dumping. The new business bled cash as soon as he set up an of-fice. Fortunately, Alice, his assistant, had agreed to come back to work for him part time after he let the business slide over losing the aforemen-tioned girl. Unfortunately, he had used most of his savings since leaving the police force in Houston and his few small investigation gigs. If he didn't get a client in the next week he'd need to start checking out cafe barista jobs and put the Airstream up for sale.

"I'm sure you're swamped with work, Nick, but I've got a client for you. Between you and me, he's a bit of a poser asshole—all hat and no cattle, if you know what I mean—but I bet he'll pay pretty well."

Nick decided to leave Charlie with the assumption he had clients fall-ing all over themselves to use his services, especially after the word "pay" caught his attention.

"I might be interested. How do you know he'll pay well for the work?"

"I work on his Ferrari. Brand new. He won't trust it to the dealer, only to his personal mechanic."

"And that's you."

"Afraid so. Like I said, he's a bit of a pain, but I've made a pretty good living off of him. He drives a lot of high end stuff, so other than dealing with him, it's fun for me and I can charge premium prices."

"Do you know what this is about?"

"Tell you what. Can you be at 2002 Island Palms Cove in an hour? It's over by Mount Bonnell."

"That's the other side of town, Charlie. Don't know with the traffic, but I can give it a shot. So, you going to tell me what this is about?"

"Not sure myself. Something about his Ferrari being destroyed. Hell, I'd drive across town just to see what that looks like."

"Okay. Tell your guy, what's his name?"

"Hoyt. Dan Hoyt."

Nick had heard of this guy. Besides being a Texas tabloid playboy and a douche bag, he had made his fortune in commercial real estate before the age of thirty. Lately he had been on a bit of a losing streak. He started a controversial gated community for adults under fifty-five without children — kind of a little suburban City of Sin— which kept his lawyers continuously busy. In the middle of multiple lawsuits, he built a towering condo in downtown Austin with so many engineering issues the City Council finally had the building pulled down. Then Nick thought he had read something about the guy buying up land on the Gulf Coast in the last couple of years. The speculation around his most recent activity ranged from a massive beachfront condo to an oil refinery.

"The commercial real estate Dan Hoyt?"

"That's the one. I'll meet you there." Nick shoved the phone into his pocket.

Well Nick, I guess it's time to dance with the devil.

www.ingramcontent.com/pod-product-compliance
Lightning Source LLC
Chambersburg PA
CBHW031323170626
46807CB00002B/545